Deceived

In for $100K Large

Deceived

In for $100K Large

By

Zena Rodriguez
&
Hope McKim

BEARHEAD PUBLISHING

- BhP -

Louisville, Kentucky
www.bearheadpublishing.com/hope.html

Deceived

In for $100K Large

By
Zena Rodriguez
&
Hope McKim

Cover Design by *Bearhead Publishing*

Cover Concept by Hope McKim & Zena Rodriguez

Cover Photography by Rob Delp, *Delp Video*, Jeffersonville, Indiana

Author Photo (Hope McKim) by Rob Delp, *Delp Video*, Jeffersonville, Indiana

First Printing - August 2006
ISBN: 0-9776260-5-9

Disclaimer

This book is a work of fiction. The characters, names, places, and incidents are used fictitiously and are a product of the author's imagination. Any resemblance to actual persons, living or dead, is entirely coincidental.

Proudly printed in the United States of America

To my father for always encouraging me to write.

Zena Rodriguez

To my brother for his suggestions and support.
To our readers who make telling the story what it's all about.
And, to my dad who said: "The story was an exercise
of imagination for my entertainment and hopefully yours."

Hope McKim

PROLOGUE

Covington, Rhode Island
Friday, April 9th, 1999

All the lights in the stores that lined Antique Promenade had gone off an hour ago. *ANNA'S ATTIC* was the only one still lit. A small Tiffany lamp emitted a warm peaceful glow from the front window. It was deceiving because there was anything but peace inside the little antique shop.

It was Friday and the end of a difficult day. Too many people had been tramping in and out of the shop. Uniformed police officers, a fingerprint duster and a forensic photographer. All of them asking their questions, but answering none of hers. Now they were gone. Only the white tape that outlined where her dead grandmother's body had fallen remained. The yellow plastic crime scene tape was still up outside the shop showing where the outside perimeter had been. But it was meaningless. The lieutenant in charge of the case had told her they were done. All alone now, she sighed. It would be a while before anyone could answer her biggest question: why?

Antonia Stanton would never forget the frantic phone call she had received from Joyce, her grandmother's only employee. Antonia instantly knew something was wrong. Why else would the Caller ID register the name of her grandmother's shop at seven o'clock in the morning?

"Antonia, it's Joyce," the older woman blurted in a panic. "There's been an accident. You have to come to the shop right now!"

"Joyce, what's going on? What's happening? Where's Nana?" Antonia gripped the receiver tightly.

"Please, just hurry. I need you here right now!" Before Antonia could say anything, Joyce had hung up.

Antonia had never driven so fast in her life. You just didn't speed in Covington, Rhode Island. As she swerved onto Antique Promenade, she was greeted with her worst nightmare. Red and blue lights flashed from the two patrol cars and the only rescue truck of the volunteer fire department that were parked on the street in front of *Anna's Attic*. Antonia barely remembers parking her car. She does remember the strong arms that held her as she tried to run into the shop past the police officer stationed at the door.

" Let me go! My grandmother is in there," she struggled to break free.

"Ma'am, you shouldn't go in there."

"Let me go! Joyce! Joyce! Are you in there?" Antonia yelled into the shop.

Joyce appeared in the doorway. Upon seeing her face, Antonia abruptly stopped struggling and went limp in the officer's arms. Something terrible had happened.

The rest of the day was a blur. Antonia's grandmother, Anna Dewitt, was dead. It appeared she had fallen, hitting her head on the corner of an 18th century mahogany Chippendale desk. Joyce had gone home early on Thursday, and found Anna's body when she opened the shop Friday morning. The police report filled out by the lieutenant, who responded to the scene, stated the death was an accident. Anna was an old lady so her fall was not something out of the ordinary. Antonia was not convinced. Her grandmother was anything but ordinary. Antonia had decided that a call to Mayor Boyce of Covington was in order. He had known her grandparents for many years, and would lean on the Chief of Police to conduct an investigation.

Antonia breathed in the familiar smell of her grandmother's antique shop. She looked around at the treasures her grandparents had collected over the years. Surrounded by art, antiques and jewelry, each piece said something special about its previous owner. The antiques in the shop were rich with history, much like her family. The walls were covered with tapestries and mirrors; dark warm colors gave the feeling of comfort. She wondered what would become of these treasures her grandparents had collected from all over the world.

Walking over to the large, picture window, Antonia looked outside at what had been a mild breezy spring day. The words *ANNA'S ATTIC* arced in gold letters across the window, and reflected the glow from the Tiffany lamp. Underneath, the words *Antiques & Fine Furnishings,* also in gold, were stretched across the window in a straight line. Whether she was standing inside or outside the shop, her grandmother's name could be read correctly. Antonia touched the cool glass where the first letter A was painted. "A-N-N-A," she spelled as she traced each of the letters. She leaned her forehead against the glass and tried desperately to control the wave of sadness that threatened to engulf her. Spring was supposed to be the time of new beginnings, the promise of a new year. Winter had ended, and the trees that lined Antique Promenade had sprouted new leaves and flower buds. To Antonia it felt more like an end than a beginning. She had lost her last living grandparent.

Anna and Kurt DeWitt had opened their antique and collectibles shop in 1945, shortly after their marriage. Anna's parents had been hesitant to give their blessing when Kurt had asked for Anna's hand in marriage. Although Anna was only eighteen at the time, she was a serious and quiet young lady. Although Natalia Ivanova and Anton Simonov thought their daughter was too young to get married, they finally gave in. Kurt came from a respectable New England family with old money. He had assured Natalia and Anton that he'd be able to provide for their only child, Anna, and support her in a comfortable lifestyle.

The opening of *Anna's Attic* heralded the end of World War II, and a time of renewed prosperity. The DeWitts loved searching for items for their shop and buying special pieces for customers. Anna kept a journal, where she would record customer's names along with the items they wanted. She carried the book with her on every shopping trip. Kurt had teased her about being too young to have a poor memory, but she stood her ground and used the book faithfully so nothing would be forgotten.

Antonia's mother, Ashley, was born shortly after the shop opened, and then Joel a couple of years later. Living above the antique store enabled Anna to care for the children and still help Kurt run the shop.

"Oh, Nana, I miss you already." Tears welled up in Antonia's eyes as she pulled back from the window. "Who could have done this?"

"We DeWitt women, we laugh in the face of adversity," Nana used to say.

"But Nana, I'm not a DeWitt. Remember. Daddy is a Stanton," Antonia would always answer.

"Ah, but the DeWitt blood runs deep within you, child; just as it did in your mother."

"Hmph," Antonia snorted. "This isn't adversity it's more like downright hostility. Nana was a quiet old woman born and raised in Covington, Rhode Island. She owned an antique shop for God's sake!" Her voice echoed through the empty shop. Had she really raised it that loudly?

Antonia picked her way slowly around the pieces of furniture that dotted the antique shop showroom. She glanced at her reflection in the French provincial mirror that hung on the wall by the stairs. The burgundy velvet stanchion that usually roped off the stairs, was hanging in a loop on one side. All five feet five inches of her looked exhausted, aging her beyond her thirty-five years. Her long brown hair hung limply down her back. She had run her hands through it so many times during the day it was now tangled and mussed. Swollen red lids from the tears she had shed surrounded her green eyes. Her skin was paler than usual. She had inherited porcelain white skin from her father's side of the family. Right now her skin looked ashen.

She was wearing her favorite sweatshirt and sweatpants. They were dark blue to match her mood. Nana had hated them. She'd said they hid Antonia's lovely feminine figure because they were large and sloppy.

"Antonia, child, why do you wear such things? You are so beautiful, yet you hide yourself behind such large clothing. Why?" She'd lost count of the times Nana had repeated those exact words. Nana never failed to remind her that Toni's great grandmother, Natalia Ivanova had once been a confidante of the Grand Duchess Olga, daughter of Tsar Nicholas II of Russia. She would never have approved of Toni's 1990's casual attire. After all, Natalia had instilled an impeccable sense of appearance in Anna, who had in turn instilled that same haute couture in her daughter Ashley. Ashley would have wanted to pass this tradition on to Toni, and Anna had tried, but had failed miserably.

One tradition had been successfully passed down to Toni. All DeWitt women had names beginning with the letter "A". Toni had always tried to think of names that began with "A" for her daughter whenever she had one. Nana would have insisted on it. But now Nana was gone. Toni had lost her parents Ashley and Randolph Stanton in a car accident twenty-six years ago. Would there be anybody left to care whether or not she gave her daughter a name that began with an "A"?

Toni shook her head, not wanting to deal with any more sad memories tonight. She desperately wanted to lose herself in a warm bath, and soak away the stress. She knew this was the first day of a long road she'd have to travel alone. Her only remaining relatives were her uncle and aunt, living in Monte Carlo, and a cousin in Las Vegas. They would lend little support from their faraway homes. Not being a people-person, Toni hadn't forged the close friendships a woman her age might otherwise have. She didn't even have a boyfriend. She was truly alone, and not looking forward to what the next few weeks would bring.

Toni dragged herself up the stairs to her grandmother's apartment. She'd decided to stay the night here because she didn't trust herself behind the wheel of her car.

After her bath, she lay in Anna's bed with the flannel sheets and quilt pulled up to her chin. The bed held so many memories. After her parents' untimely death, Nana would cuddle with her in this bed when the nightmares wouldn't go away. Nana would regale her with stories of family members she had never met. Toni allowed herself to remember the stories about her great grandmother, Natalia Ivanova.

Comforted, she began to doze off, thinking about Natalia's life in Russia.

PART I

CHAPTER 1

Petrograd, Russia
January, 1917

Natalia Ivanova Gubina Simonova rubbed the back of her neck with both hands. She tried rotating her neck a couple of times in both directions. Nothing was helping the stiffness she was feeling. She desperately wanted to lie down. To close her eyes for a few hours and forget the horrors she saw everyday. Rest was not an option right now. She leaned her head on the frame of the doorway she was standing in, hoping not to hear the sound of the metal wheels clanging on the road. The sound always brought a lump to her throat because it signaled the arrival of more wounded soldiers.

Although her shift as a surgical nurse had officially ended twenty minutes ago, Natalia had been given extra work to do. The rumors that the Empress and the Grand Duchesses were coming to work at the hospital as surgery assistants had been confirmed.

Natalia needed to help the other nurses make Petrograd Hospital more presentable for the arrival of the Empress Alexandra and her two older daughters, The Grand

Duchesses Olga and Tatiana. The war had forced everyone into action, even the Imperial family.

Natalia knew that the Empress had built some hospitals with her own money, but she still had some misgivings about members of the Imperial family knowing how to treat wounded soldiers. She was excited about meeting royalty for the first time, yet apprehensive about their ability to perform adequately. Was this the Empress' way of regaining support from the Russian people or was she truly trying to help?

Natalia had always wanted to be a nurse. She enjoyed helping others and was brimming with excitement when, at eighteen, she began working at the local clinic of her hometown. It was run by the devastatingly handsome Anton Antonovich Simonov, a twenty-four year old doctor who wanted to escape the hustle and bustle of a big city hospital by opening a small clinic in a small town.

For two years, under Anton's tutelage she learned how to stitch up and dress open wounds, dispense proper medication, and comfort those who were in pain. Anton valued her ability to anticipate his needs during difficult surgeries as well as her ability to nurse the patients once the surgery was over. She and Anton had worked so closely together that it was only natural for them to develop a personal relationship as well.

They were making wedding plans when the call came from Petrograd Hospital. The hospital was in dire need of doctors and surgical nurses. The "Great War" that had begun two years ago in 1914, had taken its toll on the larger hospitals of Russia. Wounded soldiers were pouring in from all over the country. Large city hospitals became severely understaffed and began sending messages out to all the smaller hospitals, local clinics, and even medical schools begging for extra workers. Anton and Natalia could not ignore the call. They felt it was their duty to go to Petrograd to work at the hospital there.

They were married the very next morning and by nightfall were on a train to Petrograd. They took up residence in one of the small apartments given to doctors by the administrators of Petrograd Hospital.

That was three months ago. Although neither Natalia nor Anton regretted their decision to help, they were both overwhelmed by the demands made on their time and bodies by the constant influx of wounded men. The work was hard and exhausting. There was little time for meals and even less for rest. All day and long into the night, injured men were brought in for medical treatment or surgery. Some were lying on stretchers moaning in unrelieved pain. Others, less serious were sitting on cots waiting to be triaged. Army medics on the frontlines had bandaged some of the men the best they could and then moved them onto the carts to be transported to area hospitals.

As one of the surgical nurses, it was Natalia's duty to assess each man's condition and identify which were surgical candidates. Only those men who had a chance to survive were taken into surgery. The ones who were morbidly wounded and unlikely to survive surgery were made as comfortable as possible. These unfortunate men would probably die soon. Supplies, drugs, anesthesia, and medical equipment were in short supply. But it seemed there was no shortage of wounded soldiers.

Days began to blend in with nights. To most of the other nurses, the faces of the wounded soldiers became a blur. Their names were no longer relevant. They became the amputee in Bed 6, the blinded young one, and the one dying in Bed 3. But, to Natalia they were like members of a family to her. She cared for them with a compassion few had seen before. She had become one of the favorite nurses at Petrograd Hospital. Many dying men asked her to hold their hands as they closed their eyes for the last time. And she did, smiling stoically, trying desperately not to cry as the hand in hers went limp.

A voice spoke to her as if from far away. "Nurse Ivanova, are you alright?"

Natalia woke with a start. She had actually fallen asleep standing up. One of the junior nurses, Valentina Petrovna, was standing in front of her with a concerned look on her face.

"Yes, yes. I was just resting my head for a moment. Is there much left to do to prepare the surgical unit for the Empress' visit?" Natalia asked, hoping the answer was no.

She was in luck. "Not much, Nurse. The operating room is being tidied and then I am going to mop the floor. The ward looks as good as it is going to. But we are having trouble with the soldiers who are waiting in the hallway. We simply have nowhere to put them," Valentina replied.

"I will see what I can do, Valentina."

"Thank you, Nurse Ivanova. Have a good afternoon." Valentina walked through the doorway on which Natalia had fallen asleep on and disappeared into the broom closet, no doubt looking for a mop and bucket.

Natalia readjusted the nurse's cap she wore on her head. It sat just so on the bun she always pulled her long brown hair into when she was working. She ran her hands down the starched white uniform covering her small figure. She opened and closed her green eyes a few times to moisten them. Then she rotated her neck twice and forced herself to focus on what she needed to do.

The surgical unit she and Anton worked in was located on the second floor of the hospital, and consisted of an operating room, a ward, and a lounge. She had fallen asleep in the doorway that led to the lounge. It had been furnished with a dining table surrounded by chairs. There were also three sofas in the room placed there for those who wished to rest. Needless to say they had not been used very much recently. Next to her was the small broom closet and next to that was the staircase. On the other side of the stairs was the operating room. It had rows of tables where doctors and surgical nurses worked over the wounded soldiers. There was no privacy, no dividers. Everyone was in one big room. Lighting had been brought in and lamps were hung from the ceiling to light each area where an operation was performed. Across the hallway was the ward, which took up the entire length of the second floor. After surgery, the men were placed there in beds, lined up in rows.

Natalia headed towards the soldiers Valentina had spoken of. There were five of them near the stairs talking softy amongst themselves. Two of them were sitting on the top step smoking. The other three were leaning against the wall. All of them had torn and bloody uniforms. These were the soldiers who were not seriously injured, and did not require a bed. Most of them would be returning to the frontlines as soon as they were attended to.

As Natalia neared them, she saw Anton leave the operating room and head for the soldiers too. Their eyes caught for a moment. Anton smiled and Natalia's heart did that funny little pitter-patter it always did whenever she saw her husband. Valentina exited the broom closet at that moment carrying a mop and bucket, breaking the spell. She gave Natalia a sigh and made her way towards the operating room. Natalia followed her and stopped when she reached the soldiers. Anton, clad in a white lab coat, joined them.

"Natushka, is there nowhere to put these men? The Empress will be arriving at any moment," Anton said.

"There are no available beds or even chairs in the ward," Natalia replied. "We can put them in the lounge until they can be looked after."

One of the seated soldiers looked up at her with an arched eyebrow. "A lounge? Do they serve Vodka?" The others laughed. So did Natalia and Anton.

"No, but it is a lot more comfortable than this staircase," she replied. "This way please."

Anton stopped her. "I don't think the Empress will appreciate having patients in the lounge. What if she wishes to retire there?" he questioned.

"Anton, the Empress and the Grand Duchesses are here to work. They have been going from hospital to hospital working as surgical nurses since the war began. I do not think they will be retiring anywhere at any time. They are compassionate women. They will understand our need to put the lounge to good use. I am sure of it."

"Very well. Gentlemen, if you would follow Nurse Ivanova, please."

The soldiers moved wearily away from the stairs and followed Natalia into the lounge. The two smokers sat at the table while the other three plopped down on the sofas.

"We shall return to make your injuries more comfortable shortly," Anton said.

"Take your time," one of the soldiers on a couch said. "They are quite comfortable at the moment."

Natalia and Anton walked out of the lounge together leaving the laughing soldiers behind them.

"At least they can still laugh," Natalia said.

"They are the lucky ones," Anton sighed. "They will be back in the action soon. The poor men lying in those beds in the ward are the unlucky ones."

"Those in the lounge may end up in a bed in the ward soon enough."

"Natushka, one day I will take you away from all of this. I promise."

"I will hold you to that promise. However, now we must prepare ourselves for the Empress' arrival," Natalia responded as she linked her arm through his and led him towards the ward. They did not make it beyond the staircase.

"They've arrived. The Imperials have arrived!" Voices resonated up the stairs and echoed through the halls.

Valentina came scurrying out of the operating room carrying the mop and bucket she had been using. "I can hardly breathe. The Empress and the Grand Duchesses. Here!"

Within seconds the hallway filled with the other nurses and doctors who worked in the surgical unit. For a few minutes a mild panic ensued. The once professional medical personnel, who had spent countless hours saving lives and limbs, were star struck. They all began talking excitedly at the same time.

"Everyone, everyone," Anton yelled, "Please, settle yourselves. Our visitors will be ascending these stairs momentarily. It would not do for them to find us gathered in the hallway while our patients are lying in their beds unattended. Nurse Petrovna, dispose of the mop and bucket immediately. Everyone else return to your posts." Their sanity restored, the gatherers scattered to follow Anton's orders. Natalia gave her husband a quick kiss and entered the ward. She looked up and down the rows of beds occupied by soldiers. Some of the men were asleep, others were reading, still others were staring into space. Nurses walked back and forth stopping occasionally to tuck in a sheet here, fluff a pillow there. A sense of serenity had descended on the ward.

Natalia had received word that the Imperials did not expect a formal reception. They wanted to enter the hospital and find everyone going about their daily tasks. *The Empress will be satisfied*, Natalia thought.

Almost as if she had summoned her with her thoughts, the Empress entered the ward. Immediately, Natalia was struck by a sense of something so much larger than herself. She was in the presence of royalty. Tsar Nicholas the Second's wife was a beautiful woman. Her long brown hair had been gathered at the top of her head in a soft bun. Her facial features were soft and delicate. She was of average height and weight. Natalia was surprised to see the Empress clad in a nurse's uniform much like the one she had on. She was devoid of jewels and adornments. Clearly, the Tsarina Alexandra was here to work. Natalia's feet seemed rooted to the ground. She could neither move nor speak.

The Empress broke the ice. She stepped forward and extended her right hand. "Nurse, it is a pleasure to make your acquaintance."

Natalia found her voice. "Your Majesty, the pleasure is all mine. My name is Natalia Ivanova. I am the head nurse of this surgical unit," she said as she took the Empress' hand and curtsied.

"Allow me to present my two elder daughters, Princess Olga and Princess Tatiana," Empress Alexandra said as she gestured behind her to where her daughters were standing.

Tatiana smiled and stepped forward first. She was about the same age as Natalia and breathtakingly beautiful. Natalia had seen many photographs of the Grand Duchess. The black and white images paled in comparison to the real thing.

Tatiana's hair was a rich dark brown, which contrasted well with her flawless porcelain skin. Her gray eyes sparkled beneath dark lashes. Like her mother she too was wearing a nurse's uniform. She was rather thin, but her posture was unmistakably regal.

Tatiana extended her right hand. "Pleased to meet you, Nurse Ivanova. I am honored to be working with you for the next month."

"It is I who am honored, Your Highness. And please call me Natalia," Natalia said, curtseying again.

"Only if you call me Tatiana. Our work here leaves little room for formalities." She turned her attention to her sister. "This is my older sister, Olga."

Grand Duchess Olga stepped forward with her right hand outstretched. She too was dressed in a nurse's uniform. Like her sister, her movements were graceful and delicate, most definitely those of a princess. Unlike her sister, however, Olga Nicolaievna's hair was a dark blonde and her eyes were a striking blue. She was not as beautiful as Tatiana, but she was certainly appealing to look at.

Natalie curtsied a third time. "Pleased to meet you, Highness."

"Olga. And it's good to meet you."

She's rather willowy this one, Natalia thought. *I wonder if she will be able to handle the amount of hard work that will be required of her.*

"We have arranged a tour of the surgical wing for you, if you are not too tired," she said out loud.

Tsarina Alexandra answered for all of them. "No, we are quite looking forward to a tour."

"If you will come right this way, I will…" Natalia did not get the chance to finish her sentence. The distinct sound of the metal wheels clanging on the road below stopped her.

More wounded soldiers were being brought in. The ward seemed to come alive. Doctors and nurses sprang into action. Raised voices sounded from the street, the hospital hallways, everywhere. Natalia was unsure of how to proceed. She wanted to run to the operating room and join Anton in surgery, yet she could not leave her Imperial visitors standing in the ward.

Alexandra solved the problem for her. She turned to her daughters. "Olga, Tatiana, we have work to do. Natalia, we will follow you to the operating room and prepare for the arrival of the wounded."

CHAPTER 2

Petrograd, Russia
February, 1917

To Natalia, a month for the Imperials to work at Petrograd Hospital had seemed like a long time. But, as the days turned into weeks, the month was almost over before she knew it. After the initial awe had worn off and the Empress Alexandra and Grand Duchesses Olga and Tatiana had worked side by side with the staff everyday, no one gave another thought to their Imperial status. They were just three more of the medical team.

Natalia and Olga, the elder of the two Grand Duchesses, had quickly formed a bond of friendship. If someone of Natalia's position could be a friend to a Duchess, she surely was. Few knew the true Olga, a compassionate and kind-hearted person. Her friends were not part of Imperial circles, yet they were very important to her. She valued their support and often used them to keep her connected to the world outside the palace.

To others, Olga was a stubborn and strong-willed young lady. She was impatient and her bad temper had a tendency to flare and cause her to be curt. At times she was unaware of the hurtful nature of her words. Most of the other surgical nurses quickly learned to give her a wide berth. They seldom invited her to socialize with them for fear of saying or doing the wrong thing and upsetting her. They preferred to spend their time with the more congenial Tatiana.

Natalia knew differently. She had managed to break through the façade by simply being patient and kind towards the Grand Duchess. Olga in turn began to confide in Natalia. Whenever there was a break from patients, they could be found chatting in the hallway outside the ward or operatory.

The newspapers were full of stories about the insensitive Imperial Family. Reports of the excessiveness of the Imperial Family during a time when the Russian people were starving, painted an unpleasant picture of them. Natalia would see the look on Olga's face whenever she read one of these reports. The pain in Olga's eyes would move Natalia to lay a gentle hand on her shoulder to offer comfort to her friend. She knew it could not be easy to read such stories about Tsar Nicholas. It was well known that Olga adored her father and missed him terribly since the family hadn't been together in months. Natalia knew that Olga was worried that her family was in grave danger. She often told Natalia she feared for their lives. All Natalia could do was listen and be there for her friend. It was these qualities that made her invaluable to Olga.

On Wednesday of the fourth week, Alexandra announced that she and the Duchesses would be leaving Petrograd Hospital at the end of the week.

Natalia hadn't realized how attached she had become to Olga until she heard the Empress say they were leaving. She confided in Anton that night that she was saddened by Olga's impending departure. Even though it had only been a month since they had met, their relationship had developed into a closeness she hadn't expected. They had come to depend on each other to help get through the miseries they saw everyday. Anton was a gentle compassionate man and when he saw how upset his Natushka was, he took her in his arms and held her to comfort her.

The day before the Imperials were to leave, Olga pulled Natalia into the broom closet and whispered, "Natalia, there is something I must do before we leave. Something very important. May I come to your apartment this afternoon? I know Anton has to meet with the hospital administrators at three o'clock. Will you be free then?"

"You are being so secretive, Olga, you're scaring me."

"I'm sorry, I can't say more now. Can we meet later? We leave tomorrow and I must see you alone," Olga insisted.

"Yes, I can meet you at our apartment by four o'clock," Natalia said, giving herself an hour to walk home and make sure the apartment was presentable.

Olga nodded and left the broom closet without another word. Natalia remained in the closet trying to digest this turn of events for a few thoughtful moments.

At three o'clock Natalia found Anton and explained she had to go home for a while. She told him she would see him later, gave him a quick kiss and hurried out of the hospital.

Walking home, Natalia pulled her coat tightly around her uniform to protect herself from the cold wintry February afternoon. She couldn't help wondering why Olga would want to meet her at home privately. What could be that important or private?

The small second floor apartment that she and Anton had been assigned was plain but neat with all the essentials. Natalia knew it was not meant for entertaining Imperials and it wouldn't be as grand as the palace that Olga called home.

The wooden floor was bare and there was only one window in the sitting room. Pale cotton curtains hung on a thin metal rod at the top of the window frame. Natalia had not had time to make new ones since their arrival and long hours at the hospital. A divider screen separated the sitting room from the sleeping area. There was a small mahogany writing table with a straight back chair and a floor lamp nearby. The sofa was next to the wall and a matching chair, which Anton found comfortable and had adopted after a hard days work, was across from it. Behind the screen was a sturdy iron bed with a firm but comfortable mattress. A night table with a bronze lamp provided light for late night reading. A marble-topped washstand and a two-door wardrobe completed the bedroom furniture. There was no bathroom in the apartment. Anton and Natalia shared a common lavatory down the hall with other medical staff.

Natalia hurried around the apartment to straighten up before Olga's arrival. Not long after she was satisfied with the way the apartment looked, she heard a light tap on the door and knew it would be Olga.

Opening the door Natalia was taken aback to see a figure standing there wearing a black cloak with the hood pulled up over the head. It was obvious the cloak was meant to disguise the wearer's identity. She breathed a sigh of relief when the figure removed the hood to reveal Olga Romanova.

Natalia greeted Olga more formally than usual, "Your Highness, please come in."

"Thank you, Natalia, it is very cold outside."

"It's not too much warmer in here I'm afraid. The building is not kept very warm. Please, sit down."

Olga selected Anton's chair but did not remove her coat since she was still chilled from the walk. Natalia sat across from her on the sofa.

"I hope you didn't come here alone?" Natalia asked.

"Yes. What of it?" Olga answered with a shrug.

"Olga, we are a country at war. You, a member of the Royal family, have no business walking the streets alone. After all, what if one of your father's enemies were to see you. You could have been hurt, or worse," Natalia reprimanded her.

"Oh, pooh, pooh. I am a master at sneaking out of the house. I've been doing it for years now. Besides, who can tell who I am in this cloak?"

"Dear Olga. Always so impulsive."

Olga chose to ignore Natalia's rebuke. "Natalia, I'm going to come right to the reason for my visit. The Empress is very concerned about the lack of adequate medical supplies here at Petrograd Hospital in view of the influx of wounded soldiers," Olga said.

"Yes, we are aware that we need more supplies and medicines. All of the doctors and nurses have discussed the situation many times, but there is not enough money and, even if we had money, there are shortages because of the war," Natalia replied.

"I have decided to give you some pieces of jewelry that you can sell so you can purchase supplies for the hospital," Olga said.

"Olga, stop. I can't possibly take jewelry from you. What would I do with it? How would I sell it?" Natalia said.

"I want you to have it. I am in the habit of giving what I can when I can to help those in need. I have done it many times in the past. I value your friendship greatly and I trust you. With the revolution and the war we don't know what will happen to our family or our fortunes. Things are very uncertain these days, and we haven't heard from my father for a long time. Please take these and use them to buy what you can for the hospital," Olga pleaded.

Olga lifted the hem of her dress and Natalia could see it contained something heavy. As Olga removed the thread that held up the hem, Natalia gasped. The matching set of jewelry that Olga revealed was breathtaking. In her hands she held magnificent earrings, a necklace, and a bracelet. The necklace was made of small, flat, rectangular gold links that were covered with diamonds, and had a pendant attached in the center. The teardrop emerald in the pendant was the size of her thumb, and was encircled by diamonds. It was attached to the necklace by a gold-rimmed accent piece encrusted with diamonds. The emerald earrings matched the pendant in every way except they were a smaller carat. The bracelet mirrored the style of the necklace, but had no emeralds in it.

"Olga, this is the most beautiful jewelry I've ever seen. I can't take these," Natalia said.

"My father had them made for me for my sixteenth birthday. They are the most precious of my jewelry. I cannot think of a more worthy person or place to give them to. You must take them. They are of no use to me now. I would hate to see them fall into the wrong hands. I would rather you sell them for supplies than have the Duma take them." She held them out for Natalia to take.

Natalia gingerly took the four pieces and stared at them in disbelief. She was actually holding jewelry that belonged to the Imperial Family. Olga closed Natalia's hands around the jewelry, keeping her own hands wrapped around her friend's. Tears welled up in Natalia's eyes, as she looked up at Olga. From somewhere deep in their hearts, they both knew this would be the last time their paths would cross. Neither spoke nor moved their hands. They both leaned forward, drawing their foreheads closer until they touched gently. It was a moment Natalia would never forget.

Two weeks later, on March 15th, 1917, Tsar Nicholas II was forced to abdicate the throne. The next day all of the Imperial family was arrested including Alexandra, Olga, and Tatiana. They were being held prisoner by the transitional government that had signed the Treaty of Brest-Litovsk pulling Russia out of the war. The Imperials were moved from one secure location to another until they ended up in a secluded cabin in Ekaterinburg a year later.

Even though Olga had wanted Natalia to use the money from selling the jewelry for the hospital, Anton convinced Natalia it was too dangerous for her to be caught selling it. They too could be arrested as sympathizers of the Imperial Family. The situation in Russia was so bad now that Russians were flocking to Paris and Belgium to escape the tyranny. They were taking their fortunes in jewels with them. These fabulous treasures, family heirlooms of many generations would be sold to ensure their lifestyle in Europe.

One day, Anton said to Natalia as they were sitting in their little apartment, "Natalia, do you remember I promised to take you away one day from all of this?"

"Yes."

"Well, my Natushka, I think now is that time. I have secured passage for us through Belgium to America. Take all that is important to you, for we will not be returning to this country ever again."

As Natalia began packing, she wondered how she was going to get the jewelry out of Russia. She remembered how Olga had carried it into the apartment. Natalia sewed the necklace, earrings, and bracelet into the hem of the dress she wore when she left their apartment for the last time.

On July 17th, 1918, at breakfast, Anton quietly passed The *Covington Chronicle* to Natalia. He watched the tears spill down her face as she read that the Romanovs: Tsar Nicholas, Tsarina Alexandra, Tsaritsas Olga, Tatiana, Maria, Anastasia, and Tsarevich Alexei were led into a room where Bolshevik Secret Police opened fire, and murdered them all. Nicholas and Alexei died instantly. It took longer for the Empress and the Grand Duchesses to die because the bullets seemed to bounce off them. Once they were dead it was revealed that they had sewn all their jewelry into the seams of their dresses.

CHAPTER 3

Moscow, Russia
October, 1992

The big heavy door clanged shut, leaving the older, portly man dressed in a black overcoat alone surrounded by volumes of books and dust. The sound of the museum curator's footsteps receded into nothingness. Only a deafening silence remained in the musty basement.

Boris Mikhailovich Rashovsky tried to take in a deep breath and ended up coughing instead. The dust, combined with the dampness, did nothing for his asthma. *What am I doing here?* He thought. *I am a professor of history, not a detective.* Rashovsky knew he was really the only man for this job. He just wasn't pleased with having to spend yet another day in the basement of the Museum of Moscow to sift through piles of old documents looking for lost treasures. Resigned to his mission, Rashovsky unbuttoned his overcoat, and taking the only chair at the large library table, set to work.

It was almost a year ago today, when the Communist government in the Soviet Union crumbled. Rashovsky, a well-respected professor at the University of Moscow, had a fascination with the overthrow of the Romanovs by the Reds. He spent much of his spare time researching their lives; using whatever limited information the Communist government doled out to him. Rashovsky had befriended the museum's curator, Ivan, in the hopes that the latter would allow him access to documents hidden from the public. He knew the museum's basement housed many secrets in the form of letters, diaries, photographs, etc., that the Communist regime felt necessary to hide. Rashovsky hoped Ivan would throw caution to the wind, and entrust him with the secrets locked in the vaults under the museum. He was wrong. Ivan was intimidated by the prospect of imprisonment if it were discovered that he opened the vaults without orders, and therefore refused to allow Rashovsky into the basement. Now that the Communists were gone, Ivan capitulated.

Rashovsky was thrilled at first. He hoped to capitalize on his findings, by selling them to Western magazines and newspapers that were hungry for any new information on Russian history. Once again, Ivan foiled his plans. The snively curator had told the museum's owners what Rashovsky's plans were, and they, believing it was a brilliant idea to bring more revenues to the museum, made it public that Rashovsky was working for *them*. He was officially commissioned to bring back all treasures of the Romanov dynasty that had been scattered around the world.

Rashovsky was on his eighth day of research. He had already gone through a number of the volumes. This morning, he had chosen to tackle one of the boxes that contained an assortment of papers and envelopes. Upon further inspection, Rashovsky ascertained that this particular box held the letters written by the soldiers who had guarded the Imperial Family when they were imprisoned at Ekaterinburg. It wasn't very clear to Rashovsky whether these letters had actually been mailed, or if the regime had kept them from reaching their destinations. It was apparent from the letters that the soldiers had befriended the Grand Duchesses. Many of the young men's letters painted a different picture of the Imperial Family than the one portrayed in the press. In fact, some letters clearly showed disapproval of the imprisonment of the Duchesses.

Rashovsky rubbed his eyes. The dim light in the basement was forcing him to squint, bringing on a headache. He decided to read one more letter, and then call it a day. He reached deep into the box, and pulled out an unopened envelope. The letter was addressed to a Mr. and Mrs. Patroskova in Kiev. Carefully lifting the flap, Rashovsky removed the pages for the first time since the writer had inserted them almost eight decades ago.

The letter, written by a soldier named Sergei, told of a blossoming friendship between Tsaritsa Olga and him. Sergei fancied himself in love, and was relating to his parents the long conversations he and Olga had shared. The majority of the letter was filled with the fanciful writings of a man enamored with a princess he would otherwise have never met. He recounted almost verbatim the things she told him. Rashovsky was about to toss the letter back into the box, when the word "jewelry" jumped out at him.

Skipping down to the paragraph containing that word, Rashovsky read on, his bushy eyebrows arching, his eyes widening in surprise. Sergei was trying to show his family that Olga was not the spoiled rich princess everyone thought she was. He related stories of her generosity towards him and the other soldiers. 'She even went as far as giving the jewelry she had received for her birthday to a nurse at Petrograd Hospital to sell in exchange for much needed supplies.'

Putting the letter down, Rashovsky smiled to himself. He had finally found something to go on. The wheels in his head began to churn. Rashovsky thought that if he could find these jewels, and return them to Moscow, he would be recognized as a hero. His employers would then see the need to hire more people to look through the archives in this basement, rather than one lone man. *He* would be put in charge of this research team, and *he* would reap the benefits of their laboring over these books and boxes.

Boris Rashovsky alighted from the car he had hired to drive him to Petrograd Hospital. He stood on the cobbled driveway of the hospital's main entrance and looked up at the four-story building. The sky was a brilliant blue, unusual for this time of year. Pulling his overcoat tighter around his ample waist, he headed towards the double glass doors. His walking stick clicked on the stairs as he ascended them. The doors swooshed open, revealing a circular waiting room, at the end of which sat a security guard behind a long counter.

After identifying himself and the reason for his visit, he was asked to sign in. He was then directed to one of the inner offices to meet with the administrator he had an appointment with. Rashovsky had waited two long days for this meeting, and was anxious to see what information, if any, the administrator had uncovered.

"Thank you for agreeing to meet with me, Mr. Karinsky," Rashovsky began, after shaking hands and sitting down. "As I mentioned on the telephone, I am researching the whereabouts of an old friend of my mother's who had once worked for this hospital during the First World War."

"Mr. Rashovsky, you are a lucky man. As I stated in our telephone conversation, employee records are rarely kept for this length of time. I was doubtful I would be able to find anything dating back to the early 1900s. Essentially I was correct. I didn't find anything, except one file from 1917. It seems my predecessors had kept this file because of its historical significance. That was the year the women of the Imperial Family worked here."

Rashovsky could barely contain his excitement. He wanted to leap across the desk and kiss Karinsky. Instead he said, "I appreciate your dedication to my request. Although I am not sure this file is useful, I would like to inspect it. If there is anything useful, I will make copies for myself."

"I am afraid I cannot let you do that. The documents are old and I fear the photocopying process may damage them. However, you are more than welcome to make notes. I am also requesting you do your inspecting in this office."

"I understand completely. May I see the file?"

The file contained lists of surgeries performed by various surgeons, and any nurses in attendance. Rashovsky noted that on many occasions the nurses in attendance were members of the Imperial Family. He carefully jotted down the names of the doctors and nurses in a notepad, making sure to spell all the names correctly.

Pushing the file back across the desk, Rashovsky stood, thanked Karinsky, and returned to the car that was waiting for him. He directed the driver to take him to a nearby hotel where he had secured a room.

Sitting in his hotel room, Boris Rashovsky shifted the receiver from one ear to the other as he waited for someone to pick up the phone on the other end of the line. Last week, when he had left Petrograd Hospital, he had been elated. He was positive one of the names on his list would yield useful information. Less than elated today, after more than a dozen phone calls that were nothing but dead ends, he impatiently tapped the end of his pencil on the table.

Having used his connections through the University and the Museum, Rashovsky had obtained the names and telephone numbers for just about all the remaining family members of the people on his list. Luck had been on his side because many of the hospital's employees had stayed in the Petrograd area after the war. Unfortunately, they were all dead, and, so far, their descendants knew nothing that would further his research.

Still hearing the ringing of the phone, and thinking about the events of the past few weeks, brought on more frustration than he had felt back in the museum's basement. Rashovsky cradled the receiver on his shoulder, and grasped the pencil in both hands with such force that it snapped in half. Startled, Rashovsky sat up quickly. The receiver slipped off his shoulder, clattered on the table and dangled towards the floor. Cursing, he grabbed the receiver just as a woman's voice finally came on the line.

Regaining his composure, Rashovsky reverted to his suave manner. "May I speak to Katrina Lipova, please?"

"Speaking. Who is calling, please?"

"Allow me to introduce myself. My name is Boris Rashovsky. I am a professor at the University of Moscow, conducting research on the nurses who served our country during the First World War. Your mother's name was given to me as one who may have worked at Petrograd Hospital at that time. Am I correct?"

After a short pause, Katrina answered with a hesitant, 'yes.'

"Let me assure you that my work is legitimate. I have been commissioned by the Museum of Moscow to find any and all information that would lead to the recovery of the

Romanov fortune. I am in the process of speaking to the family members of any one who had worked in Petrograd Hospital and may have come in contact with the Imperial Family."

"Mr. Rashovsky, my mother, Valentina Petrovna, did indeed work at that hospital. However, neither she nor I would have any knowledge of the whereabouts of the Romanov fortune."

"Miss Lipova, I wouldn't expect you to know where the fortune is. I would just like to ask you to recount for me any stories your mother may have shared with you about her experiences. This may help me find the next piece of the puzzle that may ultimately lead to the recovery of the fortune. There may even be some compensation for you, if your information is useful." Rashovsky knew that was a lie however, he hoped it would provide an incentive for her.

He was rewarded with a twenty-minute rhetoric about the struggles Valentina Petrovna had faced, the honor of having worked with the Imperials, and the conditions in the hospital in general. Rashovsky scribbled furiously on his notepad as he listened to Katrina Lipova. This woman had been able to provide him with more information than all the other relatives combined.

The most intriguing piece of information dealt with the head nurse, Natalia Ivanova, and Grand Duchess Olga. Apparently, they had become very close friends, often sharing quiet conversations during coffee breaks in the lounge area. Valentina had commented that they looked like two young school girls when they were together, which made quite an impression on her since she was younger than both of them.

After their goodbyes, Rashovsky noted that he did not have any information for Natalia Ivanova. She was one of the employees that his contacts had been unable to trace. Along with her husband Anton, she seemed to have vanished into thin air. Rashovsky was undaunted. He knew from his previous research that many wealthier Russians had fled the country illegally and made their way to Belgium. There they had obtained documents for travel to the United States.

Rashovsky had a few more names to call, but he decided to call his friend Desmond Todd at Columbia University instead. Desmond would help him gain any available information from the Ellis Island archives about the Simonovs.

The following week, a large brown envelope appeared in Rashovsky's mailbox at the University. Holding the envelope close to his chest, Rashovsky rode the small faculty elevator up to the fourth floor, where his office was located. He knew from the return address that it was from Desmond Todd and probably contained information about the Simonovs. And not a moment too soon. As he unlocked the door to his office, Rashovsky recalled the telephone conversation he'd had with one of the Museum's owners yesterday. Actually, the conversation was rather one-sided. The owner was reprimanding Rashovsky because he hadn't gotten anywhere and hadn't recovered anything and was wasting time and money, blah, blah, blah. Rashovsky was perturbed to say the least. Hanging up his coat, Rashovsky sat at his large desk, tore open the envelope with more force than necessary, and poured its contents onto his blotter.

Spread out on his desk were a list that looked like it came from Ellis Island, a handwritten letter, and some copies of newspaper stories. Rashovsky was disappointed. He was expecting more. Pushing back his chair, he stood with his hands in the pockets of his suit pants, and stared out of his window. It was another bleak October day in Moscow;

unusually windy for this time of year. *It's going to be a harsh winter*, he thought, *in more ways than one.*

Outside, students and faculty were rushing from building to building with their shoulders hunched up burying their faces into their scarves. The trees were bare, having lost their leaves weeks ago. The grass had turned an ugly brown, and the birds that usually frequented this side of the campus were long gone. Looking up at the overcast sky, Rashovsky cursed the young television meteorologist who had assured Muscovites that the sun would be shining today.

Turning back to his desk, Rashovsky dropped back into his desk chair and rested his chin on his hands. His mood matched the weather outside. Distractedly, he picked up the handwritten letter and began to read it. It was from Todd in New York saying there was little information on the Simonovs. They had arrived at Ellis Island in 1917, settled in Covington, Rhode Island, and had one child, Anna. Todd apologized for not being able to provide any further information, but he did include newspaper articles about their descendants.

Rashovsky looked through the articles, and made notes on what he read.

1917: Anton Simonov and Natalia Ivanova arrive NY
1925: Anna Simonova born
1943: Anna Simonova marries Kurt DeWitt
1945: Ashley DeWitt born
1947: Joel DeWitt born
1963: Ashley DeWitt marries Randolph Stanton
1964: Antonia Stanton born
1965: Joel DeWitt marries Jessica Hayes
1967: Carlton DeWitt born
1972: Kurt DeWitt dies
1973: Ashley and Randolph Stanton die in car accident

Two of the articles came from the local newspaper and included photographs. Rashovsky noted that they were the wedding photos of the DeWitts and the Stantons. Something in both photographs looked familiar to him. Having never seen these people before in his life, Rashovsky studied the photos closely trying to figure out what it was that was gnawing at him. And then it hit him like a Siberian blizzard; the two brides were wearing an identical necklace, and, more intriguing, he had seen it before. Racking his brain, Rashovsky tried to visualize where. He closed his eyes, concentrating.

Seemingly out of nowhere, Olga Romanova's face swam into his mind's eye. Rashovsky's eyes snapped open. He shot out of his chair and retrieved his Romanov research from the bookshelf across the room. Furiously, he began flipping through the pages searching for photographs. With a loud hoot, he found what he was looking for: a photograph of the Imperial Family taken on Tsaritsa Olga's sixteenth birthday. She was wearing a necklace identical to the one worn by Anna and Ashley.

Rashovsky spent the rest of the morning scrutinizing the Simonov and Romanov information. By the time the lunch cart arrived at his door, he had concluded that the jewelry, an emerald and diamond necklace, matching earrings, and diamond bracelet, which once belonged to Olga Romanova, were now in the possession of Anna DeWitt of Covington, Rhode Island.

Boris Rashovsky vowed he would do whatever it takes to return the jewelry to Russia, and effectively secure his financial future.

CHAPTER 4

Las Vegas, Nevada
Sunday, April 4th, 1999

Carlton DeWitt was desperate when he stepped out of the Tropical Casino Sunday morning. A wall of heat blasted him in the face as he walked through the revolving door. It was like a furnace in Las Vegas today, which was unusual for this time of year. His blue silk shirt and beige dress pants were already beginning to cling to his skin as he perspired in the morning heat. It was the day after his birthday, and he had spent Saturday night alone in the cool, dark casino trying to win enough money to cover the fifty thousand dollar gambling note he still owed.

A man wearing a large black cowboy hat jostled Carlton. Glancing back irritably, Carlton recognized him from the Black Jack table. They had been sitting side-by-side for most of the evening, and had even bought each other drinks.

"Sorry 'bout that Partner," the man said tipping his hat.

"Not a problem. I was in the way," Carlton responded.

"I was referrin' to the scene created by the manager at the table," the man continued with a Southern drawl. "Must have been down right embarrassin' bein' asked to leave like that."

Carlton shrugged. "Just a game we play, the manager and me. Keeps the place honest."

The man laughed. He patted Carlton on the back, "Sure thing Partner. Whatever you say." With that the man walked away.

"Damn it!" Carlton cursed. *If only it were really just a game.* To be honest, Max, the manager, hadn't really caused a scene. Managers were trained not to do that. They simply walk over to you and quietly *ask* you to come with them. The two security guards they have with them make it difficult not to comply.

Once away from the table, Max steered Carlton into a tiny private room whose door was hidden from view of the casino floor. "DeWitt, we have a problem," he said motioning for Carlton to sit on the one chair in the room.

"Yeah, Max, I know, I know. I've run into a bit of bad luck tonight. But you know I'm good for it. I've always kept my account up-to-date and always paid back the notes you extend to me. Tonight's no different."

Max, a short portly balding man, leaned against the wall, and crossed his arms. "You bet tonight is different. You're in for a hundred large."

Shit! I spent that much. Carlton knew he had stayed longer than he should have, but he hadn't realized he had stayed *that* long. Out loud he said, "Aw, come on Max. It's my birthday."

"Your birthday was yesterday. It's already Sunday morning, 11 A.M. to be precise."

"Come on. You're going to argue over a few hours. Max, we're friends. Buddies. We go back a long way." Carlton began to worry that their friendship was not worth a hundred thousand dollars.

"Look DeWitt. I like you. You bring a lot of rich women in here to gamble their money away. Unfortunately I'm still the manager, and I kinda like it here. Sorry, but I gotta do what's right for the casino. That's what they pay me the big bucks for."

"You're kidding me. There's nothing you can do." Carlton began fidgeting with the collar of his shirt.

"Like what? You owe this money. You have to pay it back in order to gamble here again." Max reached into the inside pocket of his black suit and pulled out a folded sheet of paper. "Here," he said, handing the paper to Carlton, "sign."

Carlton looked at the paper as if it were a poisonous snake. "What is that?"

"It's a promissory note stating you will pay one hundred thousand dollars within thirty days."

"Thirty days? That's it?"

"Hey, it was the best I could do. My boss wanted to give you two weeks, but I convinced him to make it thirty days. He did it as a favor for one of my best customers. You could always get a job."

"Yeah, and you could hit the Jack Pot. And if I can't get it in thirty days?" Carlton asked raising one eyebrow. When Max didn't answer, Carlton gasped for air. "You're not going to send someone to break my knees, are you?"

"This ain't the Maffia. We'll just have you arrested. Hurry and sign. I gotta get back to work."

Carlton's palms became sweaty and he could feel perspiration dripping down his back. "I don't have a pen," he said dejectedly.

Max produced a pen from his jacket pocket which Carlton used to shakily sign his name. Max then initialed the signature, folded the paper, and returned it to his pocket. "You can leave now DeWitt. See you in thirty days."

As Carlton squinted in the bright sunlight, he knew he was in more trouble than he had ever been in before. He had no idea of how he was going to pay back the money. He knew Max was being serious when he said they'd have him arrested. It wasn't a threat, but a promise.

His weekly stint to the casino supported him well enough that he didn't want a full time job. The money he won went towards his living expenses that were in no way extravagant. In his divorce, his ex-wife was lucky enough to have gotten a judge who had no sympathy for gamblers. The judge ruled in her favor awarding her the house and half of the money they had in the bank, which wasn't much anyway. Carlton had no regular source of income and no family to turn to. He no longer spoke to his parents after they cut off his allowance when he had been expelled from college in 1988, for gambling. Not interested in working for a living, he sold what little he had, and moved to Las Vegas. He considered himself a lucky gambler since he had won easily and often in college. He now realized that, at a casino, the odds were not to be in his favor.

Carlton didn't consider himself to be a ladies' man. He had had his share of women since he'd moved to Vegas, but he was no Don Juan. Six feet tall and slim with chiseled facial features, he could hold his own against most guys. He was well built and sported his clothes as well as any male model. No love handles or beer belly for him. When he wasn't in the casinos, he worked out at a local health club to stay in shape. He always looked like he'd just stepped from the pages of a fashion magazine. Every dark hair in place, clean-shaven and neatly attired, he made sure that his clothes were dry-cleaned and pressed often to make a good impression. When he walked into a casino he didn't want to look like a gambling bum. He was no GQ type but heads did turn when he entered the room. On a good night he could be a force to reckon with. Other gamblers and spectators lined up two and three deep to watch when he was on a winning streak.

Carlton realized he was still standing in the way when several hotel patrons had to walk around him. He was barely outside of the gold trimmed revolving door. The doormen were busy unloading luggage from cars, and people were milling about waiting for the runners to bring their cars from the parking garage. Carlton thought to himself, *I have no idea what I'm going to do to get myself out of this mess.*

He headed away from the crowd that had formed around the front entrance of the hotel, passed the hotel's signature fountain, onto the sidewalk. He walked the short distance to his apartment a few blocks behind the strip. His stomach growled reminding him that hadn't eaten since yesterday afternoon. He hoped Daphne was up and had lunch ready for him. Daphne. Carlton's lip curled into a slight smile. They had met a few weeks ago and clicked. Unfortunately her job as a dealer made it hard for her to enjoy going to casinos on her days off, a recurring source of friction in their relationship.

Carlton took the outside stairs up to his second floor apartment. As he entered the apartment, he almost tripped over the duffle bag sitting by the door. Confused, he called, "Daphne."

"I'm in the bathroom, Carl." Daphne's voice had a strange tone to it. Crossing his small shabby living room, Carlton made his way through the apartment's only bedroom into its only bathroom. The only other room in the place was the hole in the wall kitchen. Stopping in the bathroom doorway, Carlton was surprised to see Daphne, a leggy blonde, throwing cosmetics into a plastic bag. "Cleaning up?" he asked, trying to sound nonchalant.

"More like clearing out," she replied in a monotone.

"What?"

"You heard me." Daphne continued her task without looking up.

"Daphne, what's going on?"

Finally looking up, Daphne placed her hands on her hips. "I've had it, Carl. With your gambling, with your womanizing, your drinking, your unemployment. All I wanted to do last night was go out to a nice dinner to celebrate your birthday and maybe see a movie. You know, something normal couples do. But no, *you* prefer to sit on your ass, drink like a fish and gamble. You're too old to live like this. Look at this place. It's nothing. It's a dump," her voice got louder with each word. "No wonder your ex-wife left you. You walk around like you're the Sultan of Brunei, when you're nothing but a guy from Rhode Island whose own family disowned him."

"Are you finished?" Carlton responded, raising both eyebrows. *Who the hell does this chick think she is?*

"Yes. I am. With you."

"Don't let the door hit you on your ass on your way out." Carlton stomped into the kitchen to get a beer.

"Asshole!" Daphne screeched as she slammed the bathroom door.

Carlton walked out of the jalousie door onto the tiny landing just outside the kitchen. He purposely left the door open so he could hear Daphne leave to avoid another confrontation at all cost, which was his policy. Finishing his beer he aimed for the dumpster that was below him and threw the bottle, lay-up style, into it. He threw up both arms, "Nothing but net!"

Carlton returned to the living room and flopped onto his couch. He was really quite sorry to see Daphne go. He liked her, but he liked gambling better. He knew he'd miss her for a few days, and then move on. Right now he had more pressing matters on his mind. Mainly, how to come up with one hundred grand in the next month.

Looking around the room his eyes fell on the key Daphne had obviously left. She had placed it on top of the mail so he wouldn't miss it. Daphne had been after him to open his mail for days. She hated the fact that he would let it pile up until there was little room left on the coffee table for anything else. Sighing, Carlton felt he owed it to her to go through the pile. There among the usual bills and advertising was a blue envelope postmarked from Rhode Island. It had been forwarded from his last address. He hadn't thought about his grandmother since his last birthday. She was the only member of his family that had faithfully sent him a birthday card every year. *I might have gotten a check this year*, he thought. *Grandmother Anna's getting along in years and she might be feeling sentimental. That would come in handy right about now.*

Tearing open the letter he recognized his grandmother's handwriting on the card. She had written her usual newsy note that brought him up to date on her antique shop and invited him for a visit. *I haven't seen the old lady in such a long time; it would be interesting to see her again.*

It would give me a chance to get out of town for a while and figure out how to cover my gambling debt. Maybe she'll take pity on me and lend me some money. She's well off now and the antique shop is probably doing well. I'll take off in the morning, he reasoned.

Carlton rummaged through his desk to find an envelope and paper so he could mail a note to his grandmother before leaving in the morning. *If I drive straight through and sleep in my car, I should reach Rhode Island in four days. I hope my letter will arrive before I do. That will give me enough time to work out a way to convince Grandmother to loan me some money again. If Grandmother doesn't come through,* he thought, *there's always cousin Antonia.*

CHAPTER 5

Carlton DeWitt sat in his '88 Mustang convertible and stared across the street at *Anna's Attic*. It was only 5:20 P.M. but it was beginning to get dark because rain was on the way. The lights were on inside the antique shop. He could see his grandmother, Anna still talking to a woman he assumed was a customer. They had spent the last ten minutes looking at something Carlton couldn't see. The Victorian couch and the two wing chairs Anna had near the picture window were blocking his view. Quite frankly he didn't care what they were looking at. All Carlton cared about at the moment was getting out of his car and surprising Anna when she was locking up her shop. In all of her birthday letters, Anna had told Carlton that she always closed promptly at 5:30 P.M.

Carlton wrapped his leather jacket around himself more tightly; glad he had thrown it into the backseat at the last minute. It was cold and drafty inside his little ragtop. He had turned off the engine when he had pulled up about twenty minutes ago. Although he didn't want to go into the shop when someone else was there, he was cold and hungry, and his jeans and Polo shirt were doing little to keep him warm. Having driven straight through from the Pennsylvania border to get to Covington before 5:30, he was now desperate to get out of the confines of his little car.

"The hell with it!" Carlton cursed. He flung open the wide door and poured himself out of his car. His back muscles tightened and his legs almost buckled. Four days in a two-door sports car did little for his thirty-something body. Slowly, he began walking, and was halfway across the two-lane street when he saw his grandmother and the woman head towards the front door of the shop. He hesitated a moment debating whether to crouch down behind the nearest car parked on the street. The way his luck had been going so far, the car would probably belong to the woman leaving the shop. *No,* he thought, *the best thing would be to just walk up to Gram and act natural.*

"Thank you again, Anna," he heard the woman say as she paused in the open doorway. "Winston is going to be so happy when the tea table is delivered. He's had his eye on it for a while."

"You're very welcome, Roslyn. I promise it will be delivered the day after you return from your cruise. Winston's a lucky man. A cruise and an antique table for his birthday. You'll have to tell me his reaction when he sees the table. Have a wonderful trip."

"Thank you. I'll be in touch when we return from Europe."

Anna was about to say something when she spotted Carlton walking towards them.

"Carlton! What a pleasant surprise. Roslyn, this is my grandson, Carlton. Carlton, may I introduce one of my best friends, Roslyn Smythe-Burns." Anna was beaming as she introduced them.

Carlton shook Roslyn's hand. He immediately noticed the perfectly coiffed blonde hair, and manicured nails. *She must be in her late sixties*, he thought. The size of the diamonds in her ring as well as the full-length mink coat she was wearing told him she was also filthy rich. "It's a pleasure to meet you," Carlton said, flashing his most charming smile.

"Anna, you never told me your grandson was so handsome. You have two fine looking grandchildren. Carlton, I know your cousin Antonia well, I hope you and I can get to know each other also."

Well, what do you know? If Gram doesn't shell out some dough maybe I can get this rich broad to, Carlton thought slyly.

When Carlton didn't respond Roslyn said, "Winston is waiting for me. Ta ta."

"Carlton come in, come in. Let me look at you. It's been such a long time since we've seen each other. Come here and give your old grandmother a hug."

Carlton pulled away from his grandmother keeping one arm draped around her shoulders, "Gram, I'm starving, can I take my favorite grandmother out for dinner?" Carlton had no intention of taking her anywhere. Knowing his grandmother, he knew she'd offer to cook his favorite meal instead.

"Oh, Carlton, I'm your only grandmother. You're such a charmer, just like your father."

"Must we bring him up so early in our visit?" Carlton chided her.

Anna sighed, "I see some things never change." She paused. "We have so much to catch up on. Let me make us dinner here and you can treat me to dinner out another time. Just give me a minute to lock up and we can go upstairs."

Relieved at not having to spend money he didn't have, Carlton looked around the shop as Anna went through her closing up routine. The antiques in the shop were different than those he remembered, but the layout was still the same, and the prices were more outrageous than ever. He snorted at the price of a four-inch perfume bottle. *Twenty-six hundred dollars for something that can fit in my pocket.* He walked towards the stairs at the back of the shop and hung his jacket on the banister. He fingered the velvet stanchion then unhooked it. The lights in the shop went off around him plunging him into semi-darkness. He turned and saw Anna walking towards him as if she could see in the dark. She obviously knew her way around the shop very well.

Upstairs Anna entered the kitchen and offered Carlton one of the four chairs at the table and a glass of cranberry juice. Carlton thought about asking Anna if she had any vodka to go with the cranberry juice, but decided that wouldn't be a good idea right now. He also decided that revealing the real reason he was here would have to wait. *I shouldn't expose my hidden agenda yet*, he thought. *Gram needs to be lulled into a false sense of security just like every other woman. It's the only way to get what I want out of her.*

She began to prepare the spaghetti dinner she knew was his favorite. *She looks pretty good for being in her seventies*, he thought, as she wrapped an apron around herself to protect the flowered dress she was wearing. *Maybe she goes up the stairs a little more slowly but she's still sharp as a tack mentally. Her hair is grayer and shorter now and she's plumper than I remembered, but she still has that kindly smile and warm sparkling brown eyes.*

Anna pressed a garlic clove through the press and spread it on some bread. As the bread went into the oven, the water in the Dutch oven began to boil, and Anna plopped in the box of angel hair pasta. Spaghetti had always been Carlton's favorite, and his ego inflated a little knowing his grandmother had remembered. The sauce had started to bubble and would be ready when the pasta tested al dente. As they waited for all the food to finish cooking, Anna set the table. She placed a bowl in the center of it that she had filled with mixed salad greens and sprinkled with a grated Parmesan/Romano cheese blend that she also used for the pasta. Carlton couldn't wait to dig in.

As Carlton and Anna ate their salads, Anna told Carlton all the interesting events that had happened since he left Covington. Carlton appeared to listen attentively asking a question here and there to show he was interested in the same things as his grandmother. He even remembered to ask how his cousin Antonia was.

The timer buzzed indicating the pasta was done. Anna began to serve the steaming hot pasta with the thick red sauce spread over it. The little kitchen was filled with the aroma of the garlic bread and sauce. When they both had plates piled high, she sat down to enjoy the meal.

"Carlton, enough about me. Tell me, how have you been holding up since your divorce?" Anna said.

"Oh, Gram, it hasn't been easy being alone. You know Tracy got the house and half our money. It's been difficult just trying to make ends meet."

"Where are you working now?"

Carlton shifted in his seat. "Well, you see, I'm in between jobs at the moment."

Anna pinned him with one of her looks. "Carlton, don't try to put one over on me. I know you don't like working, but I was hoping that after Tracy left you, you would have changed your habits."

"How do you know why Tracy left me?" Carlton asked.

"I can only guess. But, I saw the way she looked at you at your wedding. For her to leave you, it must have been over something she couldn't live with anymore." Anna raised an eyebrow. "Carlton, are you still gambling?"

Oh shit! Now what? Carlton thought.

"I take your silence as a yes." When he still didn't answer, Anna sighed and leaned back in her seat. "Carlton, we all make choices in life. Most of us learn from our mistakes so we don't repeat them. Obviously, this is not the case with you." Anna abruptly scraped her chair back and got up to clear the empty plates.

Carlton could tell she was upset with him. This was not going according to his plan. "Gram, it's been so long since we've seen each other. Let's not argue."

She appeared to soften a little. "Now that you're here, what are your plans for the next few days?" Anna asked as she washed the dinner dishes. There was no dishwasher in the little apartment-sized kitchen and she washed everything by hand.

"I really don't have anything specific planned," he replied.

Would you like to see Antonia?" Anna asked.

"Mmmmm. I don't know. Let me think about it," he said.

"You know she'd love to see you again. She is actually in town for a few days."

"My cousin, the traveling gypsy. Never in one place long enough to connect with anyone. We're not so different, she and I."

Anna stiffened. "Antonia has made a good life for herself."

"Unlike me, you mean?"

"Oh Carl, you live so differently than the rest of your family. We just don't understand the choices you've made. We all wish you'd move back here and settle down. Your parents are willing to let the past go. You're their only son. You cannot imagine how dear you are to them. Especially now..." Anna trailed off.

"What do you mean, especially now?"

"Your mother is ill, Carlton. She's been under the care of a physician, but no one seems to know what's wrong with her."

"Maybe she's the one that should move back here and settle down."

"Young man, you have no right to speak about your mother that way."

The awkward silence that followed made Carlton uncomfortable. "You got anything for dessert?"

"Since we haven't seen each other for so long, I'm going to allow you to change the subject. So, I've made a little coffee cake, would you like it with a cup of coffee or tea?" Anna asked.

"Coffee cake and coffee sound terrific," he answered.

Anna busied herself cutting the cake and preparing the coffee. She sat down at the table as the coffee brewed. This gave Carlton the opportunity to start talking.

"To answer your question, after my divorce, I was feeling pretty low and didn't have much money to get a place to live. I took what money I had and went to one of the casinos in Vegas to try to win some more so I could rent a decent apartment and buy some furniture. I did pretty well that first time and came away with enough to set myself up comfortably, not extravagantly but comfortably. I know you're thinking about my gambling in college and how it got me into trouble. But wait to hear me out before you judge me. I enjoyed being around the casino atmosphere. Everyone was upbeat and running on adrenaline thinking they could be the next big winner. This really helped pull me out of my depression. After a few weeks, I was like a drug addict and needed to go to the casino to get my high even if I didn't gamble. Eventually, I did play cards and I won more than I lost and it was enough to cover rent, food, and other expenses so I didn't bother to look for a job," Carlton explained. He finished the piece of cake on his plate and took a swig of coffee. Anna got up and refilled his cup. That was his second since he had started spilling his guts to his grandmother.

"Carlton, I'm not going to judge you. You live your life how you choose by the choices you make. You're my grandson and I love you. Of course I would like to see you be successful in whatever you do and most importantly I would like you to be happy," Anna said.

"Gram, I haven't told you the worst yet. Right before your card arrived, my luck started to go south and I began to lose more than win. Since I've been a regular at my favorite casino for several years I have a line of credit set up. Over the last few weeks I've used it up and then I borrowed to try to win back enough to cover the balance plus get ahead. It didn't work, and now I'm in the hole even more," he said looking down into his cup.

"Carlton, how much do you owe?" Anna asked.

"You don't wanna know, Gram," he answered.

"Yes I do or I wouldn't have asked," she said forcefully.

Carlton hesitated, *should I tell the truth?* "$100,000," he blurted out.

"Carlton, you owe $100,000 to a casino?" Anna asked in disbelief. "Are you crazy?"

"Calm down, Gram,"

"I don't know what to say. That's a lot of money," she said.

"I know it is. When your card arrived with the invitation to visit you I thought I'd come east to see you and maybe you would help me get out of this mess."

"Again? Carlton, I refused to …"

Carlton interrupted, "Before you go on, there's more. I didn't tell you, I have thirty days to settle the balance or other arrangements will have to be made with the casino."

"What kind of other arrangements?" Anna asked as she squinted at him.

"Use your imagination. What do you think they do with people who owe them money?" He thought, *if I make the situation sound dangerous, she might be more willing to help me.*

"So what are *you* going to do?" Anna asked pointing a finger at him.

"Gram, you havta help me. You have to lend me the money," Carlton whined.

"Carlton, I can't do that. Your grandfather and I worked very hard here and the money I've saved is for my retirement and care. Your grandfather would never forgive me if I gave that money to you to cover a gambling debt. Neither would your parents forgive me if I gave you any money let alone $100,000," Anna said emphatically.

"But Gram, the thirty days will almost be up by the time I get back to Vegas and I have to pay off the note. You've got to help me, I'm broke," he continued to whine and then he surprised himself as well as Anna when he banged his fist on the table in frustration.

"Well, Carlton, you should have thought about that before you got yourself into this mess," she said uncaringly as she got up from the table and went to the sink to clean up the cake dishes and coffee cups. Her kind, warm, smiling eyes had turned cold and unfeeling. Now she remembered who Carlton DeWitt was and how he operated.

"Gram…" he started.

"Carlton," she turned sending a hard look his way. "I think it's time for you to leave. Our visit is over," she said dismissing him.

Carlton wasn't used to being dismissed like this. He could feel his temper begin flare. "Gram, how can you let me leave like this? I drove all the way from Vegas to see you, and this is what I get?" he yelled.

"You and I both know the real reason you came here. You didn't come to visit me. You came to beg for money," she said as she walked out of the kitchen and down the stairs. She could see his jacket hanging at the bottom of the staircase and heard him following her.

"Gram, you're making me very upset. I thought I could count on you. You're my last resort. Now I see that Toni was your favorite and you'd do anything for her but not me. If she asked you for help you'd be right there for her wouldn't you?" He was red faced and the veins on his neck were bulging.

Anna was well into the showroom. She flicked on the lights and swung around to confront him. "Carlton, this has nothing to do with Antonia, this is about *your* gambling and *your* asking me for money that I can't give you." She couldn't disguise the disdain in her voice.

Carlton yanked his jacket off the banister and shoved his arms into it. He stalked towards his grandmother and grabbed her left arm. "Gram, you gotta help me. I only have a few hundred dollars to my name. I'm really broke. Please, you're the only one I can ask."

Anna shook her arm free. "Carlton, you need to leave now," the tremor in her voice was unmistakable. Carlton grabbed Anna by both shoulders. He had to make her understand the severity of his situation. He couldn't face jail time. He'd rather die first. She broke free. "If you grab me one more time, I will call the police." She turned to escort him to the door.

Desperation set in. Carlton grabbed Anna's forearm and twisted her around to face him. She lost her balance and fell against him. Carlton hadn't expected her to turn so easily and he had pulled a little too hard on her elderly body. He immediately let go of her arm and braced her so she wouldn't fall to the floor.

Anna struggled to get way from him. "That's it. I'm calling the police!" she shrieked.

"Oh no you don't!" Carlton pushed his grandmother intending for her to fall on the couch behind her. He had pushed too hard. She missed the couch and with a strangled cry fell backwards hitting her head on the Chippendale desk. Carlton lunged forward to try to stop her from falling. He watched as if the actions were happening in slow motion, but it happened in a second. He hadn't reacted quickly enough. He watched her body go limp and slump to the floor.

Immediately Carlton bent down to check on his grandmother. He thought she was unconscious from hitting her head. "Gram, Gram, are you okay?" He asked frantically.

Anna DeWitt didn't answer. She was lying there motionless. After several anxious minutes when Anna didn't wake up, Carlton decided he better check for her pulse. He couldn't find a pulse in her wrist. Maybe her wrist pulse wasn't strong enough for him to feel. He put his index and middle fingers together and gently touched her neck. Nothing. His heart was pounding in his chest and stomach. Now he was really frantic.

Carlton stood up abruptly and paced back and forth near Anna's body trying to decide what to do. He could see a dark red pool of blood forming on the floor. It was oozing out in a circle around her head and shoulders. As he paced he made a fist from his right hand and pounded it into the palm of his left hand. Not that this made him think any better, but it gave him something to do with his hands. What happened was an accident; he hadn't meant to hurt his grandmother but who would believe him. *I've gotta get out of here fast,* he thought.

He made for the front door. As he reached for the doorknob, reality set in. He stopped short. He turned and surveyed the showroom. The lights were blazing as if reminding him that he had just killed his grandmother. He knew he had to erase all evidence of his visit.

He took the stairs two at a time. The dishes in the kitchen were all washed and sitting in the wire drainer. The table had been cleared and only the tablecloth remained. He grabbed one of the damp dishcloths that Anna had used only a few minutes earlier and looked around the kitchen. *I need to find anything I touched and wipe away my fingerprints*, he thought. *I think everything I touched has been washed. The chair, I touched the chair when I sat down.* He hurriedly wiped the chair arms. *The handrail by the stairs, I touched it on the way up and again on the way down.*

He ran out of the kitchen and wiped the railing along the top and sides with the cloth. Once at the bottom of the staircase, he hurried nervously back to where his grandmother lay. He checked for a pulse once more but there was none. He hastily looked around the shop to see if he had touched anything downstairs. He decided he hadn't. All that was left was to turn off the lights and wipe both sides of the knob on the front door. He couldn't recall if he had actually touched the knob, but he would have to touch it to open the door when he left. He stuffed the end of the dishcloth into his pants pocket and it hung down by the side of his leg. After turning off the lights, he stood in the darkness frantically searching his mind. What else? What else? His eyes darted all around the darkened shop.

The streetlight outside dimly lit the showroom. He could see his car across the street. His only escape. All of a sudden he remembered Anna had invited him to visit and he didn't know who else knew that. Had she told Toni? He had sent her his reply by letter. His letter saying he was driving east, he had to find it. He ran to Anna's little office and clicked on the desk lamp using the dishcloth wrapped around his fingers. There was a pile of mail on the desk and he carefully pushed the letters around with a pencil. He didn't want to touch anything. All that was in the pile was bills. Off to the side he saw another group of envelopes. His lay among them unopened. He grabbed his letter and stuffed it into his jacket pocket. Before he put down the pencil he wiped it with the dishcloth and clicked off the light protecting his fingers and stuffed the dishcloth back into his pants pocket.

Carlton headed for the door. He looked back one more time and saw his grandmother still lying where she had fallen. A stab of regret pierced through him. He shrugged it off. Nothing he could do now. He wiped the doorknob, opened the door and pushed in the button to lock it. He was about to close the door behind him when the realization that he had no money and nowhere to go hit him. He stepped back into the showroom, and cursed. *There's gotta be something here I can...the perfume bottle!* Leaving the door open, he quickly grabbed the bottle, and then keeping the dishcloth wrapped around his right hand, he exited closing the door behind him. He gave the outside knob a quick wipe. He had no way to lock the deadbolt so he hoped the bottom lock was enough for security in Covington.

Taking a long deep breath, he pulled the collar of his leather jacket up to protect his neck from the rain that had begun falling while he was with his grandmother. He walked across the street and got into his car. Carlton sat there in disbelief for a few minutes and then started the engine. He realized he still had the dishcloth wrapped around his hand when he put the car in gear. *I need to throw this away but not here*, he thought.

Pulling away from the curb he didn't have a plan or know where he was going. Covington wasn't a very large town and he drove around trying to decide what to do. Since Anna hadn't yet opened his letter, the only person who knew he was in Covington was Anna's customer Roslyn. But she would be away on a cruise to Europe. Hopefully, by the time she got back, this would have all blown over. This small town police department will probably think this was just an accident. Just another old woman who tripped in the dark and hit her head. His comfort had come recently by being around people in casinos when he was depressed. *Where are there casinos in the east? Ah, Atlantic City. I'll drive to Atlantic City and get myself together there. On the way I'm sure I'll find another antique dealer that'll buy this bottle. In a few days I can come back to Covington to see what's going on and find out who knows what about my grandmother. By then the police will have done their thing and it might be over.*

Carlton headed out of town and south to New Jersey. He would drive for a while on the Interstate and then nap at a rest stop and be in Atlantic City sometime Friday. There was no hurry. The dealers would be there whenever he arrived.

PART II

CHAPTER 6

Covington, Rhode Island
Saturday April 10th, 1999

Sergeant Ian Monroe of the Covington Police Department had been transferred to homicide about five years ago to work as a detective after being a uniformed officer for a short time after his return from New York. He had never been assigned to investigate the death of someone like Anna DeWitt. *I don't know why I'm being ordered to look into the death of a seventy-four year old woman*, he thought. *Who would want to kill her?* When he'd received the call to start working the case, he had tried to reason with his captain that this could wait until Monday. Ian was told that the mayor had gotten involved and was leaning on the captain to perform a forensic autopsy. While he was getting dressed, Ian's fax machine began receiving the lieutenant's report the captain had sent over.

As Ian waited for the whole fax to print, he thought, *I'll go over to the shop, look around, go through the motions and wrap this up today. There won't be any reason to drag this out longer than one day. The scene has been contaminated by now and whatever the forensic guys didn't get is probably ruined. If they didn't find anything that points to a homicide I'm not going to find it a day later.*

An hour later he knocked on the door to *Anna's Attic* and waited for someone to open it. The white sign with blue trim that hung on the glass door said, "Closed". He knocked again, harder.

Antonia, sleeping upstairs, awoke with a start. She thought she heard knocking coming from downstairs. For a moment she was disoriented having been awakened abruptly from a sound sleep, and figured she must have been dreaming. Then, she heard the knocking again, so loud and insistent she had to investigate.

Quickly throwing a robe over her knee length nightshirt, she padded down the stairs in her bare feet to find a man standing at the front door. He was wearing gray slacks, a black turtleneck sweater, and a black windbreaker. As she moved closer to the door, she noticed the police badge he was holding up. This stranger was about six feet two inches tall, with light brown hair that had traces of gray in it giving him a distinguished look. Almost at the door, Toni couldn't help being impressed by his physique. Even through the layers of clothing, it was obvious the man worked out regularly. Reaching the door, she was struck by the most beautiful blue eyes she had ever seen. She thought he was as good looking as a young Clint Eastwood, her first crush. She opened the door tentatively.

"Yes, can I help you?" she asked.

"Ma'am, I'm Sergeant Ian Monroe from the Homicide Unit, Covington Police Department. I've been assigned to investigate the death of Anna DeWitt. May I come in?"

"Yes, of course Sergeant, please come in." Antonia was surprised at how early he was there. "I'm Antonia Stanton, Anna DeWitt's granddaughter."

"My captain called me at home this morning. The mayor has requested we open an investigation into your grandmother's death, so the coroner will be performing an autopsy on Monday. Apparently you're well connected, and that's why I'm here. I've been *asked* to meet with you," he said looking around the showroom.

"Sergeant Monroe," Toni began belligerently, "my grandmother lived in Covington all of her life, and she was a well respected and prominent citizen here. When your lieutenant told me yesterday there would be no inquiry into her death, I called the mayor who has known my grandparents for years. Apparently he requested an investigation, and that's why you're here," she finished folding her arms across her chest.

They stared at each other for a few seconds, neither willing to back down. Toni's stubborn streak would have held her rooted to her spot, had it not been for the cold air creeping up her bare legs. She gave an involuntary shiver that had more to do with the way he was looking at her than with the cold. The half smile on his face as he looked her up and down made her self-conscious. Under other circumstances, she would have admonished him. However, standing there in only a nightshirt and robe, she could hardly blame him.

"Sergeant, how about a cup of coffee?"

"Sure Miss Stanton, lead the way."

In the kitchenette, Toni clumsily prepared the coffee maker, while Ian leaned on the counter watching her. He unnerved her, and he knew it. When she missed the filter sending coffee grounds onto the floor, the half smile broadened into an impish grin. He seemed to be amused by her futile attempt to keep her nightshirt from riding up while she cleaned the floor. Frustration ate at her so that as soon as she could smell the aroma of the freshly brewed coffee, she excused herself and tore up the stairs.

Toni was feeling a little uncomfortable about leaving a complete stranger alone downstairs, but, she had to make herself look more presentable. After washing her face and brushing her teeth, she donned a trendy pair of jeans and a burgundy cashmere sweater. She took the time to run a brush through her hair, and apply some make-up. Toni chose to wear her black leather high-heeled boots, feeling the need for additional height. Satisfied with her appearance, she went back downstairs and found Ian standing over the spot where her grandmother had fallen.

"How do you take your coffee?" she asked casually. She didn't miss the look of appreciation that replaced the half smile on his face when he turned towards her.

"Black," he answered gruffly.

Geez, friendly guy. Just what I need around today. Sighing, she went to pour the coffee. He must have followed her, because when she turned she was startled to see him standing in the doorway of the kitchenette. Hot coffee sloshed out of the mug she was carrying onto her hand. Swearing, she swung back towards the counter, hastily put the mug down and ran cool water over her hand. She felt the tears well up in her eyes, and held onto the sink trying to compose herself.

"Are you all right?" Was it her imagination or had his voice softened a little.

"Yes, yes, I'll be fine, thank you." Turning to face him she continued, "I guess I'm still shook up from yesterday."

"Quite understandable. Let's sit and talk. I'll get the coffee."

Deciding that it would be easier to allow him to take control, she took a seat at the little kitchen table.

"Tell me, Miss Stanton, why do you think your grandmother's death needs to be investigated?" He asked, placing a full mug in front of her.

"Although my grandmother was seventy-four years old, she was in perfect health. I'm positive she did not fall and hit her head. She had no medical history of any kind that would cause her to fall. She could find her way through the showroom in the dark if she had to. Someone had to have pushed her, which caused her to fall."

"Miss Stanton…"

"Please call me Toni. We're going to be working together for a while and it will make it a lot easier than Miss Stanton every time you want to say something."

"All right, Toni, I'm going to be honest with you. The lieutenant's report clearly states that he believes this was an accident. I tend to agree with him. I don't think there is a reason to open a full-blown investigation. Can you tell me something specific that would change my mind?"

"Sergeant, my grandmother didn't deserve to die a violent death. She should have died with her family around her." Tears began to form again in Toni's eyes, and she was having trouble holding back the pent up emotions from the day before. She started to sob softly. She knew this might bother him, but she didn't care.

"Miss Stanton, Toni, it's okay. You've been through a lot."

Between sniffling, wiping her eyes and blowing her nose she managed to say, "My grandmother bought many valuable items for this shop, when she attended estate sales and auctions. It's possible she outbid someone or bought something that someone else really wanted. There is fierce competition in this business, you know. Some buyers can be aggressive by trying to intimidate others to get what they want. I've even heard stories that smugglers bring diamonds into the country by hiding them inside antiques. Maybe she unknowingly bought something that was meant for another dealer. I don't know."

"Toni, I think you're grasping at straws here. Lieutenant Weldon is a professional. He knows an accident when he sees one."

"And I *know* this was no accident. Sergeant, I know my grandmother well enough to know she does not go around falling over furniture she has positioned herself. She was an alert, intelligent woman. She brought me up for God's sake!"

"She did? What happened to your parents?" he asked.

"They died in a car accident when I was eight. I came to live with Nana because my Uncle Joel and Aunt Jessica had their hands full with my cousin Carlton."

"It seems you're alone here. Where's the rest of your family?"

"My aunt and uncle have retired to live in Monte Carlo, and Carl lives in Las Vegas. I am planning to call him later today. He doesn't ever get up this early."

"Does he own one of the hotels there?" asked Ian sarcastically.

"Sergeant Monroe, obviously I come from a privileged background. How else would I know the mayor?" she responded with equal sarcasm.

Impressed by her wittiness especially after what she had been through, Ian decided to switch tactics. "Toni, I want you to tell me all about your family history. Maybe it will help you remember something I can use."

He sat down opposite her on the vinyl covered dinette chair. Toni had always hated these chairs. "Where shall I begin, Sergeant?"

"Please call me Ian."

Toni looked directly into those blue eyes. *Wow! He is even better looking up close.* She noticed a small scar that ran along his left jaw line, and found herself wondering how he had gotten it. Her gaze automatically shifted to his left hand, which was wrapped around the coffee mug. She surprised herself by being pleased that his ring finger was bare. *That doesn't mean anything,* she chided herself, *many men don't wear their wedding bands. Although if I were married to this fine specimen I would make sure other women knew he was unavailable.* She could have slapped herself. *What am I thinking? I'm supposed to be in mourning and here I am daydreaming about this guy.* Toni looked back at Ian's face, and was embarrassed to see the hint of a smile on it. He had caught her checking him out. *Damn it! I need to stay focused.*

"My great-grandparents chose to settle in Covington when they fled Russia after the Russian Revolution in 1917. My grandmother was born in 1925. From what I've been told she was a beautiful young lady that many men wanted to marry. My grandfather Kurt was the lucky guy, and after they got married they opened this shop. They lived in the apartment upstairs until they could afford to buy a house. In the meantime they had two kids. My mother and my Uncle Joel. Eventually, they grew up and moved out leaving my grandparents in that big house all by themselves. After my grandfather died, Nana wanted to sell the house, but then my parents died and she didn't want me growing up in an apartment above an antique shop."

"Why didn't you go to live with your uncle?" Ian asked.

"As I mentioned, my uncle was married to my Aunt Jessica and their son Carlton was quite a handful. My Aunt had had trouble getting pregnant and when Carlton was finally born she spoiled him so rotten that by the time he was five years old no one could control him. They did offer to take me in, but Nana wouldn't hear of it. I always suspected that I was her favorite grandchild. She never short-changed Carlton, but there was something different in the ways she treated us. Maybe it was because my parents were dead. I don't know. It was just a feeling."

"Did your cousin also believe you were the favorite?"

"I don't know," she said with a sigh. "Carlton is a tough one to figure out." She debated telling Ian about Carlton's indiscretions, but decided not to. She wasn't sure why. "Anyway, I lived with Nana until I graduated from college and got my own place. Nana sold the house and moved back into the apartment upstairs. By then, Uncle Joel had retired to Monte Carlo and Carlton had moved out to Las Vegas. We rarely keep in touch with each other. We exchange cards on special occasions, and that's about it. I know we don't sound like much of a family, but you have to understand, a lot changed when my parents died. My uncle and my mother were extremely close and I think it hurt him too much to hang around me. I can't blame him. All my life, people have told me that I am my mother all over again."

"Your father was Randolph Stanton, right?"

Toni cocked her head to one side. "Yeah. Why do you ask?"

"The Stantons were very well known around these parts. If I'm not mistaken, my parents knew your parents way back when."

"Really? You sure about that?"

"Why? Because I'm just a lowly police detective, our parents couldn't have known each other?"

"I didn't mean it like that. All I know about my parents is what Nana has told me over the years. I know they were active in the Covington Country Club. My father's law practice was flourishing, so he was able to personally handle only the important clients. This left him a lot of time to spend with my mom and me. I have no idea who their friends were."

"My parents were also members of the country club. I vaguely remember my mother telling my father about the death of Ashley and Randolph Stanton. I think I was about fourteen. It was a big deal around here. I didn't know they had any children," Ian explained.

"What a small world it is. Are you still a member?" Toni asked.

"Never was. Wasn't my kind of thing. How about you?"

"Me neither. I can't fathom paying their exorbitant membership fees," she shrugged.

"My parents are still trying to get me to join. They're hoping I might meet a woman there that will make me give up my desire to be a policeman and live up to their expectations of me."

"Your parents don't approve of your line of work?"

"Um, no. My father is a plastic surgeon, my mother the consummate socialite," Ian said wryly.

"Oh dear, sounds like a conflict of interests to me."

"You don't know the half of it."

"You must really like your job."

He pinned her with an intent look. "It's the hunt I like."

CHAPTER 7

Covington, Rhode Island
Saturday April 10th, 1999

Ian sat in his car for a few minutes thinking about Toni and her family before driving away from Antique Promenade. He made a left onto Taylor Road, which led him to Circle Street. City Hall, where the precinct was located, loomed in front of him as he followed the circular road. He chose instead to make a right onto Grant, and headed home.

He had stayed a lot longer than he had planned. As he waited for the security gate at River Chase Townhouses to open, he thought about his initial impression of just going through the motions and wrapping up his investigation in one day. But, after having met Toni and listening to her, he didn't think he could walk away that easily.

He pulled into his designated parking space in front of his townhouse, and took his key out of the ignition. The doors on his new black Corvette unlocked automatically. Again, he sat in his car thinking about Toni. *What was it about that woman that had him so preoccupied? She was certainly not his type. He preferred blonde, leggy, model types. They were not a reminder of the woman who broke his heart years ago.*

With a click the car doors relocked reminding him how long he had been sitting there.

As he walked up to his townhouse he could hear his telephone ringing. He hurriedly fumbled for his door key and quickly headed for the kitchen wall phone. Just as he put his hand on it, it stopped ringing. *Darn it! It's times like this that I wish I had Caller ID.*

Tossing his house keys on the counter, Ian headed back out to his mailbox, and brought in his mail. He picked up the phone and pressed the buttons to call his captain. Knowing the conversation would be one-sided, he sifted through his mail as he half-listened to the captain's words. Ian checked over his Visa statement as the captain went on about satisfying Toni's suspicions that this was not an accident. Ian was required to put on a good show of police work only to reach the same conclusion the lieutenant had. The captain made it clear that he did not want to receive another call from the mayor.

"Do whatever it takes to make the granddaughter satisfied," Ian repeated the captain's exact words to himself. "That gives a whole new meaning to police work. This is one case I'm gonna enjoy." *Oh quit it*, he thought. *I don't think the captain meant any sexual innuendo.* It struck him that the captain didn't mention calling earlier. *I guess it wasn't him.*

Ian went into the living room, grabbed the TV remote and sat down on the arm of his recliner. His townhouse was a bachelor pad in the true sense of the word. No fru fru. It was neat and he took pride in the fact that it was always presentable when someone visited. Ian had bought this townhouse because his master bedroom and his den were both upstairs. He valued his privacy, and liked the idea that a guest had no reason to go upstairs; unless *she* was invited.

The townhouse complex was a source of great controversy when it was being built. The residents of Covington, most of which were from old money, were unsettled by the idea that yuppies were about to infiltrate their small town. However, the builder was a close friend of the mayor at that time, and he had convinced him how good the new townhouses could be for Covington businesses. Turns out he was right. River Chase made Covington affordable for young couples looking to live in a quaint Rhode Island town. And Covington was just that; everything was within walking distance of everything else.

There was a small downtown area that housed the town's municipal buildings: City Hall, Volunteer Fire Department, etc. The *Covington Chronicle* also made its home downtown, along with other businesses. The whole area was shaped like a wheel, earning the street the name, Circle Street. There were three main streets off of Circle, Grant to the east, Jackson to the west, and Taylor to the south. It was Taylor that visitors knew the best since heading south, one could bear right to shop or keep going to The Estates. The Estates, as residents referred to the area south of downtown, was where Covington society lived in mansions that sat on sprawling acreage. Naturally, Covington Country Club was located there. Those not fortunate enough to have been born into wealth made their home in modest houses and apartment buildings, which dotted the small side streets of Covington.

Ian turned on the TV in the lighted entertainment center. Along with the 48" television, was a surround sound system, a DVD player, a VHS recorder, a stereo, and movie library most guys would kill to own. A beige velvet pit sofa and chairs that could comfortably seat ten faced the entertainment center. On the wall by the door he had bookshelves from ceiling to floor that held an eclectic reading selection. He had read them all; novels, biographies, autobiographies, history books, and gourmet cook books for all cuisines. He was a culinary master, movie buff, and an avid reader; a woman's dream.

Flipping through channels, he found his mind being haunted by the fact that Toni was so certain her grandmother didn't die accidentally. He flopped himself into the recliner leaving one leg draped over the arm. As usual, there was nothing to hold his interest on any channel. He stopped on the Food Network and watched the chef du jour prepare a romantic dinner for two. It reminded Ian that when he cooked, it was for one.

Ian was single, never married. He had been engaged once to a woman much different from Toni; blonde, statuesque, flighty, and much younger than he. At thirty-five, Ian was beginning to think about settling down and maybe transferring to a smaller department.

The catalyst came when he had been shot in the shoulder while with the NYPD. Taking a leave of absence to recover at his parents' home in Covington, Ian rediscovered his small town roots. Meeting Julianna helped him make the decision to not return to New York. They had met at the restaurant where she worked as a hostess, and had a whirlwind courtship. Although Juli was ten years his junior, Ian had fallen in love with her, or so he thought, and proposed four months into their relationship. Juli had accepted, anticipating the romantic life of an NYPD policeman's wife. Unbeknownst to her, Ian had quit his job in New York and had accepted a position with the Covington Police Department.

For six months Juli had tried to convince him that a life in New York was so much more exciting than the one they would have in Covington. Ian had had enough excitement to last him a lifetime, and just wanted to settle down and start a family as soon as possible. Their argument had escalated until one day Julianna broke off the engagement and moved to Atlantic City within the week. Since then he had dated casually, no one serious. He still held out hope that he would meet the right woman soon. At forty he wasn't getting any younger and all his friends kept reminding him it's no fun growing old alone.

This Toni Stanton was intriguing. She was educated. Probably had a successful career, and came from a family rooted here in Covington. He recalled during their meeting catching her staring at him. He knew he was an attractive man, but somehow he thought Toni would think he was not in her league. Although his family was no less prominent than hers, he was still just a working grunt. Having grown up around Covington society all his life, Ian knew a working person was not a member of the "in" crowd. What people didn't realize about him, was that he had no desire to be a member of the "in" crowd. Much to his mother's chagrin, Ian chose to work hard for a living, and not just live off his trust fund. He found detective work stimulating.

Ian flipped through the movie channels, and landed on one showing a movie he was unfamiliar with. The actress on the screen reminded him of Toni. She appeared to be a psychic trying to read the mind of a criminal. *You don't have to be psychic to read people's minds*, he thought. *All you have to do is look at their faces.* He had learned to read people's expressions through his years of police work.

He found himself surprised when he realized that Toni appeared to like what she was seeing when she looked at him. He hated to admit it, but he also liked what he saw. Toni was not what one would call a classic beauty, but there was something about her big green eyes and long brown hair that attracted him to her. Maybe it was seeing her for the first time wearing a nightshirt. There's something intimate about seeing a woman in her sleepwear; especially when it was obvious she was not wearing anything underneath. He allowed his imagination to wander as he pictured what she would look like standing in front of him naked. Her skin, he had noted, looked so soft and pure he had to control himself to not reach out and touch her. When she broke down in tears he had to summon all his willpower to stop himself from wrapping his arms around her and consoling her. After all, he was a cop on an investigation. The stirrings of an emotional attachment began to arouse a physical desire deep within him for Toni. *Stop it*, he thought. *She's not your type, man*, he reminded himself. *Keep telling yourself that.*

Ian gave up on the television and decided to immerse himself in his favorite Clint Eastwood flick, *The Gauntlet.* He had often been told that he resembled Clint Eastwood so he envisioned himself as a toned down Dirty Harry.

Ian Monroe was hoping the movie would take his mind off Antonia Stanton and the web she had managed to spin around his mind.

Toni had closed the door behind Ian and turned back into the shop. Now she was feeling irritated and depressed. The fact that she had slept fitfully the night before didn't help her mood. She wasn't looking forward to spending the rest of the weekend alone. There would be no progress on the investigation until Monday.

She aimlessly walked around the shop letting her fingers touch the fabric on the antique furniture. Picking up the small antiques that lay around the shop and looking at them, only served to make her feel more sentimental. These were her grandmother's precious possessions, lovingly cared for until they could be passed to their next owner. Concentrating was out of the question.

I'll go home now and make some phone calls, Toni thought. *I haven't thought about work since this began and I need to let my editor know I won't be able to take on any new assignments until I get answers to my questions about Nana. I should call Joyce too, and Uncle Joel, and Carlton.* Before leaving she popped her head into the kitchenette to make sure she'd turned off the coffee maker. The two mugs sat in the sink side by side reminding her of the coffee she'd shared with Ian earlier. A brief thought of him ran through her head making her wonder where he went and what he would do this weekend.

Locking the door to the shop with her own key, Toni walked to her Lexus SUV now occupying a parking space in front of the shop. She drove to the end of Antique Promenade, made a right onto Taylor and then took her second left onto Village Way in a trance like state. Her car knew its way home by heart, having made this trip often. Sliding into her designated parking spot, she hardly remembered how she got there.

Inside her spacious apartment she looked around at the familiar furnishings and sat down on the chaise part of her sofa, kicking off her boots and stretching her legs out. The sun was starting to set and light coming in through the windows danced shadows on the walls and hardwood floor.

Her building on Village Way, a trendy address for apartment owners, would be considered upscale by most standards and it was reflected in the mortgage Toni paid each month. With her career as a freelance photojournalist well established, she felt she could afford to treat herself to a nice place to live. When she traveled on assignments there was no telling what type of accommodations would be available, especially in foreign countries. Coming home after a week or more away she deserved a comfortable refuge. Although she loved her grandmother's antiques, Toni's two-bedroom apartment had only contemporary furniture. She had picked a country décor featuring apples when the decorator had asked for a theme. The wallpaper border had red apples of different sizes along with green leaves and small dots in red and various shades of green.

Walking in the apartment front door one was greeted with a lighted atrium on the left side with glass shelving and live plants positioned at different levels. Shiny dark green bromeliads filled the bottom of the atrium, which was followed immediately by a mirror to the end of the wall. The living room was on the right with a tan leather sofa and chairs surrounding a coffee table. The table was a low one and its large square top had small neat piles of books on it. There were a number of magazines in the compartments underneath. The stereo was on a table in the corner and a lighted glass-shelving unit rounded out the furniture. The living room opened onto a dining room with the kitchen through a doorway to the right. Off the short hallway was a den on the left with the master bedroom and bathroom on the right. Toni had convinced Hans, her decorator, to adorn the walls with photographs she had taken.

Toni usually watched TV propped up in her queen size bed. The only other furniture in the bedroom was a night table. The louvered closet doors, which covered one wall, hid a nine-drawer dresser; her shoes were stacked on slanted wire shelving, and her clothes were hung neatly. The wall opposite the closet was a sliding glass door that opened onto a small brick paved balcony surrounded by a privacy fence made of lattice. The ivy Toni had planted a few years ago had grown up over the lattice and sheltered the area. Drapes, that matched the comforter, provided additional privacy.

For convenience, Toni had set up the master bathroom as her dark room, leaving the one outside her bedroom as the only usable bathroom in the apartment. Since she rarely had overnight guests, this arrangement suited her well. Hans had decorated the bathroom with a border paper of large purplish blue seashells, a matching shower curtain and thick white bath towels. Her white velour terrycloth robe hung on the back of the door. The floor had a large rectangular purplish blue plush rug that matched the toilet seat cover. A large square mirror with six fat sammy makeup lights that screwed into a stainless steel housing covered the wall by the sink. The sink top held body oil, lotions and her favorite fragrances. She could shower or take a bath in the garden tub. This was truly her refuge from the world of stress, irritation, fear, and anxiety.

Toni awoke to the click of the timer turning on the living room lights. She had dozed off shortly after reclining on the chaise. Stretching and slowly getting up she could feel the tension in her neck and shoulders. *I should schedule a massage*, she thought. *It's been a while and I sure could use one after Friday.*

Being an organized person, Toni decided to make a "to do list." It would help her focus and keep her mind off her grandmother for a while longer. She wrote:

> 1.Call Joyce.
> 2.Call editor.
> 3.Call Uncle Joel.
> 4.Call Carlton.
> 5.Meet with detective Monday.
> 6.Nana's shop?

Toni was stuck at this point. She knew there was so much more to do but she couldn't think of anything else to write. She decided to take a shower and come back to the list later. In the shower, as the hot steamy water hit the top of her head, a sense of utter despair hit her. Toni finally realized she was all alone in this. There was no one to help her do all the things that are required after someone dies. As the water streamed over her neck and shoulders, tears streamed down her face. She put her face in her hands and began sobbing uncontrollably. Her body began shaking visibly. Toni hugged herself and leaned against the tiled wall, letting the emotion of the last two days out. She stayed like that until she felt the hot water turn cool.

Stepping out of the tub, she reached for her bathrobe, and wrapped herself in its comfort. She unrolled the cuff on the right sleeve and used it to defog the mirror and stared at her reflection watching as the mirror clouded up again. She tried to remember how she felt when she was eight years old and her parents had died. As a child the loss of her parents had saddened her, but she didn't understand the full impact of their death. Nana had always been there for her. Now, Nana was gone too. Who would be there for her now?

Toni's stomach growled. She realized she hadn't eaten anything yet, and decided to prepare some supper. She would make her phone calls after she ate. Toni always thought better on a full stomach. *Pizza. I'll order pizza*, she thought. *Hawaiian. I wonder if that's Ian Monroe's favorite? Now, where did that thought come from? Sure, he's kinda cute. Okay, he's gorgeous, I admit it. A guy like that probably has women lined up at his front door. Women I could never compete with. So, I'm going to leave this bathroom, and get dressed before I freeze to death or die of hunger.*

Half an hour later, Toni sat in her dining room eating her pizza, reading a travel magazine, and wishing desperately that she was anywhere but there.

CHAPTER 8

Covington, Rhode Island
Sunday April 11th, 1999

"Sweetheart, how can you be sure it was not an accident?"

Antonia gripped the telephone a little tighter. After having to tell Uncle Joel his mother was dead, she didn't feel like being told by yet another person that she was grasping at straws. "I don't know, Uncle Joel. It's just a strong feeling I have."

"But Toni, if the police say it was an accident, then it must be. They are professionals, Little Ant, they must know what they're doing," her uncle's soft voice came over the line clearly, using the name he had called her since she was a child.

Toni had called Uncle Joel first knowing there was a six-hour difference between Rhode Island and Monte Carlo. She knew he would take the news stoically, so she had just come right out and told him. He was silent for a few minutes no doubt dealing with the rush of sadness that must have washed over him. Then he asked the inevitable question: How? Toni had taken a deep breath and told him how her grandmother had died. When she confided her suspicions to him, she was hoping he would agree that an investigation was warranted. Obviously, she was wrong.

"But Nana knew this place so well. It's impossible that she would have tripped over a couch, Uncle Joel. Anyway, the autopsy report will be ready tomorrow. Then I'll know for sure if it wasn't a natural death."

"Toni, why are you putting yourself through this? She's gone and none of this can bring her back."

"But if someone killed her, wouldn't you want to know?" she asked.

Uncle Joel sighed, "Where are you getting this from? Who in the world would want your grandmother dead? Is there something you haven't told me?"

"No, no, no. I've told you everything I know. I just truly believe that Nana did not trip. Once the autopsy report is released maybe I'll change my mind. But if there is no investigation, the unanswered questions will gnaw at me for the rest of my life."

"You're an intelligent woman, Toni. Do what you have to do for yourself. I did the same thing to satisfy myself when your parents died. I needed proof that their deaths were accidental. It gave me the closure I needed to get on with my life. I miss your mother terribly, but at least I know no one killed her," Uncle Joel paused. "Toni, there's something I have to tell you. I wasn't going to tell you until we had definite information, but with this turn of events I know you are expecting your aunt and me to come to Rhode Island. Unfortunately, Aunt Jessica can't travel right now. She's very ill, but no one seems to know what the problem is. We've been seeing specialist after specialist trying to find out what's wrong. She's weak, she has dizzy spells and her stomach is always upset. A trip to the States would be too stressful for her right now. I hope you understand," Uncle Joel finished quietly.

"Oh no, Uncle Joel. I understand totally. I can handle everything on my own. Please give my love to Aunt Jess and tell her I love her. And please let me know as soon as you find out what's wrong with her."

"I'll call you tomorrow to find out what the report said. I love you, Little Ant."

"I love you too. Bye for now."

Toni rolled over in her bed and hung up the phone. Her mother's smiling face looked back at her from the frame on her nightstand. The smile was almost as brilliant as the sun that was shinning in on her own face. She could feel the warmth through the glass doors. She propped herself up on a couple of pillows and thought about it being Sunday. She rarely attended church, but briefly considered going to the service at Covington United Methodist. Her grandmother was a member there and she would ask the senior pastor who knew Anna for many years to conduct the funeral service. Toni decided she wasn't up to dealing with people and questions today and would wait until after the autopsy results to talk to Pastor Kevin about arrangements for Anna's service.

Knowing the funeral home would take care of the obituary, she mentally went through the other things she would have to take care of. The magnitude of making the funeral arrangements alone was beginning to hit her. Up until now she had only thought about the shop and Nana being gone. She would have to call Chapman Funeral Home after the autopsy so they could collect Anna's body and prepare it for the funeral. They were a compassionate family who had handled the funerals of her grandfather and her parents. *Anna's body......*Toni cringed, *not Nana, but Anna's body*. It brought tears to her eyes thinking of her grandmother as a body.

After lying in bed a little while longer to compose herself, Toni got up and went to the kitchen to make a pot of coffee. A few slices of last night's pizza remained in the square, red, white, and blue box. She wrapped them and put them into the refrigerator. As she closed the door she recalled when she had painstakingly shopped for the appliance and had labored over the sizes, brands, and styles and then if she should buy the pricey one she really wanted and liked. She finally selected a double door stainless steel model with icemaker and water in the door to match her electric range. It was massive in the little kitchen, but she loved it and wasn't sorry she splurged on it.

As the coffee brewed, Toni stood staring at nothing in particular waiting to pour her first cup. *I'll get dressed and go to the shop this morning*, she thought. *I'll look through Nana's office to see if I can find anything that might be important. I'm not in the mood to be around anybody so when I call Joyce I'll tell her not to come in until Tuesday.* Toni decided to skip breakfast and have another cup of coffee instead. She sipped her second cup as she put on her jeans and her gray Smith College fleece sweatshirt. She pulled her sneakers out from under the bed, drained the remnants of her coffee, and headed out the door.

Turning her key in the lock, Toni went into the shop and locked the door behind her. She heard the open/closed plastic sign tap against the door a few times as it settled down from the movement of the door. She left it showing "closed" and walked slowly to the back of the shop. It was eerily quiet, only a little creak of the wooden floor as she walked. No cheery greeting from her grandmother.

Toni turned on the light in Anna's office and sat down in her grandmother's chair. She scooted forward towards the desk. For a few minutes she just sat and looked at the piles of paper, letters, and catalogs. She had not helped Anna run the shop and was feeling at a loss as to where to start. *Maybe I'll put everything on the desk into a box and then look through it one piece at a time. That will be less overwhelming*, she thought.

Toni went into the back room that Anna had used as a storage and utility area. She found a sturdy box with a lid and took it back to the office. In one fell swoop she cleared the desktop and slid everything into the carton. Sitting down again with the box on the floor next to her, she started taking papers out one by one, reading them, and sorting them into piles by category: Bills, paid and unpaid, letters, catalogs, and miscellaneous. She wasn't sure where she was going in this process but it would organize everything and keep her focused on doing something productive. On Tuesday she and Joyce could figure out what to keep and what to throw away or file.

She would tackle the file cabinet drawers later, after lunch. Toni figured it would take the rest of the morning to get through everything that had been on the desk.

Carlton DeWitt took the Jackson exit off the Interstate, reaching the outskirts of Covington early Sunday morning. He pulled into a park and sat in his car thinking about his strategy when he got to the shop. *Who would be there? Perhaps Toni or Joyce or maybe nobody. The shop would be closed to customers,* he was sure about that. *I'll go to the shop first around eleven, if no one's there I'll go to Toni's apartment and look for her there,* he thought.

His two-day stint in Atlantic City was the best therapy to take his mind off his troubles. After leaving Covington, Thursday night he had made it only as far as Hope Valley, a small town fifteen miles south of Covington. He was exhausted and he didn't trust himself to drive farther. Forced to sleep in his car for another night, he made it his mission on Friday morning to find a buyer for the perfume bottle. Sandoval Pratt of *Hope Valley Antiques & Collectibles* was currently the proud owner of a Quezal perfume bottle.

Carlton didn't care what the name of the bottle was, he was just happy with the two thousand dollars it had netted him. He'd used the money to impress one of the female dealers in Atlantic City and ended up spending Friday and Saturday with her. Carlton had left her sleeping when he snuck out very early this morning, helping himself to the cash he found in her purse. By the time she woke up, he'd be long gone and, not having told her his last name, the police would be hard pressed to find him.

Carlton pushed open the glass door to the coffee shop across from the park and was greeted by a plump matronly looking woman.

"Good morning. Can I get you a coffee?" she asked.

"Sure. I'll sit here at the counter." The shop was empty except for the cook and the waitress. He could have taken any seat, but decided on the counter. He glanced at the menu while taking gulps of the steamy hot black coffee.

Betty, according to the name badge on her uniform, hovered around Carlton. "Haven't seen you in here. Are you new in town?" she asked.

"No." Carlton didn't want to talk.

"Just passing through?" Betty kept on.

"No, just visiting."

"Friends?" Betty persisted.

"Family." Carlton wished she would leave him alone.

"Parents? Brother? Sister?"

"Grandmother," he responded wishing he had taken a seat at one of the tables instead.

"Really, and who would she be?"

It was obvious to Carlton that Betty was looking for a conversation. He decided to appease her. "Anna DeWitt. She owns Anna's Attic on Antique Promenade."

"Lord, Jesus, Joseph and Mary, don't you know?"

"Know what?" Carlton asked finally making eye contact with her.

"I'm sorry to be the one to tell you. Your grandmother died Thursday night. It's been all over the news. She was a very prominent person in Covington."

"Oh no! What happened? Why is it in the news? Do they always report on deaths of elderly women?" Carlton felt panic begin to rise. His mind was racing with questions. *Did I leave something behind? Did I make some sort of mistake?*

Seemingly oblivious to his agitation, Betty continued, "According to the reporters who talked to the police, the mayor has requested an investigation. The police think she fell, but her granddaughter doesn't think so, and being who she is, she pulled some strings."

"I've gotto go look for my cousin," Carlton stood up quickly. He threw a couple of dollars onto the counter, took the last swallow of coffee and left the coffee shop. *No sense hanging around here. Betty might wonder why I don't know about this already.*

Carlton drove east on Jackson until he reached Spring Street. Bearing right he took it to Antique Promenade. He parked in a spot in front of the shop, jumped out and knocked on the front door. He looked through the glass door and could see a light on in the back of the shop. He waited, and then knocked again. He saw the closed sign, but if someone were inside they would surely answer if there were a knock.

Toni heard someone knocking and was trying to decide if she would go to the door. *It could be Ian, no, he said Monday.* A customer would see the closed sign and not stop. She should have put a sign in the window "closed due to death of owner", no "due to death of Anna DeWitt", but she hadn't thought of that and it was too late now.

Toni walked to the front of the store and was surprised to see her cousin, Carlton, standing on the sidewalk looking up and down the street. He was dressed in black slacks, and was wearing a leather jacket. She opened the door and he turned around. "Carlton, what are you doing here?" she asked suspiciously.

"I'm here to visit Gram. Can I come in?"

"I'm sorry, certainly, come in." As she held the door open for Carlton, Toni couldn't help feeling a tiny bit glad to see him. "Carl, I am so glad you're here. I was beginning to feel so alone. Come in, sit down, I've got something to tell you." She led him to an area of the showroom that had been set up with matching living room furniture. She took a seat on the sofa and motioned for Carlton to sit next to her.

She took a deep breath, but before she could begin, Carlton spoke up. "I know. I stopped at a coffee shop just now and the waitress told me Gram is dead. I can't believe it. What happened?"

"I don't know for sure. Nana hit her head on the corner of that desk over there, Thursday night. Joyce found her on Friday and called the police. They say it was an accident. But, I requested an autopsy. The report will be ready tomorrow."

"Autopsy? Why? What for?"

"Because I don't believe it was an accident. I think someone deliberately pushed Nana into that desk. I have no proof. Just a feeling."

"Maybe you're right," Carlton said looking away.

Antonia's spirits soared. *Finally, someone agrees with me.*

"Who is helping you with the arrangements?" Carlton asked looking back at her.

"No one. I'm doing it alone."

"What about my parents? I'm sure they will be willing to help. So would I. Only problem is you know we can't be in the same room together."

Toni reached for Carlton's hand. "Carl, I seem to have nothing but bad news to give you. Aunt Jess is sick and can't travel. So, yes, I am alone."

"I'm sorry to hear that my mother is sick but, you can't be alone at a time like this. Let me help you. You need family with you. I know we haven't been close but I'm here now. How can I help?"

Toni was so grateful to Carlton that she almost hugged him. She decided to forgive the debts he owed her and the lies he'd told her. She needed a friend and Carlton was the only one available. "I'm going through the things that were on Nana's desk and then I planned to go through the file cabinet."

"Look it's almost time for lunch. Have you anything to eat? All I've had is coffee and I'm hungry. Let's get something to eat and talk about what we're going to do."

Carlton was acting like he was taking charge. Toni let him. She was done dealing with this on her own. "OK. OK. I'm not going to fight with you. I need the help and if you're willing we'll do it together," she said.

"I don't have to be back in Vegas for another three weeks. I can do whatever needs to be done around here. Whatever you need, I'm here for you. It's time I started acting like a real cousin."

"Carlton, we may have had our differences over the years, but I'm willing to put it behind us. I know Nana loved us both very much, and if anything, she can rest easy knowing that her death brought us back together." Toni eyes began to water.

Carlton reached for her hand and squeezed it. "Hey, now. None of that. There'll be time for tears later. Right now, we have much to do. But first, lunch. Second, a hotel."

"Hotel?"

"If I'm going to be here for three weeks, I'm going to need a place to stay."

"Oh please! I know I live in a one bedroom, but it's quite roomy. And I promise you my couch is large and comfortable."

"Are you sure it won't be an imposition?"

"It's not up for discussion. Besides I could use the company... especially now."

Carlton pulled Toni into his arms and hugged her. He felt her relax against him. He had gained her trust. Now he would find a way to pilfer enough of his grandmother's smaller expensive antiques to pay back his debts and then some.

CHAPTER 9

Covington, Rhode Island
Monday April 12th, 1999

Antonia stood in the doorway of Nana's office on Monday morning watching Carlton. He was sitting cross-legged on the floor sorting the papers from the bottom drawer of the five-drawer file cabinet. *I can't believe he's come through for me*, Toni thought. *After all the years of borrowing money from me and never paying me back. The promises he made and never kept. If only Nana had lived long enough to see this change in him.*

Carlton looked up and caught Toni staring at him. He smiled at her and bent back to his work. Toni moved into the office and surveyed their progress. After lunch yesterday, they had managed to go through Nana's desk and all but two of the file cabinet drawers. It had taken all of Sunday, but they had managed to figure out Nana's filing system. All that remained was a small pile of papers that they'd left on Nana's chair that Toni needed to ask Joyce about.

Toni sent up a silent prayer of thanks for her cousin. His presence helped her immensely. She had someone to talk to and, most importantly, someone to take her mind off her grandmother. They had spent last night watching Toni's two favorite movies, *Charade* and *Breakfast at Tiffany's*, and eating Chinese food. Carlton had regaled her with stories of his casino days and the kinds of people he encountered in Las Vegas. He didn't tell her much about his personal life, but Toni thought nothing of it.

All she cared about was that he was here and he was keeping her occupied. *If it hadn't been for Carl*, she thought, *I'd have spent yesterday pacing in anticipation of today. I can't wait to see what the autopsy shows*. Toni didn't admit to herself that she was also anticipating seeing Ian again. Although she had dressed in her typical jeans and sneakers, she had opted for a red cable knit sweater. She had even taken the time to apply some light makeup and pull her hair back with a clip.

The ringing phone brought Toni back to the present. She answered it the way she had heard her grandmother do so many times before. "Anna's Attic, how can I help you?"

"Miss Antonia Stanton, please," said a deep, booming voice she didn't recognize.

"Speaking," she responded tentatively. "Who is this?" Out of the corner of her eye, Toni noticed Carlton stand up and come to stand next to her. She gave him an appreciative look.

"Miss Stanton," the voice continued, "my name is Morris Jameson. I am…was Anna's lawyer."

Toni sagged in relief. She had herself convinced he was the Medical Examiner calling about the autopsy.

"What can I do for you, Mr. Jameson?" Toni asked.

"First, please accept my condolences on the loss of your grandmother. She was an exceptional woman."

"Yes, she was. Thank you," Toni's throat constricted.

"Miss Stanton, I was wondering if I might impose on you to come to my office. I know this is a difficult time for you, but there is much to do regarding Anna's legal affairs."

"Oh yes, of course, Mr. Jameson. I hadn't even thought about any of that. I…" Toni stopped talking abruptly because someone was banging on the front door of the shop.

"I'll get it," Carlton mouthed.

As he exited the office, Toni returned to her telephone conversation. "I'm sorry, Mr. Jameson, someone was banging on the door."

"Okay. I will hold on if you wish to answer it," Mr. Jameson said.

"It's alright. My cousin went to get it."

"Your cousin?" Mr. Jameson asked. "Surely you're not referring to Carlton DeWitt, Joel's son."

"Why of course, Mr. Jameson. He's the only cousin I've got," Toni chuckled.

Morris Jameson didn't sound amused when he said, "Oh dear. Well that's an interesting turn of events."

"Isn't it just? I know it's sort of out of the blue, him showing up. But quite frankly I'm glad he's here. He's been very supportive, and, believe me, I need all the support I can get right now."

"I understand, Miss Stanton. When can you meet with me?"

"How about tomorrow?"

"Tomorrow is just fine. Does ten in the morning suit you?" the lawyer asked.

"Ten o'clock is good. Is there something I should bring with me?"

"No, Miss Stanton."

"Alright then," Toni said. "I'll see you tomorrow morning then."

"Oh and Miss Stanton…."

"Yes, Mr. Jameson."

"I would prefer it if you came by yourself."

"Uh, okay, Mr. Jameson. 'Till tomorrow."

"Good day, Miss Stanton."

That was interesting, Toni thought. *I wonder why he doesn't want Carl there. Oh well. Lawyers are a different breed.*

Ian Monroe banged on the front door of the antique shop again. *What's taking her so long?* He asked himself. *I know she's in there, I can see the light coming from the office. Who the hell is this?* Ian was quite taken aback when he saw Carlton walking towards the door. A stab of jealousy went through him. He'd never considered the fact that Antonia could have a boyfriend. And a good-looking one at that.

"Can I help you?" Carlton asked after he had opened the door.

"I'm here to see Antonia," Ian said dryly.

"And who would you be?" Carlton was looking at Ian as if he'd grown a second head.

"Sergeant Ian Monroe, Covington PD. Is she here?"

"Carl, who is it?" Toni called as she walked into the showroom. When she saw Ian standing outside she stopped and stared. Dressed in a navy blue turtleneck and gray slacks, he looked better than she remembered. "Carl, don't leave him standing out there. Let him in."

Ian entered the shop and stood toe to toe with Carlton. To Toni, it looked like they were sizing each other up. It gave her a feeling of guilty pleasure. She knew she should be introducing them to each other, but hesitated for a minute. Ian however wasn't going to let the uncomfortable moment last any longer.

"I am here on official police business," he said to Carlton. "Who would *you* be?"

"I'm sorry. Where are my manners?" Antonia said as she stepped closer to them. "Carlton DeWitt, Ian Monroe." The men shook hands.

"DeWitt?" asked Ian looking at Toni. "Any relation to Anna?"

"He's my cousin," Toni responded.

"Ah, the elusive Las Vegas tycoon," Ian's sarcasm was unmistakable.

"Huh?" was all Carlton could say.

"It's a long story, Carl," Toni said giving Ian a nasty look. "I'll explain after *Detective Monroe* leaves." She turned on her heel and stalked to the kitchenette.

"So, tell me DeWitt, was this a planned visit or one hell of a coincidence?" Ian asked with one eyebrow raised.

Carlton responded coolly, "I don't know what you mean."

"Did Toni ask you to come?"

"I'm always welcome as far as my cousin is concerned," Carlton hedged.

"Are you deliberately not answering my question?" Ian's suspicions began growing.

"No. Toni did not ask me to come. However, I've been planning to visit my grandmother for awhile now, and I just managed to get some time off from work, so I called and kinda invited myself, and of course Gram was more than happy to hear that I was coming east to see her so then I told her I'd be here Thursday," Carlton rambled.

Ian's eyebrows shot up. "Thursday? The day your grandmother died?"

"Um, I mean, um, no, it…" Carlton realized his mistake and had to do some quick thinking. Remembering the small plane crash that had stopped traffic on the Strip last month he decided to use that as an excuse for his delay. A small town cop like this one would never know that it had been cleared in a matter of hours. "I was *planning* to be here on Thursday, but some moron decided to crash his plane on the Strip stopping all traffic flow in and out Vegas. So that's how come I didn't arrive until yesterday."

Ian chose not to let Carlton see that he knew he was being bullshitted. Instead, he murmured a few words of acknowledgement and made a mental note to check out Carlton's story.

Entering the kitchenette, Ian detected the strong smell of the coffee Toni had brewed that morning. But, Toni did not offer Ian a cup. Nor did she offer him a seat as she and Carlton sat down. Having developed a feeling of kinship with Carlton, she was irked by Ian's comment. He had no right to make fun of her cousin. Ian took the chair he had occupied the last time he was in the kitchenette. He placed a manila folder on the table in front of him and folded his hands over it. Ian paused for what to Toni seemed like an eternity. "Antonia, I'd like to talk to you alone," he said suddenly becoming serious.

"Why?" She asked tensing at his use of her given name.

"I'd like to go over the autopsy with you."

"Ian, my cousin is staying. He can hear whatever you have to say. He's the only family I have here and I need him with me on this." Toni was firm but not rude.

"O.K. It's your choice. Do you remember on Saturday you repeatedly told me you had a feeling your grandmother did not die accidentally? And I kept telling you I needed evidence? A cop can work on gut feelings during an investigation, but when it comes down to it, there has to be real evidence to back up the feelings. Remember I asked you if you could give me something specific that would point to foul play and you couldn't?"

"Yes, I remember all those things. Ian, come on just tell me what the autopsy says." Toni moved toward the front edge of her chair in anticipation of the worst.

"I have the autopsy and police reports in this folder. We already know the police called Anna's death accidental. I've read the autopsy and I now know...."

"Wait!" Toni blurted out, not sure she wanted to hear what Ian was about to say.

"Toni, it's O.K. the autopsy shows your feeling was correct."

Toni's eyes widened in disbelief. Deep down she had hoped it was an accident. "Oh my God," she gasped. All of a sudden she couldn't get enough air into her lungs.

"Are you okay?" Toni wasn't sure who had asked her that question.

"I don't know if... then that means someone murdered Nana." The realization of what she had just said hit home.

"I'll tell you what the coroner has written. 'Anna DeWitt, seventy-four year old white female died of causes consistent with non-accidental circumstances.' There's a general description of the findings that I'll skip, but the last line is what we're focusing on: 'defensive bruises bilaterally on dorsal hands, forearms, and shoulders; and areas of hemorrhage in the brain.'"

"Wait a minute, what does this all mean?" Carlton interjected as he began fiddling with the collar of his yellow Polo shirt.

"In layman's terms this means she did struggle with someone who probably grabbed her in the areas where there's bruising. The report is pretty graphic about what happened next. I'm not sure if you want to hear it."

Steeling herself for the worst, Toni told him she wanted to know everything.

Sighing, Ian continued. "The fact that blood vessels in her brain were broken may mean she was shaken or pushed hard before she hit her head on the desk. When the brain hits inside the skull from trauma before death, we see the damage on autopsy. If she had tripped and fallen, hitting her head on the desk, the coroner would have found a different scenario in the brain and other types of conditions in her skull than we're seeing."

Toni stared at Ian, horrified. While he was speaking she had clutched her stomach as if she was going to be physically ill. In her heart of hearts she had wanted to be wrong. She had wanted her grandmother to have died a natural death. Not a death fighting off someone. She was numb and unable to say anything. Carlton broke the silence.

"Detective, you still haven't told us what this all means?"

"Carlton, it means we now have a homicide investigation."

Toni had somewhat regained her composure and asked out loud to neither of them in particular, "What happens now?"

"This is when I earn my money. I look for clues and interview people to gather as much information as I can so I can come up with answers as to what happened. Someone is bound to have seen something or know something. It's just finding that person and getting them to remember what they saw. I'll need a list of names from Anna's files. All her customers and anyone she had done business with for the shop. Will you be able to get that for me?" Ian asked.

"Joyce, my grandmother's assistant will be here tomorrow morning. I'll have her start getting the names for you as soon as she gets here," Toni said in an unsteady voice.

"I'll be here around ten tomorrow. That would also be a good time to get elimination fingerprints from you, Joyce, and Carlton," Ian said.

"Why me? Why do I need to give you fingerprints? I wasn't even here until yesterday," Carlton looked as agitated as he sounded.

Ian's gut instinct told him that Carlton DeWitt was not behaving like a grieving grandson, and that he was more uneasy than could be expected. "I understand that. However, unless you've been wearing gloves since you arrived *yesterday,* you've left prints behind."

"Carl," Toni laid a hand his arm, "it's not that big a deal. Please don't turn it into one."

"Whatever."

"Ian, I'll leave Joyce a message today so she knows to get the list ready, and I'll tell her to give you anything else you might think of that will help. I hope you know you'll have our full cooperation," Toni said, glaring at Carlton, who had creased the collar of his shirt by now, looking for agreement.

Ian looked at Carlton. "What about you, can I count on your full cooperation too?"

"Sure. Sure," Carlton said. "Whatever you need."

"I may not be here in the morning, but Carlton and Joyce will be."

"And where will you be?" his detective mode kicking in as he asked suspiciously.

"I have an appointment. I'll talk to you tomorrow when I get back." Toni decided to skip telling Ian about the phone call from her grandmother's attorney since Carlton was being excluded from the meeting and she didn't know why yet.

Covington's Mayor, Jacob Boyce, was fit to be tied. He slammed the police report down on his desk and stood up, placing his hands on his hips. "This is absolutely unacceptable!" He thundered. "How could such a mistake have been made?"

The Mayor's question was directed at Lieutenant Albert Weldon, a short heavy man in his late fifties. Weldon and Ian had been summoned to the Mayor's office after Anna's autopsy report was released. "I assure you, Mayor Boyce, I followed standard procedure. There was no sign of forced entry, the door was locked from the inside, and Mrs. DeWitt was on the floor. It was a classic case of accidental death."

"Apparently not, Lieutenant Weldon," Boyce's face got redder. "Someone murdered Anna DeWitt, and it took her granddaughter's insistence to confirm that it was not an accident."

"Sir, I assure you, it looked like the old lady tripped and hit her head. Case closed."

"You should have made sure," Boyce bellowed. "When such an influential member of the community is found dead, we conduct an investigation!"

Ian watched Weldon squirm. Both men knew the Lieutenant was in hot water. Ian wasn't sure why he'd been asked to attend this meeting. He just knew he wasn't going to say anything until Boyce was finished with Weldon.

"I apologize for the oversight, Mayor Boyce. I will do whatever it takes to rectify the situation."

"You're damn right you will. And you'll start by taking yourself off this case."

"Sir?" Weldon said, surprised.

"You heard me. Antonia Stanton does not want you within one hundred feet of her. And I suggest you work on your approach the next time you are dealing with members of this community."

"I beg your pardon, Sir?"

"According to Miss Stanton, you were condescending and short, which did not reflect positively on the Covington Police Department."

"So, who are you putting in charge of the case?" Weldon asked, looking over at Ian.

"You guessed it, Lieutenant. Sergeant Ian Monroe will run point from now on. He will report directly to the captain."

Weldon stood. "If that's all, Sir." Without waiting for a response, he stormed out of the mayor's office.

Jacob Boyce sat down. *He looks like a typical politician*, Ian thought. *Well groomed and polished, with a million dollar smile*. Not that he was smiling at the moment.

Ian shifted in his chair. He looked across Boyce's desk at the man who had just given him the authority over this case. Ian knew this was not just a vote of confidence. Boyce had something up his sleeve. He wished his captain was there but his superior was at home battling a bout with bronchitis. When the call came in about Anna's death, Lieutenant Weldon had responded knowing that simply sending a Detective wouldn't do.

"Sergeant Monroe, I'm sure you are aware of Anna DeWitt's position in this community. Weldon made a sound decision when he went to the scene instead of sending you. Well, then he blew it.

"I'm sorry to hear that, sir." If Boyce was expecting Ian to bad mouth his superior he was wrong. Ian understood that loyalty to your fellow officers was imperative within any police department.

"By ignoring the details, Weldon managed to upset one of my influential constituents."

"I wasn't aware of Miss Stanton's standing in the community," Ian said. He was confused. Toni intimated to him that she wasn't into Covington society. Had she lied? Had he misjudged her character?

"Well, it's not her I'm really worried about. It's Anna's friends. If they feel that Antonia has been discounted they will certainly let me know by the next election." Boyce looked at Ian pointedly.

Oh, great. Ian thought. *Now I have this guy's politics to add to my list, but at least Toni was genuine.* "Mayor Boyce, I will do my best to ensure that Miss Stanton is satisfied." *Now that's a loaded statement,* he thought. Satisfaction comes in many forms.

"Your best is not good enough. This will be your only case until it is solved. And I have your Captain's assurance that you are up to the task. I understand you were instrumental in solving many of the cases you worked in New York City, and I expect you to use your expertise to do the same here. I cannot impress enough upon you the importance of this investigation. Leave no stone unturned, follow every lead, no matter how insignificant you think it is."

Now this guy's telling me how to do my job. Ian felt like asking Mayor Boyce how much experience he had in law enforcement, but chose to keep quiet. *Let the man say his piece, and let me get on with my job. I don't have any open cases anyway.*

Jacob Boyce sensed Ian's impatience. He didn't want Monroe to miss the point; however he didn't want to alienate him either. "Sergeant Monroe, Ian, if you will give me a few more minutes of your time, I would like to give you some background on your victim. It will help you understand why I am being so insistent."

"Mayor, I am at your disposal." *Especially since it's your signature on my paycheck*, Ian thought.

"Kurt DeWitt, Anna's husband, did much for this town. He had made it his life's work to ensure Covington's prosperity well into the future. After his death, Anna continued her husband's philanthropy. I'm sure you're aware of the DeWitt Trauma Center in Covington Regional Hospital. Anna set up the endowment shortly after her daughter and son-in-law were killed. Even though they couldn't be saved, she wanted the critical care unit for others."

"I've been there. It's state-of-the-art. Many lives have been saved thanks to the CCU. Mayor, you don't need to convince me, remember who my parents are."

"I know, I know. You left Covington right out of high school and only returned a few years ago. You may not be aware of what Anna has been doing for Covington."

Ian realized there was no getting out of hearing what the Mayor had to say. He took out a notepad, and faked an interested look as the Mayor launched into his speech.

"Anna loved the children of Covington. She supported many of their fund raising activities and youth programs. She bought ads in all the programs, yearbooks, etc. Even though she did not need the publicity. Whenever any charitable organization needed funds, Anna was first to donate and managed to get others to donate also. She would even donate valuable items from her shop for auctions. She was a member of many community associations simply because her opinion was valued by many. That's what makes this such a tragedy. Anna DeWitt was real. Her humility allowed her to connect with the elite as well as the average person. There is no one in Covington that did not cherish Anna."

Ian was impressed. Having attended an exclusive private school, he was insulated from the programs the public school kids participated in. He knew his parents lent their support for many youth organizations which was why he always made time to go to Covington High to talk to the students about drugs, alcohol, drunk driving, etc. The school's Career Day was one of his favorites. He felt an immediate kinship with Anna. He would do everything in his power to bring her killer to justice. Once he solved the case, Toni's gratitude would be an added bonus.

Mayor Boyce was speaking again. *Boy this guy loves the sound of his own voice,* Ian thought. *Does he expect me to conduct an investigation from his office?* Since Mayor Boyce was a typical politician who could talk ad nauseam about nothing Ian waited for a pause and interjected, "I appreciate your confidence in my abilities and I am anxious to get the ball rolling. If there's nothing else, I'd like to excuse myself now."

"Of course, of course." Mayor Boyce stood and extended his hand. As Ian took it, the Mayor clapped him on the shoulder, "You understand that I expect to be kept in the loop. My secretary will set up a meeting for us to discuss your progress on Friday. Make sure you have some good news for me."

Anyone else may have been intimidated by the Mayor's edict, but Ian was amused. Once a politician, always a politician. Boyce wanted this thing gone so he could go on with his campaigning.

Stopping by the deli Ian ordered a sandwich and thumbed through a local publication as he ate. He thought about his years in New York City. He jealously protected his excellent work ethic. He believed that a job worth doing was worth doing right. Besides, he didn't want to share Weldon's fate. Monroe or not, Mayor Boyce would have no qualms about replacing him.

CHAPTER 10

Covington, Rhode Island
Tuesday April 13th, 1999

Joyce Parsons took a deep breath before pushing the door to *Anna's Attic* open. *Toni must have changed her mind and come in early*, she thought. When they had spoken on the phone last night, Toni had said she wouldn't be in until noonish. She'd also shocked Joyce with the news of Carlton's impromptu visit. The older woman didn't know what to make of that bit of news.

Standing in the showroom, the familiar surroundings sent a wave of sadness through her. She hadn't been here since she'd found Anna dead on the floor four days ago. She shuddered as her eyes fell on the spot where Anna had fallen. "That fool Lieutenant. I knew this was no accident!" She said to no one in particular.

"Who's there?" an unfamiliar voice spoke from the storeroom next to the office.

"Joyce Parsons. Show yourself." A gasp escaped her as she took in the man who emerged from the back of the shop. Her eyes narrowed "Carlton Joel DeWitt, what in heaven's name are you doing here?"

"It's good to see you too, Joyce," Carlton responded sarcastically.

A retired schoolteacher in her sixties, Joyce Parsons' appearance was matronly. Her short gray hair, glasses, and plump figure reminded Carlton of an illustration of Mother Goose from the cover of a children's book. The older woman was dressed in her usual dark slacks, print blouse and wool cardigan. "Answer my question. What are you doing here?"

"I decided to surprise Gram with a visit. Only it was I who was in for a surprise. Kinda worked out, though. Toni really needs me here during this time. She's a mess."

That girl hasn't needed a man in her life, Joyce thought. Out loud she said, "I meant what are you doing here, in the shop?"

"Toni let me in on her way to some appointment. I think she's meeting her boss or something."

"Oh I see…" was all she could think of to say. Joyce knew Toni had an appointment with Morris Jamison, Anna's lawyer. She was happy to see that Toni had kept that information from Carlton, what bothered her was that Carlton had been left here alone with all this valuable merchandise. *What was Antonia thinking?* "I have to prepare a list for the detective. I believe he'll be here shortly. Perhaps you can help me? My eyes aren't what they used to be." Her eyes were just fine, she just needed Carlton where she could keep an eye on him.

Carlton shrugged and followed Joyce to the office. He could continue looking for more small things to sell later. He had made a tidy sum off the perfume bottle he had sold to Sandoval Pratt, and Carlton hoped the watch, hair comb and stick pin sitting in the inside pocket of his leather jacket would prove equally lucrative. The money people paid for this old crap never ceased to amaze him. He hoped no one noticed that he had rearranged some of the items on the shelves so it didn't look like anything was missing. He considered wearing his jacket instead of leaving it wrapped around the back of one of the chairs in the showroom, but decided that would be too obvious. He didn't want to arouse Joyce's suspicions. He knew from past experience that she was as sharp as a tack.

They spent the next forty-five minutes compiling a list of the shop's regular customers. Anna had made a file folder for each person and had carefully catalogued all their purchases. Some of the files dated back to the 1940s, when the shop had first opened. Refusing to join the computer revolution, Anna had insisted that all record keeping be done by hand. Carlton cursed as he got yet another paper cut. Nevertheless, he dictated the name on the last folder he'd pulled from the file cabinet to Joyce who added it to the bottom of the list of names, phone numbers, and addresses on the legal pad she was using.

"Are we finally done?" he asked, irritated.

"Yes, Carlton, we're done. And just in time, too," she checked her watch. "Ian Monroe should be here any minute."

Oh great. Super-cop. Just what I need. "Well, I'm starving. I'm gonna get something to eat. I'll be back soon." Carlton grabbed his jacket and made a hasty exit before Joyce could stall him.

With furrowed eyebrows, Joyce gaped at Carlton as he practically ran out of the shop. *Hmm,* she thought. *What was that all about?* Leaving the office, Joyce walked into the storeroom hoping Carlton hadn't disturbed anything. From the looks of it, everything was as it should be. The room, the size of a large walk-in closet, had rows of shelves on the wall facing the door that held the latest smaller antiques Anna had purchased. Two large tables faced each other in the middle of the room. It was there that Joyce and Anna had spent many hours lovingly cleaning, restoring, and pricing the treasures Anna was planning to sell. Joyce felt the sharp sting of tears behind her eyes. How could she possibly have any tears left to shed? It felt like she hadn't stopped crying since Friday. *Pull yourself together, woman,* she chided herself. *Toni needs you to be strong. There'll be time enough for grieving later.*

Joyce switched off the overhead light in the storeroom, planning to return to the office and wait for Ian's arrival. She wondered if he would remember her, his Kindergarten teacher. That was over thirty years ago, and if she remembered correctly, the boy was always in some kind of trouble. He just couldn't seem to keep his nose out of the other children's business. She used to tell his parents that he would make a great lawyer someday, never once thinking he would choose a career in law enforcement. The young men of Covington society just didn't become blue-collar workers. But, then again, Ian always marched to a different beat. Even at five years old, one could see he would never become a nine to fiver. *So much like dear Antonia,* she thought sighing. *Ah well, to each his own.*

On her way to the office, Joyce spotted something odd. Actually it was what *wasn't* there that caught her eye. The Quezal perfume bottle that normally sat on the Victorian washstand was missing. She tried to remember if Anna had mentioned it being sold. No, she was sure Anna hadn't. Strange, because a valuable item like that would have certainly given them something to talk about over their morning coffee. Quezal glass holds the same value as Tiffany's, and was hard to come by. The perfume bottle was precisely decorated green, and was iridescent even without direct light. Maybe one of the policemen who had traipsed though here on Friday had knocked it over. But, surely they would have said something. She had taught many of them, and she knew them to be honest men. No, there must be another explanation. Of course, Carlton. Everything in the showroom was priced. He would know how much he could get for all the items in here. *Oooh it makes me so angry to think that he could steal from his dead grandmother!*

A knock on the door turned her attention away from the missing item. Ian Monroe was standing just inside the open door carrying a black case and holding a large manila folder. She beamed at the sight of him. He had grown into a devilishly handsome man. Clint Eastwood like, if she wasn't mistaken.

"Mrs. Parsons," he smiled, setting the case down, "I thought that was you standing there. Do you remember me? Ian Monroe. My parents are Wallace and Catherine Monroe."

"Of course I remember you. How could I forget one of my favorite students," Joyce responded as she stepped into Ian's embrace. "It's so nice to see you again, although I wish it were under better circumstances."

"I hear you. How long have you been working for Anna?"

"I don't really work *for* Anna. That is I do work here but it's more for something to keep me occupied. Miles, Mr. Parsons, left me with more than enough to take care of myself, but I found I had so much time on my hands. Anna's business was booming and she needed an extra set of hands. And, well, mine were available," Joyce finished with a shrug.

"Oh. I see. And how's Loren?" Ian asked about Joyce's only child.

Her mother's pride was evident on her face. "Oh Ian, his practice in Providence is thriving. And he and Melissa are expecting their first child in August. I can't wait."

"Wow. That's great, Mrs. Parsons."

"Please call me Joyce. Mrs. Parsons makes me feel so old."

Ian laughed. This woman had always held a special place in his heart. She was the only one of his teachers that knew how to handle him. Strict discipline, tempered with a lot of love. He hated that they had been reunited by someone's death. Clearing his throat, Ian got to the reason for his visit. "Mrs. Parsons, I mean Joyce, Toni said you'd have a list of your customers for me."

"Yes, of course. It's in the office.'

"And if you don't mind, I'd like to take a look at the place where Mrs. DeWitt was, um, found. I have the photos taken by the forensic photographer, but seeing in person is more effective."

"I'm sure. I found Anna over there," she pointed behind her, "between the Chippendale desk and the sofa. I'll just get you that list." She hurried to the office.

Not surprised she wanted no part of this, Ian walked to the 'crime scene.' The floor where Anna's head had lain had obviously been cleaned recently. Someone had removed the white tape, but he could still see the imprint it had made on the hard wood floor. It looked like the desk had been cleaned also. The blood and hairs that had been photographed on the edge of the desk were gone. *So much for an uncontaminated crime scene*, Ian thought wryly. He had brought along a portable fingerprinting unit to take the elimination prints, but he knew they would yield no clues. He had just come up with that so he could have an excuse to see Toni again. Although DeWitt's reaction when he'd mentioned fingerprints was certainly something to think about.

Opening the case file folder, he set it down on the couch and removed two large color photographs from it. They were the clearest shots that were taken of Anna as she was found on Friday morning. Ian tried to ascertain where Anna had been standing when she'd been pushed. He moved about pretending to fall back from many different angles, all the while holding the photos up in front of him. The best he could tell, Anna had been standing very close to the couch. Maybe her assailant had been trying to push her onto the couch? Being an old woman, it would have taken her a few minutes to have pushed herself back up, giving the perpetrator time to run off. Had she surprised a burglar? No, the report said there was no forced entry. The Coroner's official time of death indicated that the shop was already closed, so Anna must have known the murderer and let them in. But who, he wondered, who would commit such an odious act?

Ian looked up, just as Carlton strode into the showroom. The latter stopped short upon seeing Ian and the two of them stared each other down for a few seconds. Ian's hand twitched. He wanted to draw his gun, and say, "Go ahead, make my day," just to see what Carlton would do. Joyce's entrance from the office dissipated the moment. When she spotted Carlton, her demeanor changed. There was no mistaking the obvious tension between Joyce and Carlton.

"Ah, Carlton, you're back just in time. I trust you've satisfied your hunger," she spoke with a less than friendly voice.

"Yeah, Joyce," Carlton's tone was equally unfriendly. To Ian he asked, "Find anything?"

"No. Maybe you can tell me what I should be looking for."

"How should I know," Carlton said defensively, "you're the cop. Isn't that what you do?"

"Yeah. It's what I do." Ian placed the photos face down on top of the case file. "And you know, I could use some help. Could you come over here and pretend to be your grandmother. I'd like to reenact her fall."

"Are you kidding me? No way! That's sick, man." Carlton's face was twisted in revulsion.

"I'll do it," Joyce said, surprising them both. "Anna and I are, were, about the same height." She walked to Ian and handed him the list of customers. "Where should I stand?" she asked bravely.

"Uh, okay. If you wouldn't mind stepping over here," Ian said gesturing towards the couch. He tossed the list onto the open case file and stood in front of Joyce. He gently placed his hands around her upper forearms. "I'm almost certain this is where Anna was standing. Now if you'd just lean back a little. Don't worry, I won't let you fall. I just need to see if the desk is close enough…"

Shit! The son-of-a-bitch got it right, Carlton cursed inwardly. *I've gotta put an end to this little presentation, and pronto.* "Stop, Monroe. I don't want Toni walking in and seeing this. She's in too fragile a state of mind to handle this."

"Toni's coming?" Ian couldn't help the flutter in his stomach. He released Joyce, who was staring at Carlton as if he'd grown a second head.

"Uh, yeah. She called my cell a few minutes ago to say she was on her way," Carlton lied.

Not wanting to cause Toni any more stress than was necessary, Ian acquiesced. He hastily threw the photographs and customer list into the folder and slammed it shut. There was little else for him to do, but fingerprint Joyce and Carlton, and wait for Toni to arrive.

Toni pushed on the brass bar and opened the glass door to the Covington National Bank Building. The directory next to the elevators showed that Mr. Jameson's office was in Suite 403. When the elevator doors opened, several men and women exited, leaving the cab empty. As the doors bumped shut, Toni breathed in a lemon fragrance that reminded her of the lemon wax she used to clean her apartment. She could feel the pressure in her ears from the rapid ascent of the elevator which matched the pressure of her mounting headache.

When the cab came to an abrupt stop, the doors slid open revealing a carpeted hallway with doors on both sides. Toni found Mr. Jameson's name on the third door on the right: *Morris Jameson, Attorney at Law*, in raised brass letters on a well-shined black door. She entered the office and was greeted by a young woman at the reception desk. She introduced herself and was told the lawyer was expecting her.

As she waited for him, Toni looked around the small outer office. It was comfortably furnished with burgundy colored overstuffed chairs, two lamps on wooden end tables, and a coffee table with an assortment of magazines on it.

The door to an inner office to the left of the receptionist's desk opened and Mr. Jameson came out. He was a tall distinguished looking man with a full head of gray hair. The dark blue business suit he was wearing, contradicted the fatherly features of his face. "Ms. Stanton, I'm Morris Jameson," he said as he shook hands with her. "It's nice to finally meet you. I'm sorry it's under these sad circumstances. Please come this way."

He led Toni through the door into a large bright office with a huge glass topped table that he was using as a desk. Behind it were ceiling to floor windows that afforded a view of the entire city. One could see the Pawtuxet River. Covington had been a quaint little town with once prosperous industries. West and central Covington were still rural, but the eastern section they lived in had grown around the textile mills that had been built along the river's edge. The towns of Quidnick, Anthony, Arkwright, Harris, Washington, Covington Center, Summit, and Greene Villages around Covington gave a view into the past. It was a picturesque land area that had been mostly agricultural and dotted with farms. As America became industrialized to meet the demand for goods, Eastern Covington had changed from farming to industry.

"Please have a seat. Can I get you something to drink?"

"No thank you, I've already had three cups of coffee this morning," Toni replied.

Before Toni sat down, she was drawn to the wall on her right that had numerous framed photographs hanging on it. She thought she recognized the people in some of the photos. She was right. One of the black and white images was of her grandparents with Mr. Jameson in their younger days; another was of Nana with Mr. Jameson and the mayor of Covington; yet another was of Nana and some people Toni didn't recognize standing on a stage holding a plaque. Wherever she looked her grandmother was there. She was so engrossed in the photographs she didn't notice Mr. Jameson had followed her until she heard his voice right behind her.

"Anna DeWitt was special to this town. Her passing will be felt by all." The silence between them was deafening. Both lost in their own sadness.

Morris Jameson cleared his throat and launched into a brief history of Covington designed to take their minds off their grief. "Your grandfather, Kurt, was instrumental in the development of Covington. During World War II, we had so much more to think about than the condition of our town. The streets had potholes, the sidewalks were cracked, and many buildings were in disrepair. After the war Kurt knew that

Covington had to be revitalized if it were to survive. He had begun a plan to market Antique Promenade to attract wealthy shoppers from Providence and other large cities. He became a one-man force that lobbied every and any town official he could find. After he died, Anna continued to help make Covington prosperous. He and your grandmother have been recognized repeatedly for their efforts on behalf of our town."

"Wow! I barely remember my grandfather. But, I know Nana missed him everyday. She always talked about him."

"Come, let's sit down," Mr. Jameson said, offering Toni one of the chairs in front of his desk before sitting behind it.

Antonia, I'll come right to the reason for this meeting. I prepared all of the legal documents for *Anna's Attic* and for your grandparents personally. I have Anna's will here and this meeting is for the purpose of reading her will. I understand your Uncle Joel is in Europe and is not able to be here."

"Yes, my Aunt Jessica is ill and they can't travel right now. Does he need to be here?"

"No. The will and its codicils cover everything and we can proceed with the reading. I'll give you an overview of Anna's will. Your grandmother's will basically leaves everything to you. There are a couple of special bequests that I need to go over with you."

"Wait a minute. What do you mean everything? What about my uncle, my cousin…" Toni leaned forward and put her arms on the desk. She was not expecting this.

"Antonia, let me explain. You are her executrix, sort of like a personal representative. You will carry out all of the legal matters for her estate and settle any debts and liquidate any assets. Since you are the only heir it will be a fairly simple estate to settle. The special bequests are to Joyce, her long time employee and your Aunt Jessica and Uncle Joel.

The bequests are for a few of the antiques that are from your grandmother's personal collection. Joel is aware of the contents of this will since he was present at the time I drafted it for Anna. He made it clear that you were to inherit everything, because he wanted you to be financially secure."

Toni sank back into the chair. She was speechless.

The lawyer continued, "I asked you to come alone because of the exclusion of Carlton DeWitt from any inheritance. That's why I was surprised when you told me he was in town. Anna had led me to believe he was the black sheep of the family and his parents had disowned him. Your grandmother has a specific clause that states Carlton is to receive only one thousand dollars and that proves she did not forget him in her will. She also has a clause that says if he challenges the will he receives nothing."

"I can't believe she did this to Carl?"

"Antonia, you know Carlton's history as well as I do. Anna's motives were mainly to protect you and all that she and your grandfather had worked so hard to achieve. If you feel the need to help Carlton by giving him more after the estate is settled, that's entirely up to you."

"This clause, can one do that?"

"Yes, that is how I counseled her to structure the will to prevent the estate and you from being sued."

"Oh."

"One more thing. There's a letter for you from your grandmother. She had instructed me to give this letter to you upon the reading of her will. It is a personal letter that I have neither seen nor read."

Mr. Jameson handed her an envelope with Anna's handwriting on the front. "Antonia Stanton" was all it said. It was sealed shut. Toni stared at the envelope for a minute trying to decide if she should open it now or wait until later.

Her hands began to shake. These would be the last words she would receive from her Nana.

"Antonia, I'll leave you alone for a few minutes to read Anna's letter." He stood up and quietly left the office leaving Toni sitting staring at the envelope in her hands.

She slid her finger under the flap and it opened easily. The glue appeared to have dried up long ago leaving a yellow stain on the envelope. She unfolded the two pages and saw her grandmother's handwriting on them. Tears immediately blurred her vision. She brushed them away and took a deep breath.

January 1973

My dearest Antonia,

If you are reading this letter, it means my attorney Morris Jameson has given it to you because something has happened to me. In the event of my death, or if I am in grave condition and unable to communicate, I have instructed Morris to give you this letter on the condition that you are already eighteen or older.

I'm writing to you after just returning home from your parents' funeral. You are down for a nap so I am taking this opportunity to write my thoughts and feelings.

My darling Toni, I promise to give you the best life I can. I can never replace your parents, but I will always be there for you. My heart is breaking at losing my daughter, but I have you to think about now. I will raise you as I know your mother would want me to. I will instill in you all the traditions my mother instilled in me that I had passed on to your mother knowing that she would pass them on to you. Unfortunately, there is one tradition that your mother, and maybe I, will not be able to pass to you. Therefore, I am writing it here.

When I was married, your great grandmother, Natalia, gave me a set of jewelry that she had received from the Russian Grand Duchess Olga. It includes an emerald and diamond necklace, emerald and diamond earrings, and a diamond bracelet. These were given to your great grandmother before she and your great grandfather fled Russia. She sewed them into the hem of the dress that she wore on the day they left Russia for Belgium and then on to America. I in turn surprised your mother with them on the day she married your father. Ashley was to do the same on your wedding day. Now that I know that will not happen, it is up to me to pass them down to you. However, I'm not sure how much longer I will live. In case I am not alive for your wedding, I am writing this now to let you know that these invaluable pieces are yours. I ask that you enjoy them and then pass them down to your daughter on her wedding day.

Toni had to put the letter down. She was overcome with emotion and couldn't continue reading. Goosebumps ran up her arms. She took a couple of tissues out of her purse and blew her nose. She wiped her eyes with her fingers. Toni sat up straight, shifted slightly in her seat, and forced herself to finish reading the letter.

If you need help with anything, please ask Mr. Jameson. He has been a trusted friend and lawyer to us for many years, and he will not steer you wrong.

Just to know that you will be reading this one-day makes me realize how sad you will be about losing me, after having lost your parents at such a young age. Antonia, I will be with you always in your heart and memories. I love you.   Nana

Toni reread the letter. She knew nothing of the jewelry her grandmother described. She didn't remember her great-grandparents as she was still a baby when they died. She had never known Natalia and Anton Simonov. Toni refolded the letter, put it back into its envelope, and into her handbag. She slowly stood up and walked to the office door. Upon opening it, she saw Mr. Jameson standing next to his receptionist's desk hanging up the phone.

"Mr. Jameson, I've finished reading the letter. If you don't mind, can we finish this later?"

"We are finished for today, Antonia. There will be some court documents that require your signature and bank account paperwork that will need done for the estate. But, that'll come later."

"Thank you, Mr. Jameson."

Mr. Jameson shook her hand and walked with her towards the outer door. "Thank you for coming, Antonia. I will be in touch. In the meantime, if there's anything I can do, please don't hesitate to call me."

CHAPTER 11

Covington, Rhode Island
Tuesday April 13th, 1999

Toni walked to her car in a trance like state trying to process all of the information she had heard and read. She had to decide how and when she would tell Joyce and her uncle about the contents of the will. A bigger problem was how she should handle telling Carlton that Nana left him only one thousand dollars. She knew Joyce didn't expect anything, and Joel and Jessica would be delighted to receive a few of her grandmother's antiques from her personal collection. But, she knew Carlton would be expecting more than he was getting.

Chewing on her bottom lip she eased her Lexus out of the parking lot. This had not been what she was expecting. She just thought she'd have to sign a few papers and be done with it. She'd never dealt with the legalities of a death before, and was unaware of the emotional strain it put on families. At least her family was financially able to cover funeral expenses with no worries.

Toni found herself pulling into her parking spot at home. "How did I get here?" she asked her empty passenger seat. *As long as I'm here,* she thought, *I might as well go in and freshen up. I don't want anyone seeing me like this.*

Inside her apartment, Toni played back the messages on her answering machine. There was one from her friend Barbara, confirming dinner plans for tomorrow; one from the dry cleaners, telling her the suit they had altered was ready; and one from Uncle Joel. At the sound of his voice, Toni broke down. She hadn't realized just how much she needed him here until now.

Tears were still streaming down her face, when he answered the phone. "Uncle Joel, it's Toni. I need to talk to you."

"Little Ant, what's wrong?"

"I just needed to hear your voice. I don't know where to begin. There's so much to do; so much going on; so many decisions I don't want to make alone. What if I screw it all up? I don't know, I don't know, I don't know."

"Calm down, Little Ant. Tell me what's been happening. I'm sure we can figure it out together," Joel said soothingly.

Toni recounted her experience at the lawyer's. She told her uncle about the money, the letter, and the jewelry. Wiping her eyes, she asked, "How do I tell Carl?"

"With everything you have going on, don't worry about Carlton. You don't have to tell him anything, since he's in Vegas and most likely won't contact you anyway. Let Jameson handle it."

"Oh! I guess I didn't tell you. Carl is here." She braced for her uncle's response.

"In Covington? Please tell me Carlton isn't in Covington," Uncle Joel's voice rose a fraction.

"Um, ah, he showed up Sunday. I had no clue he was coming. He said he was here to visit Nana."

"No doubt, coming to collect."

"Maybe Nana invited him?" Toni had stopped crying by now.

"I don't think so. Not in this lifetime," he added sarcastically.

"You know, I think he's changed. He's being so helpful, and he's even promised to stay until I don't need him anymore."

"Antonia Stanton! Don't let him fool you into giving him more money. You know how irresponsible he can be. He'll just blow through it and then come back begging for more. Why do you think your grandmother only left him one thousand dollars? It's not because she's a mean old lady. She would have loved nothing more than making sure he was comfortable for the rest of his life. But, she knew and I know the way Carlton is."

"But Uncle Joel, he hasn't asked for anything."

"Yet."

"I'm not an idiot. If Carlton's motives are not honorable, I think I'll be able to tell." Toni wanted to change the subject. "Do you know where Nana kept the jewelry?"

"I don't know. Come to think of it, I can't even hazard a guess. She didn't tell you in her letter?"

"No, she didn't. Oh well, that's not really important. I'm sure I'll find them when I clean out her apartment," she said shuddering. "I'll tackle all of that after the funeral. By the way, I'm planning to go to the funeral home today."

"Alright, Little Ant. Call me tomorrow morning, your time, and let me know what you've arranged."

After they each said I love you and goodbye, she hung up feeling somewhat better.

An unfamiliar car was parked in front of the shop when Toni arrived. A black Corvette that made her wish she had the guts to own it. She didn't need to wonder who the owner was, because she could see Ian Monroe walking around inside the shop. She was glad he was still there. From the doorstep, she watched him for a minute or so, before opening the door. He was holding some papers in his hands, and seemed to be studying the area where her grandmother had fallen. He turned when he heard the door open.

"Well, here she is," Ian announced. "It's about time you got here. We've been waiting for you."

Toni couldn't take her eyes off him. She was really beginning to like this guy. "What's wrong? I told Joyce what you needed. Wasn't she able to get the lists for you?"

"Nothing's wrong. Yes, she got the lists for me," Ian crossed his arms, and stood there looking at her.

Toni wasn't sure why he hadn't left as soon as he got the lists. She would have liked to believe that he had hung around because he wanted to see her again, but, with men these days, who knew. She decided to ask. "Excuse me if I sound rude but, why are you still here?"

"Aren't you happy to see me?"

"Yes, of course. What woman wouldn't be?" Realizing what she had just admitted, Toni blushed and turned away. "Didn't you get what you came for?"

"How do you know what I came for?" he said winking.

"Got something in your eye, or is that a permanent twitch?" Toni smiled as she blinked her eyes rapidly. She was rewarded with a boyish grin.

"Actually, I figured I'd wait for you since Carlton said you were on your way. I didn't realize you would be so long."

"Carlton said that? When?"

"Didn't you call him on his cell?"

"No… I… Mmm…"

"Toni, I didn't know you had come in," Joyce said as she entered the showroom from the little office.

Toni walked over to her grandmother's faithful employee, and gave her a hug. "Joyce, I am so glad you're here. I don't know what I'd do without you." Both women got a little misty eyed.

"My dear, you know I wouldn't leave you. You're like the daughter I never had. How have you been holding up?" Joyce asked with concern.

"Hanging in there. There's so much I have to go over with you. But not now."

"Well, I guess that's my cue to leave," Ian piped up. "Joyce, thank you for providing me with these lists." To Toni he said, "I'll be in touch so we can schedule a good time for me to get your prints." Ian was out the door before Toni could say anything.

"Joyce, where's Carl?" Toni asked peering around the showroom.

Joyce snorted. "He's rummaging in the storeroom, probably looking for something to pilfer."

"Joyce!"

"Don't be fooled. A leopard never changes his spots."

"Where is this coming from?" Toni asked.

"When you called me yesterday, I know you said Carlton was a Godsend. Toni, I've been with Anna since you came to live with her. I know Carlton well. It's difficult for me to accept that he has changed overnight. Keep an eye on him. I'm not convinced he's trustworthy."

"Why is it that everyone close to Nana thinks ill of Carl?"

"Who is everyone?" Joyce asked.

"Morris Jameson, for one. That's what I needed to talk to you about. I met with him this morning. He told me what is in Nana's will. I need to ask you some things. But, I can't do it in front of Carl," Toni had dropped her voice to a whisper.

Joyce raised an eyebrow. "Is there an errand we can send him on?"

"Let's ask him to go pick up some lunch for us. That should give us enough time to talk," Toni said continuing to whisper.

Joyce nodded, and the two women walked towards the storeroom.

With a full belly, Toni felt better able to make decisions. Nana had always told her, "No one can think on an empty stomach." While Carlton was out of the shop picking up their lunch, Toni had talked to Joyce and told her in detail about the meeting with Mr. Jameson. She also told Joyce she wasn't sure what she was going to do about *Anna's Attic*. She wanted to ask Joyce if she knew anything about the jewelry, but Carlton returned with lunch before she was able to. They decided to finish the conversation later.

Toni finished cleaning up the kitchenette, and went into the showroom. Carlton had returned to the storeroom, and Joyce had gone back to Anna's office.

Now that the autopsy was complete, Toni had to start planning Anna's funeral. She knew she had to "pull herself up by her bootstraps" as Nana was fond of telling her. So, knowing she worked best while on the floor surrounded by her photographs, Toni grabbed a notepad and pen and sat cross-legged on one of the Persian rugs. Anna had put rugs down here and there to make the furniture in the shop look more like it would in a home. She started a list of things to do:

1. Call funeral home to make arrangements
2. Make sign for shop window
3. Call Pastor Kevin at Anna's church
4. Select clothing for Anna to be buried in
5. Call Barbara, Margie, Julie, Alec, and David; cannot make weekly dinner on Wednesday.

She decided not to write anything on the list about the lawyer or the jewelry in case Carlton was to see it.

Joyce emerged from the office holding a large piece of paper. "I went ahead and made a sign for the front window. What do you think?" The paper that Joyce held up said, 'THE SHOP IS CLOSED UNTIL FURTHER NOTICE. PLEASE LEAVE A MESSAGE AT 555-6983' printed in black magic marker. "I put the number in case customers need to reach us. I'm not sure when you want to reopen the shop, so, I didn't mention it on the sign."

Toni wasn't sure what a reasonable amount of time to mourn Nana's passing away should be. She came to the conclusion that there was no reason to keep the shop closed more than a week and that her mourning the death of her grandmother was going to take a lot longer to get over than a week. "Next Tuesday. We will reopen next Tuesday."

Toni removed the plastic hanging sign, and taped Joyce's sign on the glass of the front door underneath the store hours. She went outside to inspect it from the sidewalk, and was satisfied it was large enough but still respectful.

Popping her head into the office, she asked Joyce, "I have a few phone calls to make. Will it bother you if I use the desk phone?"

"No, Toni, it won't bother me. But wouldn't you rather go upstairs so you can talk privately?"

"Mmm. That's a good idea. Oh, by the way I left some things on the desk chair for you to look at. I wasn't sure what to do with them. Do you have time to sort through them?"

"Of course, dear, I'll do that right away." She moved behind the desk, picked up the stack, and placed it on the desk. Taking a seat she sent a warm smile in Toni's direction. "Let me know what else I can do."

"Thanks, Joyce." Toni took her list and went upstairs.

After sifting through the assortment, and taking care of each item appropriately, Joyce was left with the shop sales record book. It was a beige pad that held the carbon copy receipts of any purchases made at *Anna's Attic*. A thought dawned on Joyce. Maybe Anna had indeed sold the Quezal perfume bottle and it hadn't been stolen after all. Joyce flipped through several pages going back a few weeks. There was no mention of the sale of the perfume bottle. A voice inside Joyce's head insisted the item had been stolen. But, what could a thief do with such a thing? You couldn't very well take it to a pawnshop and expect to get anywhere near its value. Since everything at the shop had a price on it, the thief would know how much the bottle was worth. Who else would know the value of it? She pondered that thought a minute and came to the only logical answer: another antique dealer.

A plan of action was taking place in Joyce's head. She would call all the dealers in the vicinity. The perfume bottle was a numbered piece and would be easy to identify. She considered telling Ian and letting *him* be the detective, but since she had no real proof of the bottle's theft, she thought he'd dismiss it as inconsequential. Satisfied that she was making the right decision, Joyce figured she would stop by the library before going home and ask for help with searching on the Internet for Rhode Island antique dealers.

I'll call Pastor Kevin first, Toni thought. She reached for Nana's personal telephone that sat on an end table next to the sofa in her grandmother's living room. He probably already knows from the news that Nana died. She pressed the buttons on the touchtone phone and heard several rings before the church secretary answered. "I'm sorry Ms. Stanton, Pastor Kevin is at the hospital now. Can I have him call you back when he returns?"

"Yes, certainly. I'll be at Anna's Attic most of the day. Let me give you my cell phone number just in case." After leaving her cell number as well as her home number, Toni hung up. She placed her next call.

"Chapman Funeral Home," a man's voice answered.

"Hello. This is Antonia Stanton, Anna DeWitt's granddaughter. I need to talk to someone about funeral arrangements for my grandmother."

"Hello Miss Stanton. This is Charles Chapman. I was very sorry to hear about Anna's passing. I am available to meet with you anytime today so we can make the arrangements."

"Mr. Chapman," Toni began hesitantly, "I've never done this before. Is there anything I need to bring with me?"

"Miss Stanton, please be assured that we will make all the arrangements and prepare the necessary paperwork. You are like family to us. Don't worry, we'll take care of everything for you. I'll see you when you come in,"

Toni was about to pick up the phone again and call her friend Barbara, when she heard a loud banging coming from the front door. She ran to the landing just as Joyce appeared at the bottom of the stairs.

"Toni, there's a man at the door. I know who he is. He's a Russian who has yet to learn manners. Your grandmother refused to do business with him for many reasons. I'm sure he's not here to pay his respects."

"Unfortunately. We can't pretend nobody's here." The banging on the front door grew more insistent. Toni became more annoyed than fearful. "He's gonna break the damn glass! I've gotta let him in."

Toni descended the stairs as Carlton came striding out of the storeroom. "What the hell is going on? What's all the racket?" he bellowed. The visitor began rattling the doorknob as if to shake the door off its hinges. "Who the hell is that?" Carlton yelled pointing towards the door.

Toni shrugged her shoulders. What she did know was that the man could see them huddled in the back of the showroom. She started to walk towards the front door, but Carlton held her back. "Let me!"

As Carlton strode towards the door, Toni shot Joyce a look of apprehension, then followed, remaining a few paces behind him. Joyce, however, was hot on *her* heels.

Carlton flung the door open. "Yeah, what?" he asked in an unpleasant voice, blocking the doorway.

"I'm here to see Anna DeWitt. We have business," the man said with a heavy Russian accent.

"She's not here. Who are you and what do you want?" Carlton continued in a gruff manner. Toni allowed him to play the role of protector. She stood behind him mutely. She didn't hear Joyce come up behind her.

"Are you in charge?"

"Listen, Mister. I don't know who you are or what you want. All I know is that you were about to break this door down. If you don't explain yourself in the next thirty seconds, I'm gonna break your face."

"This is going to get ugly," Joyce whispered into Toni's ear, prompting her to step in.

"Carlton, let's invite this gentleman in to find out what he wants," Toni suggested quietly hoping to dissipate the situation. Instead, she somehow managed to upset her cousin.

"Suit yourself," Carlton huffed. He pushed past her, deposited himself on the nearest couch, and pretended to read the day's newspaper.

The burly man entered the shop before Toni could react to Carlton's childishness. He removed his hat to reveal a head of thick dark brown hair streaked with gray and neatly trimmed. He had a graying mustache and beard and dark brown piercing eyes. Under his black trench coat, Toni saw he was dressed in a dark blue business suit.

Rashovsky launched into the spiel he had used years before when he had met Anna DeWitt for the first time. "Allow me to introduce myself. I'm Boris Rashovsky, a professor at Moscow University in Russia. I am currently employed by the Moscow Museum. I wish to have a moment of your time."

"I'm Antonia Stanton, Anna DeWitt's granddaughter. How may I help you?"

"Ah, Miss Stanton. A pleasure to make your acquaintance," the man bowed his head slightly. This was a far cry from his earlier behavior. "I am an old friend of your grandmother's. We have had many encounters in the past few years. I was distressed to learn of her passing. She was an extraordinary woman. Please accept my sincere condolences."

Joyce snorted. "Sincere my eye," she mumbled, surprising both Toni and Carlton.

Rashovsky squinted at Joyce. It was obvious to Toni that the contempt Joyce had expressed earlier was mutual.

"Miss Stanton, is there somewhere we can speak privately?"

Toni wasn't sure what was going on, but she was positive she didn't want to be alone with this man. "We're all family here, and in mourning. I would appreciate it if you would quickly state the reason for your visit."

"I will not take up too much more of your time. I would like to make an offer to purchase something that Anna owns."

Carlton's ears perked up. He continued to pretend to read the newspaper, but his ears were on Rashovsky.

It was Joyce's turn to step forward, "Boris Rashovsky, I know you. You are no friend of Anna's. You've been after Anna for years to make that purchase. She has always refused to sell it to you or anyone and you know why. It's not any different now that Anna is dead. It's not for sale!" Toni was taken aback by the aggressiveness of Joyce's tone.

Rashovsky however, ignored Joyce's outburst. "Miss Stanton, I understand that Anna did not want to sell to me when she was alive. However, she's gone. I assume that you are now in charge of this fine establishment. I see no reason why you and I cannot do business together."

"Well Mr. Rashovsky, if my grandmother was that adamant about not working with you, then why should I?"

"Because, Miss Stanton, you know little about the antique business. I am an expert in that field, and I can be of invaluable service to you."

"She's not interested in your services," Joyce stated emphatically.

"Now wait a minute, Joyce," Carlton interjected finally abandoning the newspaper. "Let's hear what this man has to offer. I mean he's right, what does Toni know about antiques?"

"Carlton! My knowledge of antiques is neither here nor there. However, this is Nana's shop, not mine. If I decide to keep this place open, it will be on her terms," Toni insisted. "Mr. Rashovsky, this is obviously not a very good time. Perhaps you could come back, but please call first."

"Miss Stanton, my time is short. I am expected back in Europe at the end of next week. Therefore, I will be direct with you. I want to buy the jewels given to your family by the Grand Duchess." He scribbled something on the back of a business card that he had taken out of a gold case and handed it to Toni. "I am staying at Covington Suites until next Friday, the number is on the back. Please think about it and call me. I have been waiting a long time to possess these jewels. I will do anything to get my hands on them." Boris Rashovsky put on his hat and walked the few steps to the door. "Good day, Miss Stanton."

The door closed behind him and Toni stood staring in disbelief at the card Mr. Rashovsky had handed her.

"What is he talking about?" Carlton broke the silence.

"It doesn't matter, Anna wouldn't sell to him," Joyce said.

"Toni, what is going on?" Carlton asked again.

"I need to sit down. Carl, would you get me a glass of water please?" Toni sat down on the nearest chair still staring at the card.

"Toni, we need to talk," Joyce whispered urgently. "There's something you need to know."

Carlton came back with the water and she sipped it slowly.

"What are these jewels this guy was talking about," Carl asked.

Toni remained silent for a few minutes. She was not looking forward to this conversation. Not so soon after she herself had learned about the jewels.

"Since that boor opened his big mouth, I suppose it's okay to tell you. It's a set of jewelry the Grand Duchess Olga of Russia gave your great grandmother. It's been passed down to each daughter on her wedding day," Joyce explained.

Toni looked at Joyce, "You knew about this?"

Carlton looked at Toni, "You knew about this?"

Joyce answered first. "Yes. Anna told me everything."

"Carl, I just found out myself. I'm still trying to digest all this. Please don't be upset with me for not telling you," she looked up at him with appealing eyes.

"Well, where is the jewelry now?" Carlton asked no one in particular.

"I don't know. Do you, Joyce?" Toni asked.

"I don't know either," Joyce responded.

"What do you mean you don't know? Weren't you Anna's confidante? You said she told you everything," Carlton grilled Joyce. It was obvious he was agitated about something.

"Carl, that's enough. If Joyce says she doesn't know, then she doesn't know. We'll just have to look for it. When we find it, I'll be damned if I'm going to sell it. It's a family heirloom, and selling it is not an option." Toni sighed. The Grandfather clock in the shop chimed the three o'clock hour. "Damn it! I have to get to the funeral home before it closes." Toni stood up and casually tossed the card onto a brass plate that sat on the end table next to the chair. "Where did I leave my keys?"

Joyce answered, "I think you left them in the office with your purse. Do you want me to go to the funeral home with you?"

"I should go," Carlton said. "I am family after all."

"Carl, do you mind driving? I'm really not feeling up to it," Toni asked wearily.

"No problem."

"And I think you should take her straight home afterwards, Carlton," Joyce said. "I will lock up. Toni, I'll call you later this evening to see how it went."

Closing the door behind them Joyce knew this would be the perfect opportunity for her to go to the library. If she was lucky, she could get information she was looking for and still have time to call around before the shops closed for the day.

CHAPTER 12

Covington, Rhode Island
Tuesday April 13th, 1999

"Carl, thanks," Toni said, breaking the silence. They were on their way to make the funeral arrangements. Chapman Funeral Home was only a few blocks west of Antique Promenade.

"For what?" Carlton asked. He was quite content with the silence, because it gave him a chance to think. So much had happened in the last twenty-four hours; he needed to come up with a plan of action. Not usually a planner, he hadn't come all this way for a family reunion.

"For everything you've done, Cuz, just thanks for being here." Toni looked at Carlton expecting some sort of a reply. When he didn't say anything she stared out the passenger side window. She was too numb to notice his preoccupation.

"I hate funerals," Carlton announced banally, as they pulled up to a red light.

"Everybody does." Toni words were drowned out by the music that suddenly filled her Lexus. She looked reproachfully at her cousin who was scanning through radio stations obviously looking for a song he liked. Toni was shocked when he began singing along with Elvis to *Hound Dog*.

Irritated she exclaimed, "How the hell can you sing at a time like this?" She punched the power button on the radio plunging the car back into silence.

Realizing he couldn't blow his chances just yet, Carlton figured he'd feign interest in what was going on. He reached out to give Toni's shoulder a slight squeeze. "How do you want to handle the funeral arrangements?"

Placated, she responded, "I don't know. Something simple yet elegant feels right. There will probably be a large turn out from the towns' people plus the mayor and his entourage. I'm positive the *Covington Chronicle* will send someone. Don't be surprised if we're on the front page the morning after. So, we need to keep it dignified and respectful. I don't want it to turn into a circus," Toni said quietly.

"Right." Carlton wasn't thrilled with the idea of having his face slathered all over the paper. But, he rationalized this is a small town paper, who in Vegas would see it. Besides, he needed Toni to think he was the world's greatest cousin. Whatever he had to do, he had to do.

Toni told Carlton to take a right on Pickering Street since the funeral home sat on the corner of Pickering and Albany. She had always liked the building. White with two round columns in the front it looked stately and peaceful. She and Carlton walked in the front door and were greeted by Mr. Chapman. His family had owned the Chapman Funeral Home for three generations. It was started by his grandfather and handed down to his father and now he was operating it for the families in Covington.

"Miss Stanton, please come in," Mr. Chapman greeted her as she and Carlton entered the main hall.

Charles Chapman was a short, portly, balding man, wearing the obligatory black suit of a funeral home director. *He must be in his mid-sixties*, Toni guessed.

"Hello, Mr. Chapman. Do you know my cousin, Carlton? He's helping me with our grandmother's affairs."

Charles Chapman looked at Carlton with raised eyebrows. A few awkward seconds passed before the older man recovered. "Ah, Mr. DeWitt, so good of you to help out during this difficult time. I'm sure your cousin appreciates your presence."

As the men shook hands, Toni sensed that Mr. Chapman's greeting to Carlton was less than genuine. *How much about Carlton's shenanigans does he know*, she wondered.

"Please come into my office. We can sit and talk awhile before you make any decisions. I'd like to get an idea of what type arrangements you're thinking about." Mr. Chapman led Toni and Carlton towards his small office off the main hall.

"Mr. Chapman, where is my grandmother?" Toni asked, her voice barely above a whisper.

Charles Chapman stopped abruptly; this was not a question he was accustomed to answering. His head turned towards a door marked "PRIVATE". "In there. The Coroner sent her remains over this morning. Let's go on into my office."

Toni gently laid her hand on Chapman's arm. "Can I see her, please?"

Once again Chapman was taken aback by her request. "I'm sorry. But, due to Health Department regulations, I cannot allow you in there. There will be opportunity to see your grandmother during the viewing. Please, let's go to my office."

Carlton, who had remained silent during this exchange, decided he'd had enough. He took Toni's arm and guided her into Chapman's office. Toni was glad Carlton had done that. She was one step away from loosing control of her emotions; one step away from a screaming, sobbing display of pure anguish.

The office was sparsely furnished with an old wooden desk in front of which were two comfortable looking chairs. A sofa sat against the wall across from the desk. There were no windows to let in sunlight. The only source of light in the room came from two lamps: one sat on the corner of the desk and the other on a table by the sofa. The room was as solemn as the mood of the people who came here to do business.

After they had sat down, Mr. Chapman pulled out a file folder with a lot of papers in it. Toni looked at the amount of paperwork and felt a rush of panic. She made a quick decision. "Mr. Chapman, you've handled my grandfather's as well as my parents' funeral arrangements. My grandmother obviously trusted you. I don't think I can handle making her funeral arrangements, so I am going to ask you to use your best judgment."

"I quite understand, my dear. Please be assured that I will take care of everything for you. Anna was a good friend to this community, her funeral will reflect that. I just have a few minor details I must discuss with you."

Carlton stared straight ahead, and allowed his mind to wander away from the conversation. He didn't want to think about funerals, caskets, or flowers. He was too busy thinking about the jewelry that the Russian had mentioned. *I must do whatever is necessary*, he thought. *Yes, I must do whatever is necessary. I will find the jewelry, which will take care of all my problems. I will be set financially for the rest of my life.* Carlton slipped his hand into his pants pocket and felt for the business card he had taken off the brass plate where Toni had tossed it. *I have to find the jewels and sell them to that Russian before anyone else finds them,* he thought. *It will be all that I need. I can pay off the Tropical Casino, and buy myself a decent car. If it's true this jewelry came from the Russian Royal Family, then it must be worth a fortune. Hell, I can probably buy the Tropical Casino. Between the jewelry and whatever I'm going to get as an inheritance, I'll be living the high life.*

Now, I just have to come up with a plan to get away from Toni long enough to search the shop and upstairs apartment. I've been stuck with her all day every day since I got here, except for when I went to pick up lunch. There has to be a reason that allows me to be at the shop without her. It really sucks that she doesn't have a boyfriend. Someone I could convince to take her away for a day or two. I don't even think she has friends. No one's called her apartment since I've been staying there. What kind of a life does my cousin lead? No friends, no sex, no parties. Damn boring!

Without turning his head Carlton stole a glance at Toni. She was looking at some papers on Chapman's desk. *She's not half bad looking either. She stays in shape and has a pretty face. She doesn't even realize what one look from those beautiful green eyes could do to a man. What's the matter with her? How can anyone live like that? I saw the way that detective was eyeing her. Even the Russian couldn't help but check her out. So, men do find her attractive. Hmmm. Wonder why she's not dating anyone? Hey, what do I care? As soon as I can get my hands on that jewelry, I'm history.*

The printer on Chapman's desk came to life, ending Carlton's musings. He heard Chapman say something about signing the contract. He guessed they were about done here. He smiled sympathetically at Toni hoping she'd think he'd been paying attention all along. When she smiled back, he squeezed her hand gently and then went right back to his plotting.

And then there's Joyce. I know she doesn't trust me because she's been watching my every move. I have a feeling she knows about the small pieces I've already helped myself to. She's making it difficult for me to take anything larger, but if I find that jewelry, I won't need to. Maybe I can sneak out after Toni falls asleep and go to the shop one of these nights. Yes, that's the only way. No one will know, so no one will be suspicious. Carlton Joel DeWitt, you're quite a guy.

"Carl, what do you think?" Toni's question startled him.

"Huh? Sorry, I missed the question."

"What do you think about Mr. Chapman's idea for Nana's funeral?" Toni looked at him quizzically.

"Sure, sure, it's okay. Whatever you decide."

"Mr. DeWitt, it's not in stone, we can change anything you don't like," Mr. Chapman interjected. "Just tell me which aspect of the arrangements you're unhappy with, and we'll discuss it."

It seemed to Carlton that Chapman knew he hadn't been paying attention. "It's okay, I'll like whatever you pick out. If Gram and Toni trust you, so do I."

"Then it's settled. I'll take care of everything as we discussed, Miss Stanton. We will advertise the visitation for Thursday from nine to one, the burial will take place immediately afterwards. The notice will appear in tomorrow's paper. Would you like me to let Pastor Kevin know about the arrangements?"

"Yes, Mr. Chapman, I would appreciate it," Toni said.

"Good. I'll see you on Thursday. Please call me if you need anything or have any questions before then." Chapman stood up and shook hands with Toni, and again with Carlton, then escorted them to the front door.

Carlton pushed the door open for Toni, and as they walked to her car, he heard her give a sigh of relief and saw her shoulders relax. "That wasn't too bad," he said as if he knew what had been decided.

"No, it wasn't. I was prepared for much worse. Mr. Chapman was very nice. I feel satisfied that he will take care of everything. I wasn't looking forward to selecting a casket and flowers. There's only one thing left to do now."

"What's that?"

"I have a beautiful photograph of Nana I took last year. I'd like to blow it up and have it displayed on an easel near the front of the room. What do you think, Carl?"

"Gee, what a great idea. You're so thoughtful," Carlton figured it wouldn't hurt to butter Toni up a little.

"Actually, I'm exhausted. I'd love a glass of wine and a really good meal. Would you mind getting dinner together?"

"Done. Your wish is my command. I'll take care of everything. Listen, I'll drop you off at your apartment, and I'll buzz by the grocery to pick up a few things. How does that sound?"

"Carl, that sounds wonderful. You're being marvelous about all this. I'm starting to feel like I'm taking advantage of you."

"Nonsense, you deserve a little pampering right now and who better to pamper you than your own family. Right?"

"Right."

Joyce Parson's always loved the look of Covington's only library. The one-story building was made of red brick and sat on the corner of Antique Promenade and Taylor.

Three young girls walked out of the library laden with books. They smiled and waved at Joyce as they passed her. "Research project," one of them announced gesturing towards the books. "And Mrs. Palmer won't let us use the Internet, can you believe?"

After a few words of encouragement, Joyce pushed through the amber glass doors and entered the darkened alcove. She paused a moment letting her eyes adjust to the darkness before entering the main room of the library. She was glad it was not very crowded. She spotted Scott Duponte sitting behind the research desk intently studying the monitor in front of him. As she approached the desk he looked up. "Hey, Mrs. Parsons, what's going on?"

"Hello, Scott. I need your help."

"Sure thing. What do you need?" Scott clicked the mouse button and moved around the desk to stand next to her. A tall, lanky, teenager, Scott was dressed in his usual baggy jeans and wrinkled T-shirt. His brown hair was unkempt like he hadn't combed it in days. Despite his appearance, Joyce knew he was one of the most helpful kids she'd come across.

"I need to look up the names and numbers of other antique dealers in the vicinity."

"Gee, Mrs. Parsons, I hope you're not planning on leaving Covington. Are they closing the shop?"

"Oh. No, no. At least not right away."

"Good. It's bad enough we're going to miss Mrs. DeWitt, it would suck if we lost you too."

"Don't worry, Scott, I'm not going anywhere. My research is business related."

Scott led Joyce to a row of computers at the back of the library. The computer lab area was set away from the shelves and reading area so that the clicking on the keyboard did not disturb those studying and reading. Scott pulled up a chair for

Joyce then took his place in front of the monitor. Within seconds the monitor displayed a list of twenty-four dealers closest to Covington. "I can expand the search parameters and get more names for you."

"No thank you, Scott. This'll do for now. Can you print this for me?"

"Done." The young man retrieved the printout and handed it to Joyce. "Anything else?"

"No. Say hello to your parents for me."

As Scott returned to his desk, Joyce scanned the list. The names of the ten or so shops on Antique Promenade were at the top of the list. The rest were order of distance away from Covington. She would begin by calling those farthest away and work her way up the list.

Checking her watch, Joyce walked home in record time. She was a woman on a mission. Entering her house she made a beeline for the telephone knowing she had only an hour to make the calls. Her first called yielded no information. The person on the phone grew indignant when Joyce mentioned she was tracking a possible stolen item. The woman made it clear that she didn't do business with thieves and then wished Joyce good day.

Joyce knew she would have to use a different approach if she wanted to get anywhere. As she waited for the next call to go through she decided she would pretend to be a private shopper working for a collector.

"Hope Valley Antiques & Collectibles, how may I help you?"

Joyce launched into her spiel. "Yes, good afternoon. My name is Joyce. I am a representative for a collector in Providence searching for Quezal items. I am actually looking for a specific item. Who am I speaking with?"

"Sandoval Pratt. I'm the proprietor. I have a few Quezal items in my showroom. What is the item you are looking for?"

"My buyer collects perfume bottles. I know Quezal bottles are rare but she wants to add to her collection."

"You're in luck, Joyce. I recently acquired one."

"Would you describe it for me, please?" Joyce asked trying to keep the excitement out of her voice.

"Certainly. It's about four inches tall, and is a green iridescent glass. It has a sterling silver hinged stopper and is numbered. I assure you it is an authentic Quezal."

"Mr. Pratt, would you mind relaying the numbering information to me?"

"Y128."

Joyce could barely contain herself. She was now positive this was the bottle taken from *Anna's Attic*. Her mind spun and she could feel her breathing getting shorter. She repeatedly circled the listing on her printout and wrote the identification number next to it. She needed to proceed carefully so as not to arouse this man's suspicion. Antique dealers become skittish when confronted with the possibility that they have purchased stolen items.

"Sir, may I inquire how you secured this item?" The silence on the other end of the phone told Joyce that she had gotten about as far as she was going to get with Sandoval Pratt. His tone when he spoke confirmed her suspicions.

"I assure you Madam, that this item was acquired legally from its previous owner. If you are interested in purchasing it, I would be more than happy to do business with you in person. Otherwise, I have customers to attend to."

"I'll be in touch. Thank you for your time."

Joyce replaced the receiver and sat in stunned silence for a few minutes. *What do I do next? Should I call Toni? No.*

She's got too much going on to worry about this. For all I know this has nothing to do with Anna's death. Maybe she did sell it and the receipt is simply missing. Next time I see Ian I'll mention it to him and see what he wants to do about it. I don't want to send the investigation in the wrong direction based on a bad lead. Finding Anna's killer is more important than a missing perfume bottle.

Joyce placed the printout on top of the side table where she usually put paperwork she wasn't finished with, and set about making herself an early dinner.

Carlton drove to the grocery store in Toni's car. He knew she kept the key to Anna's shop on the same ring as her car keys. He toyed with the idea of going by the shop to search for the jewels, but decided there wasn't enough time. He didn't want to leave Toni alone for too long in case she got suspicious about his absence. Especially after he promised he would make them dinner. There would be plenty of time in the next day or two.

Carlton stopped for a red light on Preston Avenue and stared out of the passenger side window. He spotted a leggy blonde, and watched her walk down the sidewalk past the local hardware store. A handwritten sign taped to the window read: KEYS MADE HERE. That's when it hit him. His own copy of the key to the shop would make it easier for him to carry out his plan. Without a second thought, Carlton DeWitt put on his right turn signal and maneuvered Toni's Lexus into the hardware store's parking lot.

CHAPTER 13

Covington, Rhode Island
Tuesday, April 13, 1999

The ringing telephone brought Toni back to reality with a start. *I must have dozed off* she thought. Groggily she pulled herself off the couch and almost tripped on the shoes she didn't remember kicking off. She banged her knee on the edge of the coffee table and cursed her way into the kitchen where she snatched the cordless phone from its cradle and barked, "Hello!"

"Rough day?" She didn't instantly recognize the voice on the other end.

"Who is this?" Her voice reflected her annoyance.

"Toni, it's Ian. Ian Monroe. Covington PD." Ian was suddenly insecure with his decision to call her. *Perhaps it was a mistake.* He wanted to see her again so badly he had convinced himself that asking her out on a date was a good idea.

"Oh. Yeah. Sorry about that. I almost tripped getting to the phone," she said sassily.

"I've been told I have that effect on women." When she didn't offer up a comment he continued, "I'm just kidding."

"I know. I'm sorry. It's been a trying day and I don't feel much like laughing."

"I can call you back at a more convenient time if you'd like."

"Honestly, no time is convenient. I wish I could go back to sleep and never get up again. I'm sorry, like I said it's been tough."

The strain in Toni's voice tugged at Ian's heartstrings. He felt like a heel. Here was this women dealing with a severe blow and he was trying to ask her out on a date.

"I can imagine. Please stop apologizing. I understand you're not having an easy time of it. Is there anything I can do to help?"

"Find out what happened to my grandmother," she snapped back. Realizing she had just been quite rude, she switched gears. "I apologize. I'm not quite myself as you can tell." She walked back into the living room and sat on the window seat. She watched a pregnant mother push a stroller down Village Way and sighed. *Will I ever have a family?* She wondered. The toddler in the stroller was waving its arms about, making the mother smile, lean over and say something to her child. To Toni, the scene was so perfect, so normal, that tears slipped down her cheeks.

Ian sensed that she was now crying. He wanted to be there with her. To comfort and console her. "Toni, are you still there?" Ian sounded concerned. Had he heard her crying?

"Yes, yes," she responded desperately trying to keep her voice from quivering. "I'm just...." What could she say?

"Are you alone? Would you like me to come by?" The words were out before he could stop them. He could have kicked himself. He held his breath waiting for her to send him to hell.

Ian's voice was so soft and soothing that it made her want to lean her head against his strong shoulders and let him hold her. She really wanted to say yes, but felt that would be inappropriate. Before she could change her mind she abruptly said "No." She regretted the word as soon as it came out of her mouth. She didn't want Ian to think she wasn't interested in him. There was something about him that had captured her, and she wanted to explore that feeling. But now was certainly not the right time. "I'll take a rain check though."

Ian let out his breath. *A ray of hope,* he thought, *go for it.* "How about tomorrow night? Before you say no, I have some things about the case to talk to you about."

Toni was surprised at her disappointment. She had hoped his offer to come by had been out of his wanting to be with her not about Nana's death. *Oh well, beggars can't be choosers,* she thought. *It may not be a date, but at least I get to be with him.* "Tomorrow night sounds fine. Where would you like to meet?"

Ian could barely contain his elation. He took several steadying breaths before he mentioned the name of a swanky restaurant. His only thoughts were that although this was not a date at least he could spend the evening with her. After agreeing on a time, they exchanged goodbyes and hung up.

Snapping his cellular phone shut, Ian gazed out of the driver's side window. His Corvette was parked on the curb by Mills Pond, his food sitting on the passenger seat untouched. His daily habit of eating in his car was his only salvation from the hustle and bustle of the precinct. He'd tried to eat at his desk before but was never left alone long enough to get in more than a few bites. Fed up one day, he gathered his turkey sub, Doritos, and Diet Coke, got into his Vette and drove as far from City Hall as he could. That was the beginning of what became his mealtime routine. He hated to eat inside his "baby" but a little mustard on the leather seat was better than an ulcer.

After he had retrieved the number for the restaurant from Information, he made a reservation for two and requested the best table they had. It didn't take much convincing to get the primo table after he dropped the Stanton name. It never ceased to amaze him how name-dropping worked in Covington. If you were not a member of the Covington Jet Set, you were nobody. He hoped Toni would like Annie's on the River. He had never been there himself but he had heard its praises sung by his parents, and his partner who had proposed to his wife there. Ian knew it was going to be an expensive evening, but he didn't care. He wanted to impress Toni. After all she was a member of Covington society and he didn't want her thinking she was out of his league.

Thinking about Covington society reminded Ian that he was supposed to have dinner at his parent's house that evening. He groaned inwardly at the thought of having to explain to his mother for the umpteenth time why he became a cop. As the engine roared to life Ian maneuvered his sports car onto River Road and drove the short distance to Taylor. Leaving downtown Covington behind Ian opened the sunroof and let the wind blow through his hair. Covington was experiencing unusually warm weather for this time of year.

Once past Village Way the landscape seemed to change magically. Gone were the concrete buildings and small homes, giving way to sprawling lawns and massive mansions. This area was unofficially called The Estates. It was home to Covington's elite. Successful doctors, lawyers, bankers, and politicians were the only ones who could afford to buy here. The tree-lined road was well traveled by visitors and a major part of Covington's appeal. Most of the estates were set far back from the road and guarded by large iron gates, security cameras and intercoms. If you were lucky enough to get past the main gate, a long winding driveway led you to the front door, where the family butler would meet you.

Arriving at his parent's estate Ian punched the code that opened the gate and steered his Corvette through and up the drive. Since his parents did not have a family butler, no one was there to greet him when he killed the engine and exited the car. Ian locked his gun in the glove compartment since it unnerved his mother, and donned his black blazer. It took his mother a few minutes to answer the door, but when she did he was greeted with a hug and a kiss. In her early sixties Catherine Monroe looked great as usual. Standing five feet seven inches, with short blonde hair and blue eyes she was the picture of elegance. Ian loved that his mother always looked polished, but not gaudy. Today she was wearing a knee length beige cocktail dress adorned with a diamond broach.

"Hey Mom."

"Ian, sweetheart, just in time. Your father and I were about to have a drink before dinner."

Following Catherine through the foyer, Ian barely noticed the elegant décor of the Monroe estate. He had grown up in this house and was accustomed to the ornate furnishings. His father was in the drawing room pouring drinks. Wallace Monroe turned with outstretched hand to greet his son. His once dark hair was graying rapidly. However, his blue eyes held the same twinkle that his son had inherited. At six feet tall, Wallace was dressed in a blue pinstripe suit minus the tie. He was an avid golfer and tennis player at the country club, which helped keep him in shape.

Accepting a monogrammed glass filled with Jack Daniels from his father, Ian took a seat next to Catherine on the sofa. She was already holding a martini glass, which she clinked against Ian's. Wallace sat on the matching armchair and sipped his Jack Daniels.

"Nasty business about Anna DeWitt," Wallace began. "Any leads?"

"Oh, Wallace, must we talk shop? I'd like to enjoy an evening with my son without having to discuss law enforcement."

"You're never going to forgive me for becoming a cop, are you mom?" Ian said smiling at his mother.

"No." She patted his hand letting him know she loved him anyway.

"To answer your question, Dad, no. All we know is that she was pushed after a struggle and hit her head. The scene was wiped clean and really looked like an accident at first glance. Had it not been for the autopsy, we would have never known she'd been killed."

Catherine shuddered. "That poor woman. I cannot imagine. And poor Antonia. All alone now." She finished shaking her head.

"You know Antonia?" Ian asked.

"I know of her. We knew her parents. Such good people. Such a tragedy."

"What happened to them?"

It was Wallace who answered. "They were driving home from a function at the country club. The Police believed they must have hit a patch of black ice, lost control of the car and hit a tree, killing them instantly. Damn near tore that family apart."

"Anna was devastated. The brother, Joel was never the same. He and Ashley were ever so close. I believe he left the country to escape the memories," Catherine explained. "Anna took Antonia in and raised her. Poor child was only eight. To lose one's parents at such a young age…"

Ian was touched by this story. He imagined what life must have been like for Toni growing up. He and his parents had their differences, but he couldn't imagine living without them. A few moments of silence passed and was interrupted by the housekeeper announcing dinner.

The soup was already in their bowls when they entered the dining room. Taking their usual seats, Wallace at the head, Catherine to his left and Ian to his right. The conversation made its way back to the only topic Covington residents were talking about.

"I don't know, Dad, that's just it. There was no sign of forced entry, no fingerprints anywhere. Nothing that would point to anyone."

"So then who did it?" Wallace asked. "You must have some idea. Come on, that masters degree I paid for should be coming in handy."

"Dad, I'm not some small time cop. That degree helped immensely when I was NYPD."

"Ian, your father didn't mean anything by that. We're just curious, that's all."

"Yeah, son, tell me something I can't read in the *Covington Chronicle*."

"On one condition. Mom, you won't divulge any of this at your next ladies luncheon."

"Ian! I would never."

"Yeah, sure mom." Ian heckled his mother about her role in society almost as much as she chided him about his career choice. He knew she would love nothing more than for him to give up police work.

"Your mother is sworn to secrecy," Wallace said with anticipation. He couldn't wait to hear what his son had to say. He had already bragged to the men at the club that Ian was the only detective in charge of this major case, and he had no doubt his only son would bring the killer to justice.

"Well, it seems that Anna's grandson, Carlton has resurfaced." Ian paused at his mother's sharp intake of breath.

"What, Mom?"

"Isn't that a little coincidental?" Catherine asked.

"My thoughts exactly. But I have to tread very carefully. As you know the DeWitts and the Stantons are very well connected. It seems that Antonia has called in her favors. Mayor Boyce is breathing down our necks, so I have to wrap this investigation up, but without ruffling any feathers."

"Don't let Boyce bully you. The Monroes have as much standing in this community as Antonia Stanton. She has no right to use her grandmother's name to put pressure on you. I'm sure you're doing your best," his mother stated indignantly.

Ian instinctively wanted to defend Toni. She wasn't like that he wanted to tell his mother. She'd correctly guessed that Anna's death had not been accidental, making the department look like the Keystone Cops. However, he chose not to say anything. His mother knew him well, and she would be very curious to know why he was defending Toni's honor. That would open the door to a host of questions he had no intention of answering. There was a brief lull in the conversation while the housekeeper took away their soup bowls and served the lamb chops with mint jelly.

"What can you tell me about Carlton DeWitt?" Ian dug in.

"It's all hearsay, you understand," Catherine began. "He was always a tough boy to keep a handle on. Always getting himself into some kind of trouble. He ran with a crowd of troublemakers. They were always running around at all hours of the night, wreaking havoc on the streets of Covington. His parents had no control over him. The worst of it was that whenever he was caught, his parents used their influence to get him out of trouble. The boy grew up not accepting responsibility for any of his actions."

"Do you know how he ended up in Vegas?"

"I don't think I even knew he lived in Vegas. I know his father pulled many strings to get him into college, where, of course, Carlton got himself into even more trouble. By then his parents had left the country leaving his poor grandmother to deal with him. He was so different from Antonia. She was on her way to making something of herself, and he was doing his best to bring shame to his family. Last I heard, he'd been kicked out of college for gambling. In deference to Anna, no one mentions Carlton at the club."

"Hmm. Sounds like a real winner. I'm not sure what to make of his arrival. Like you said, it's quite coincidental. But I cannot hold his past behavior against him. Just because he's a gambler, doesn't make him a murderer, no matter how inconsistent his story."

"What do you mean, inconsistent?" Wallace asked taking a sip from his French Merlot.

"Antonia tells me he arrived in Covington on Sunday, but when I was speaking to him, he said he'd arrived on Thursday. He said he'd gotten his days mixed up but I don't know…"

"You don't believe him?" Wallace asked.

"He gave me some story about a plane crash shutting the Las Vegas Strip down for days. I did some checking and apparently it did happen. But it was last month and the street closing only lasted a few hours."

"So you think he was really here on Thursday?"

"I have no proof. Call it instinct, but I'm focusing the investigation in Carlton's direction."

"Maybe someone saw him. Antique Promenade is a busy street, and those shop owners are great at watching out for each other," Catherine suggested.

"We've already checked. The day Anna was found, officers walked up and down the street and interviewed all the shop owners. No one saw anything. I was at the shop this morning, so I took the opportunity to ask again just in case someone missed something. It seems they all closed early that day due to lack of business. Anna's Attic was the only place open."

"Sounds like you've got your work cut out for you."

"Yeah, Dad, I know. I'm not looking forward to going into the precinct tomorrow. The Cap is fit to be tied."

"What's your next move, Son?"

"I was able to get a list of all of Anna's customers. So, tomorrow I'm going to start calling them and see if that gets me anywhere. And, since you guys are on the list, save me a phone call and tell me if there's anything else I should know."

"We've already told you what we know," Catherine began. "I can't think of anything else of significance."

"Well if you do, you know where to find me," Ian winked. "So Mom, what's for dessert?"

CHAPTER 14

Covington, Rhode Island
Wednesday April 14ᵗʰ, 1999

The Covington Police Department was a hubbub of activity. Located inside the City Hall building, it was made up of one large room that looked like a hodgepodge of desks, filing cabinets, and office equipment. Two small offices could be seen towards the back of the room. They were unoccupied this morning since the Captain was at home and the Lieutenant was attending a law enforcement conference in Providence. The station also housed a holding cell barely big enough to fit two grown men. In front of the cell was the fingerprinting area. The black inkpad was almost dry due to the low volume of arrests in Covington.

Ian sat at his desk staring at the closed frosted glass door of one of the offices. The blinds had been closed so that the black lettering bearing the name of Captain Nicholas Kirk was more prominent. Ian grinned to himself recalling numerous occasions the captain refused to share his first name, forcing others to call him Captain Kirk. An avid Star Trek fan, the captain even had an autographed photo of William Shatner as Captain James T. Kirk hanging on the wall of his office. Captain Kirk, not of the Enterprise, had

Ian's desk deliberately turned to face his office. That way, he could either yell Ian's name or wave at him whenever he needed him. Since Anna DeWitt's murder, he had been doing more yelling than waving.

Captain Kirk had assigned Ian one of the six uniformed officers the department employed, to work the DeWitt case. Usually, Ian had his partner of five years, Adam Ross, working with him. Unfortunately, Adam was not around for the biggest case to hit the CPD in a long time.

Adam hailed from a law enforcement family in Las Vegas, where his older brother, and father before him, had joined the LVPD. Tired of the bright lights, drunken tourists, disorderly gamblers, and the dangers of working for a metropolitan police force, Adam wanted out of the Las Vegas police department. One of his wife's sorority sisters was married to Captain Kirk, so Adam's application to the CPD was just a formality. For the past five years, Ian and Adam worked well together and formed an enduring friendship. And, boy, could Ian use a friend now. Of course, Adam was having the time of his life attending his niece's wedding in Las Vegas. Ian had also been invited to the wedding, but as Captain Kirk put it, "Hell, no. I need one of you here."

And here he was, Sergeant Ian Monroe, struggling to find clues or leads. He didn't even have a list of suspects to question. The little nagging voice inside his head kept returning to Carlton DeWitt. Although he had absolutely no evidence or proof, Ian had a gut feeling that Carlton had something to do with Anna's death. He wasn't sure if Carlton had actually killed his grandmother, but he knew more than he was letting on. Ian knew that if he kept digging, something would come up to point to Carlton's involvement. It was just a matter of some solid detective work.

Ian flipped through his phone messages. There were four of them. One from Captain Kirk, one from Mayor Boyce, one from a reporter from the *Covington Chronicle*, and one from Toni. He was hesitant about calling Toni back, afraid she'd called to cancel their dinner plans for tonight. He called Mayor Boyce's office first. He was now on a first name basis with Suzanne, Boyce's secretary, since the Mayor hadn't stopped calling him after their meeting on Monday. Thankfully, Mayor Boyce was out of the office, and Ian was spared having to tell him yet again that there was nothing new to report.

Captain Kirk answered the phone when Ian called. He was a little less aggressive than Boyce when Ian briefed him on what he knew so far. Their working relationship was such that Ian felt comfortable telling Captain Kirk that his suspicions were focused on Carlton. The Captain cautioned Ian to be one hundred percent positive about Carlton's involvement before sharing the news with the mayor. "You know how Boyce operates. He'll go straight to the media and blow the case. We have to treat everyone involved with kid gloves. I know you won't let the Department down."

"No pressure, huh?" Ian joked.

"I think you know how important this is. I'll probably see you tomorrow at the funeral."

Ian's next call was to Tom Kaneda. An old high school buddy, Tom had chosen to stay in Covington and become the Chief Investigative Reporter for the *Covington Chronicle*. An impressive title if he'd ever had to put it to use. Not much happens in Covington that requires investigating. Until now. When Tom came on the line, they exchanged pleasantries before Ian asked the reason for the call.

"Come on, Monroe, why else would I be calling? Word is Anna DeWitt was murdered. What do you have to say about that?"

"Is this on the record?"

"Hell yeah! Give me something good."

"Unfortunately, I have nothing for you. Sorry." Ian wanted to end this call as soon as possible. "As soon as I know anything I'll give you a call."

"Monroe, you're killing me. This is the break I've been waiting for. If I play my cards right, I could end up working for a major paper. Come on. Throw an old pal a bone, will ya?"

"Kaneda, you know I have no authority to speak to the press. That's Captain Kirk's job. You're going to have to talk to him. Now if you don't mind I really gotta go."

"I'll remember this, Monroe. Next time you need the press on your side, don't count on old Kaneda."

Ian knew Tom was kidding. They both had jobs to do and they rarely allowed their professional lives to overshadow their friendship. Taking a deep breath, Ian dialed Toni's home phone number. He was somewhat apprehensive and prepared himself for the letdown he was anticipating. *I can't believe this woman's gotten under my skin like this,* he thought.

"Ian, I'm glad you called. I need to tell you about something strange that happened yesterday. I don't know why it's bothering me so much. I just thought you should know," Toni started.

Relieved, Ian picked up his pen and prompted Toni to continue.

"Yesterday this man came to Anna's Attic. I've never seen him before, but apparently Nana knew him. He asked about buying some…," Toni hesitated, how much should she tell Ian? "antiques. Joyce was adamant that Nana didn't like this guy. I don't know, he gave me the creeps. He seemed too intent on making this purchase."

"What did you tell him?"

"I blew him off. He made me really nervous and was quite rude."

"Toni, did he say or do anything that can be construed as a threat?"

"He did say that he would do anything to get his hands on the stuff. Maybe I'm overreacting. But, it's too much of a coincidence that he turns up now."

"I agree." Ian was angry at this man for making Toni's already difficult day worse. Once he found him, he was going to give him a piece of his mind. "Do you know how I can get in touch with him? I'd like to talk to him."

"He said he was staying at Covington Suites. He did leave me a business card, but it seems to have disappeared. He's Russian, I think. He had an accent."

"Do you remember his name?"

"Boris something or other. I'm sorry I'm not being much help. I had a lot going on when he arrived."

"Toni, don't worry. You've given me something to go on. I'm sure I'll find him. How many guys with a Russian accent can be staying at Covington Suites?"

"Do you think he had anything to do with Nana's death?" she asked softly.

"I won't know until I find him, but I sure would like to talk to him."

"Carlton said you would. He's the reason I called you. Ever since yesterday he's been bothered by the man's demeanor. He keeps bringing him up saying that you should look into him."

Interesting. Ian thought. *Very interesting.*

"I will head over there right now."

"Thanks, Ian." After a brief pause, "I'll see you later?"

"Of course. I'm looking forward to it."

"Who was that?" Carlton asked when Toni put the cordless phone down on the coffee table.

"Ian. He was returning my call. I told him about the Russian and he's going to go talk to him now."

Good, Carlton thought. *Hopefully the Russian will say something incriminating.* "Ton, you have a phone book around here?"

"Yes, I do. What for, Carl?"

"On the drive here from Vegas my car was making a funny noise. While you were still sleeping this morning, I took it for a spin, and it seems to be getting worse. I want to have a mechanic look at it before I make the trek back to Vegas." Carl hoped he sounded convincing. His car was fine, but he needed to get away for a while.

"Carl, please tell me you're not thinking of leaving. Not now," Toni whined.

"Of course, I'm not leaving now, Silly." *I still haven't found the jewels.* "But I will have to go back to Vegas eventually. My boss is being pretty understanding because of the circumstances, but the work is just piling up. There's no one else qualified enough to do my work," Carlton fictionalized.

"Oh yes of course. I'll get you the phone book." Toni disappeared into the kitchen, and returned with the Yellow Pages. "Want some more coffee?" she asked.

"Sure." Carlton made a great show of studying the mechanics' ads in the phone book. "This looks like a good place," he said pointing to the largest ad and writing the address down. He checked his watch. "If I head out there right now, maybe they'll be able to look at it today."

Toni followed him to the foyer. "Carl, don't you think you should call first? What if they're too busy? Then you'll have just wasted your time."

Believe me, honey, this trip is no waste of time, he thought as he donned his jacket. "Don't worry. I'll call from my cell." He gave her a quick kiss on the cheek and left the apartment.

Finally, he thought. He'd been wracking his brain since yesterday trying to find an excuse to get away from Toni. He planned to return to Hope Valley and Sandoval Pratt to sell the small antiques he'd helped himself to.

Leaving Covington behind, Carlton rolled down the windows of his Mustang, which was running just fine, and sang along with the radio. The trip to Hope Valley took less than twenty minutes.

The little bell attached to the door tinkled as Carlton entered *Hope Valley Antiques and Collectibles.* Sandoval Pratt looked up from his position behind the counter. In his sixties, Pratt had lost most of his hair, and was wearing a bright red cardigan around his ample body. "Ah Carlton. Welcome back. I didn't expect you back so soon."

"Hello, Sandoval. I've brought some more things for you to look at." Carlton laid out the watch, stickpin, and hair comb on the counter.

Pratt's eyes lit up. He rubbed his hands together. By the looks of them, these items were extremely valuable. His excitement waned when he remembered the phone call he'd received about the perfume bottle. "May I ask where these items came from?"

"Why?" Carlton asked suspiciously.

"When dealing with such valuable items, I'd like to know where they came from first."

Think fast, Carlton thought. "I have a spinster aunt that recently passed away. She was an avid antique collector and left her whole collection to all us nephews and nieces. I'm sure my cousins will be here sometime in the near future. I told them how generous you were with the perfume bottle," Carlton finished with a smile.

Sounds plausible enough, Pratt thought. "I just like to make sure, you know. I have a reputation to uphold."

"Of course. I understand."

"You wouldn't happen to have proof of ownership? Receipts, perhaps?"

"Why all the questions, Sandoval?" Carlton was getting concerned. Pratt hadn't asked a single question when he'd come in with the perfume bottle. What was going on?

"I'll be honest, Carlton. There's been an inquiry made about the origins of the Quezal perfume bottle."

"What are you talking about?" Carlton was downright nervous now.

"A woman called asking about the perfume bottle. Wanted to know the authentication number, and where I'd gotten it from."

"What's an authentication number?" Carlton was having trouble reigning in his rising panic.

"When a manufacturer only makes a certain number of a particular item, they paint or etch a number on the item. It's a way of ensuring it's genuine and not a reproduction."

"And did the numbers match?"

"I had no desire to discuss that matter with her. I was confident that you were legitimate. I hope I am not wrong."

"Sandoval, Sandoval. You have nothing to worry about. I would *never* try to sell you stolen property."

Eyeing the pieces on the counter, Pratt made a decision. He could already think of two customers who would pay top dollar for these kinds of items. If anyone asked questions, he would plead ignorance. Picking up the two-inch stickpin, Pratt put his glasses on and studied it. "This is a turn of the century 14K gold, diamond and pearl stickpin. It's very elaborate and the crown and coat of arms insets give it a royalty theme." Setting the pin down, Pratt picked up the watch. "Vintage Swiss Corum, 18K gold with diamonds and sapphires. It was sold by New York City jewelers, Van Cleef & Arpels. The band is stunning, and it's in excellent shape." The last piece, the hair comb, had Pratt going to a trade book to look it up. "According to this, each of the eight stalks is individually wired so the wearer can alter the look of it. The pearls are not real, but the piece is handmade and quite intricate."

Thanks for the history lesson. "I'm a little pressed for time. How much for all three?"

Pratt wrote on the notepad he had next to the register. "I can give you two fifty for the comb, five hundred for the pin, and a thousand for the watch."

Carlton almost launched himself over the counter to hug Pratt. At most he thought this sale would net him a thousand. But he was walking away with seventeen hundred and fifty bucks. His spirits plummeted when he saw Pratt take out a checkbook. *Oh man, what good is a check gonna do me? Shit? I need cash. But if I ask for cash, Pratt's gonna get suspicious all over again.* He looked at the bank information on the check. He vaguely remembered passing a branch of the bank on his way into Hope Valley.

"It's a pleasure doing business with you, Carlton," Sandoval smiled as he handed over the check, and a yellow itemized sales receipt. "Please come back soon."

"Sure thing." They shook hands. "Just out of curiosity did you get the name of the woman who called about the perfume bottle?"

"Joyce, I believe. She didn't leave a last name."

I knew that old woman would be trouble, Carlton thought. *I'm going to have to be more careful.* Leaving Pratt's shop Carlton looked up and down the street he was facing. Spotting the bank branch he remembered seeing, he got back into his Mustang and drove towards it.

Inside the bank, Carlton waited for the attractive young teller to finish with her customer. Sidling up to the counter he flirted with her so she wouldn't question the check. Luck was on his side. The brunette was so taken with him, she simply cashed the check out and handed him an envelope full of cash. *I've still got the old charm,* Carl thought smiling.

Checking his watch, Carl estimated he'd been gone about an hour. He should be back in Covington within the next twenty minutes. The drive back would give him the opportunity to come up with a good story about his experience at the mechanic's.

CHAPTER 15

Covington, Rhode Island
Wednesday April 14th, 1999

Carlton sat on the edge of Toni's bed watching her flit around the room wearing a red silk kimono. He couldn't decide if she was bouncing around like a cat on a hot tin roof or a clown in a three-ring circus. He had never seen her like this. "Girl what's wrong with you? You're acting like a teenager on a first date."

Toni didn't answer him. She just stood in the middle of her bedroom staring into the open closet. She was too preoccupied with picking out the right dress. She wanted to choose an outfit that sent the message: flirty yet respectable. She began shifting hangers across the rod eliminating dresses. "This is my first real date in a long time," Toni finally said.

"I thought you said it wasn't a date."

"You know what I mean. It's been a long time since I've gone out with a guy," Toni responded with a wave of her hand. She pulled a red evening gown with a plunging neckline out of the closet, and held it up for Carlton to inspect.

Carlton rolled his eyes and plopped back onto the bed with his arms outstretched, untucking his maroon golf shirt.

"Okay, okay. It's a little much, I know." Toni put the dress back into the closet. "Urgh! I've got nothing to wear!" She stomped her bare foot on the carpet.

Carlton sprang up. He waved his hand towards the open closet. "You have got to be kidding me! There's no room left in that closet, honey. It's overflowing with clothes, not to mention shoes. I swear I think you have more shoes than Imelda Marcos in there."

"Carl, half of the dresses in here I've only worn once. You know how it is. Nana insisted I attend many social events with her that required a new outfit each time."

"Any excuse to go shopping."

Ignoring him, Toni gave him her back and returned to her dress dilemma. She finally decided on a spaghetti strapped cocktail length dress that had a matching wrap and strappy sandals. She had fallen in love with the dress the moment she'd seen it because it had a soft flowy ruffle that went around the bodice. The color, coral, was not one she was accustomed to wearing, but there was something about the way the dress hung on her that was very flattering.

Toni held the dress up for Carlton to see. He gave an appreciative nod. "Looks like a first date dress to me."

"Carl, I already told you, Ian called me yesterday and suggested we get together for dinner to talk about the investigation."

"Call it whatever you want. I still think it's a date."

"Alright, it's a date. Whatever. We're going to discuss the investigation anyway, might as well make it over dinner out. I'm excited that he asked me out to dinner. Maybe once the investigation is over, it could turn into more, if he's interested. I know I certainly am."

"Well what do you know? You are human," he said a little sarcastically.

"Of course I am, it just has to be the right person and time," Toni shot back.

"You barely know this guy. He's a cop investigating our grandmother's murder. How do you know he's the right person?"

"By getting to know him better. And how do you get to know someone better? By going out with him."

"But why him of all men? Don't you have other men that are interested in you?" Carlton stood up and smoothed out the legs of his khaki pants, and stretched. "Come on, Toni. Don't start thinking of him as a knight in shining armor who's going to gallop into your life on a white stallion and whisk you away."

Toni crossed her arms. "Gee, do you really think I'm that pathetic?" She sighed. "Look, I know that compared to you, I lead a boring existence. But, I choose to live this way. It works for me. Carl, you know I've always been a quiet person, not much of a party girl. Remember in High School when you used to try to get me to go out with you and your friends, and I refused? I'm not much different now."

Carlton walked over to the full-length mirror and checked himself out. He rubbed his hand over his five o'clock shadow. "Maybe that's why you're still single."

Toni walked up behind Carl and spoke to him in the mirror. "I hate to remind you, dear Cousin, so are you." They smiled at each other. "Anyway, maybe I like it that way."

Carl whirled around to face her. "Gimme a break! What woman doesn't want to tie some poor soul down?"

"Wow! You sure have a negative opinion of women. Let me ask you, what's the use in getting married just to be married? Why not wait for the right person to come along, no matter how long that takes?"

Because you might die and never find him." Oblivious to the look that crossed over Toni's face at his choice of words, he continued. "I still want to know what makes you think Monroe is the right guy?"

"I want to know why you think he's not. What do you have against him? I'm the one going on this date, not you. I need to do this to find out if he is or not. Otherwise, I may end up regretting it. Carlton, there are a lot of scumbags in this world, and I seem to keep running into them. Ian seems like a decent guy, with a decent job, from a decent family. It's been awhile since I've met someone like that. Just be happy I'm going out to dinner, and don't read too much into it."

"I'm outta here. I can't watch this anymore."

"And what are you going to do alone?"

"I dunno," he said as he shot a glance over his shoulder for a last look as Toni went into the bathroom to get herself ready.

Carlton threw himself down onto the couch and began flipping channels with the remote to the small TV Toni had set up for him. He hated the idea of Toni dating the cop; it might interfere with his plans. But for now, it suited his purpose because it got her out of the apartment. *I'll wait for fifteen minutes after Toni leaves, then I'll head over to the shop. Hopefully, I'll find the jewelry tonight, and then I won't have to worry about Monroe snooping around. I'll make up some excuse, and high tail it out of here before anyone figures out what I've done.*

Toni emerged from the bathroom dressed and ready to go. *Wow,* Carlton thought. *She looks really good. Her hair's all done, she's got makeup on, and she's actually wearing a dress. Monroe'd be a moron to let her get away.* He let out a loud wolf whistle that brought a smile to Toni's face. "Lookin' gooood. You go, girl."

Toni threw back her head and laughed. "Now if I can get a reaction like that from Ian, I'd be in business."

"He'd have to be blind not to."

"I may be back late, Carl, don't wait up for me."

"I won't. If you don't come home I'll know you've spent the night at his place."

"Carlton!"

"What?"

"I'm not that kind of girl," she said as she glided to the front door.

"Good evening, Miss," the valet said to Toni as he opened her car door. "Enjoy your dinner."

"Thank you." Toni straightened her dress as she got out of the driver's seat and walked around to the sidewalk in front of the restaurant. Suddenly she felt queasy and light headed. *I can't believe I'm getting nervous about meeting Ian. When Carl teased and then badgered me I felt defensive. But, now that the time is actually here, I feel like I have butterflies flapping their wings in my stomach and my heart is racing.*

Ian had chosen a quiet little bistro, Annie's On the River, which had white glove service and was well known in Covington for fine dining. Toni was a few minutes early and as she walked from the sidewalk up to the door she saw Ian through the glass talking to the maitre' d. She was happy to see he was already there and she wouldn't have to wait for him.

As Toni walked in, Ian turned around to see her. He let out a low whistle of approval. *Carlton was right, Ian was no moron.* "Good evening Miss Stanton. You clean up real good," he said with a grin and a wink.

Toni could feel the heat in her face and ears and wondered if Ian could tell she was blushing. "Well, thank you Sergeant Monroe. So do you." Ian was wearing gray slacks, a gray silk shirt and a sports jacket. His shirt was unbuttoned far enough for Toni to see his chest and a gold chain with an eagle pendant around his neck.

The headwaiter escorted them to their table by a window with a view of the river. After they were seated and their table waiter had left to fill their drink order, Ian surprised Toni by reaching for her hand and asking, "How are you holding up?"

"I'm okay. I'd be going nuts if Carlton weren't here though."

"He's still around?" Ian said with surprise in his voice.

"Yes. Where did you think he'd be?"

"I didn't know his plans. I'm happy he's been here for you. By the way, where is he tonight?"

"He's at my apartment. Why?"

"Oh. Just wondering. I'll need to talk to him too."

"Do you suspect my cousin of something?"

"No. But I can't leave any stone unturned."

"Am I a suspect, too?" Toni asked apprehensively.

"No. Your reaction when you learned your grandmother was dead was so real, it was obvious you had nothing to do with it."

"How do you know about that? You weren't there that day."

"Officer McConnelly told me he had a tough time holding you back. You're quite a strong woman."

"I do work out on a regular basis."

"And it shows."

Toni blushed, smiled, and looked down at the tablecloth. "What happened with the Russian?"

"He's no longer a person of interest. He showed me his plane ticket, which had him arriving Sunday evening. There's no way he could have been here last Thursday. He's an unsavory character if you ask me, but not the person we're looking for."

"Was he as rude to you as he was to us?"

"Oh, yeah. As I said, unsavory. Who's us?"

"Joyce and Carl were at the shop when he graced us with his presence."

Ian filed the information away for later use. Rashovsky had been evasive about exactly *what* he was trying to buy. Toni wasn't that forthcoming either. He was going to have to do some more digging.

"Anyway, I've been calling the customers on the list Joyce gave me." Ian continued, "There's a person I haven't been able to reach. Her maid says she and her husband are on a cruise and won't be back for another week. Roslyn something."

"Roslyn Smythe-Burns. She was a regular customer at Anna's Attic. Very wealthy and she and her husband love antiques."

"If she's not back by the time I've finished with the other interviews, I may have to call her on the ship. Since she was a regular customer, she may have important information to the investigation."

"I don't know what she could tell you," Toni said shrugging her shoulders.

"I know, you can't leave any stone unturned," they said in unison, bringing a smile to both their faces.

The waiter returned with their drinks and served them with impeccable style. He quietly removed himself from the area and left Ian and Toni alone to enjoy their cocktails.

"To happier times," Ian lifted his glass toward Toni's to make a toast.

"To the future," Toni added as she clinked her glass against Ian's.

"So what else can you tell me?" Toni asked placing her right elbow on the table, and resting her chin on the back of her hand.

"That you look beautiful, tonight."

Toni's cheeks burned as a thrill ran through her body. "I meant about the investigation."

"I was hoping you wouldn't want to talk about that all night," he teased her.

"You're right, I don't. So, let's talk about you. I've told you pretty much my family history. It's only fair that you tell me yours."

"You want to know my family history?" he asked raising an eyebrow.

"Would you prefer if I asked where you were the night of the murder?" she asked sweetly.

"Okay, Detective Stanton. I get it. Here goes. I'm forty years old. Single. Never married. No children. Only child of Ma and Pa Monroe. Graduated with a Masters in forensic science from NYU. Worked for NYPD until a few years ago. Came back to Covington. Emotionally stable, financially secure, physically fit, and one hell of a nice guy."

"You forgot name, rank, and serial number," Toni remarked, pinning him with a look.

The tension between them was broken when the waiter approached their table to take their dinner order.

After the waiter had retreated, Ian sighed. "I'm sorry. I don't like talking about myself. Remember, my job is to ask questions, not answer them."

"I understand. I don't like sharing information about myself either. I've always been a very private person. But, how are we going to get to know each other better, if we don't talk about ourselves? Unless you asked me to dinner to further your investigation and not because you liked me."

"You're right. I do like you, and I want to get to know you better. Ask whatever you want, I promise I'll answer properly."

"Most men have a wife and children by the time they are your age. How have you managed to stay single?" Toni leaned forward to study him more closely, thinking that was a good place to begin.

Ian stared intently into Toni's eyes wondering how much detail she really wanted. *I may as well give her the whole story and not hold anything back. That way, when I ask her the same question she'll be just as forthcoming.* "Believe me, it hasn't been that hard staying single. I have to be in love with the woman I'm going to share my life with, and I haven't met that woman yet. I was engaged, once. But she decided she wanted something better than a small town cop, so she broke it off."

"How awful. That must have really hurt you."

"It did at first, but then I figured out if she had been Miss Right, that wouldn't have happened. We stay in touch from time to time but I wouldn't say we're friends. She moved to Atlantic City soon after the break-up. When she left, she said something about hitting the big time."

"Sounds like something Carlton would say. I never really knew what made him move all the way to Las Vegas. I guess he wanted to get as far away from here as he possibly could. To him, that was a better choice than coming home with his tail between his legs," Toni realized too late that she had let that slip.

Ian waited for Toni to elaborate. When she didn't he said, "Now you have to tell me the rest story."

Toni paused a moment. "He was kicked out of college for gambling. Uncle Joel was so embarrassed, he pretty much disowned him. That's the whole story."

Ian pounced. "So, Carlton doesn't have access to the family fortune, huh?"

"Ian, that's a terrible thing to say."

I'm going to do a background on Carlton DeWitt first thing tomorrow morning, Ian thought. Aloud he said, "I'm sorry. Okay, where were we? Oh yeah, my singlehood. Which by the way disappoints my folks very much. They're having trouble dealing with their only child not giving them any grandchildren. They refuse to understand I'm not getting married just to have children," Ian paused, took a sip of his drink, and looked up to see if Toni was still attentive. "I am hopeful that I'll find a woman who loves me for who I am. I think I'm a romantic at heart, and I'm comfortable showing affection and emotion even though I've been told I'm hard as nails during police work. I keep that part of myself separate from my private me. I've been told I'm a good listener, I guess that comes from questioning people during investigations. I don't want to miss anything so I've learned to listen. I am a responsible man of integrity. I don't gamble and drink only occasionally. I like to have fun as much as the next guy but not at anyone's expense. I have a sense of humor but I have a serious side too. When I make a commitment to someone or something, I'm loyal to it. During our engagement I was my fiancé's best friend as well as partner in what I thought would be life for us. I like people. My coworkers think I'm tough, but for my personal life I'm easygoing. I don't like arguments or confrontations. I prefer to work out a compromise where everyone feels they've gotten what they want."

"When you open up, you really open up!" Toni was amazed by the amount of personal information Ian shared. He must have been holding all of this in just waiting for her to ask.

"Now it's my turn. Or your turn. I'll ask you the same question." Ian smiled and leaned back in his chair waiting to hear how Toni would reply.

Toni sipped her drink, put down the glass and leaned back in her chair to mirror Ian's posture. The candle in the middle of the table danced, giving off a shadowy light on Ian's face. Toni wondered if he saw the same thing on her face.

"I'm a photojournalist. I've also been accused of being a workaholic. I've been so heavily involved with my career, that some years I log more than 70,000 miles covering stories around the world. Which is probably why I'm single, and never been married or even been engaged. I have dated casually, though. Mostly because I'm in and out of town so often, it's difficult to develop any type of long-term relationship. I'm never around long enough to get intimate with someone. The few men I've dated usually move on to the next conquest long before I get back from an assignment. I have five close friends who I meet once a week for dinner, when I'm here. Obviously, I love to travel. I also like the theater, movies, and museums. I like to do as much sightseeing as I can when I'm on assignment. I know the man for me is out there but I haven't connected with him yet."

Toni smiled at Ian, hoping he might suggest the man for her was sitting across the table from her. He didn't. Embarrassed, she continued to babble. "Nana had mentioned recently, I should be thinking about settling down, reducing my traveling so I could find Mr. Right and have a family before it gets too late. She said my biological clock was ticking, loudly. Can you imagine my grandmother saying that?" Toni waited for Ian's response.

"Perhaps, your grandmother was right. And perhaps her death has brought us together," Ian suggested. "You know, the chances of our meeting would be slim since our paths would otherwise never cross."

The waiter pushed the cart with a white linen tablecloth covering it towards their table. Domed stainless steel serving containers covered each dish to keep them hot. As each was uncovered Toni and Ian could smell the delicious meals they had ordered and marveled at the beautiful presentation the Chef had arranged on their plates. The waiter then asked if they required anything else before retreating to leave them alone to enjoy their meals, and each other's company.

CHAPTER 16

Toni sighed and leaned back in her chair. "I'm stuffed." She announced. The braised pork she had for dinner was delicious and so was Ian's prime rib. They had shared portions of their meals with each other.

"No dessert?" Ian asked not wanting the evening to end so soon.

"No room," she answered smiling. Toni was thoroughly enjoying herself, allowing Ian's attention to defer reality until tomorrow. She ignored the guilt that would creep into her thoughts every now and then, reminding her that Nana's funeral was tomorrow. She didn't want to be a grieving granddaughter tonight. She was desperate for a sense of normalcy which Ian was doing his best to provide.

As they had enjoyed their entrées they had chatted amicably about events in the news, finding a common interest. Toni was surprised with Ian's knowledge and ability to converse on an eclectic group of topics. He was much more than the small town cop his ex-fiancée had accused him of being.

From the way he was looking at her Toni sensed they had made a connection that went beyond the investigation. There was obviously a physical attraction, but as Toni knew a solid relationship was built on more than sex. And Ian was certainly solid, physically and emotionally. Her eyes went to his broad shoulders and powerful arms, the results of time spent in the gym. She found herself wondering if he was sporting a six-pack, and blushed when she realized the turn her thoughts had taken. She was a woman in mourning for God's sake.

"You're blushing." Ian teased catching her off guard.

No shit. "Oops, I mean, yeah." she responded embarrassed. "You have the shoulders of a football player."

"I've been told that before."

A stab of jealousy shot through her. Had a woman told him that? "You must spend a lot of time in the gym."

"Out of necessity not vanity. I've always enjoyed working out, but now I have to in order to remain flexible and retain mobility in my shoulder."

"What happened to your shoulder?"

"About five years ago, I got shot in the left shoulder."

"Oh my God. What happened?"

"My partner and I were transporting a witness to testify, there was an attempt on the witness' life, they got me instead. It's amazing how your priorities change once you've been shot."

"I can imagine. Your fiancée must have been beside herself. Is that why you left New York?"

"Yes and no. I was given leave to recuperate, so I added my unused vacation time to give myself ample time to recover. I actually met Juli here in Covington. She's part of the reason I left the NYPD, and then she left me."

Talking about Ian's ex-fiancée was making her uncomfortable. She didn't want to think of him holding another woman. *Boy, I hope I'm not making a fool of myself over this guy. I wonder how he feels about me,* she thought. Her question was answered with Ian's next statement.

"There's a nice little piano bar inside Covington Suites. I'd like to take you there for a nightcap," Ian said expectantly.

"That sounds wonderful," Toni responded not wanting the evening to end. She excused herself to the ladies room while Ian settled the bill.

When she emerged Ian was waiting for her. "I thought we'd go in my car," he suggested. "We'll pick up your car on the way back."

Ian opened the passenger door for Toni once the valet had brought the car around. Sitting inside Ian's Corvette Toni felt a sense of intimacy. The two-seater was low to the ground and tight in proximity. As Ian put the car in gear, Toni couldn't help but notice his masculine hand wrapped around the gearshift inches from her thigh.

Ian in turn couldn't help but notice how Toni's dress had hiked up exposing part of her thighs and knees.

The piano bar was almost empty, not surprising since it was a Wednesday night. The soft tones of the piano surrounded the small bar and soothed Toni's soul as they were shown to their booth. Sitting side by side, they ordered wine for Toni, and beer for Ian. They sat in comfortable silence for a few minutes enjoying the music and their drinks.

Toni slowly tilted her head back and closed her eyes. She felt Ian begin to wrap his arm around her shoulders. Keeping her eyes closed, she allowed her head to lean on him, and shifted herself so there bodies were touching. She laid her arm along the length of his thigh enjoying the feel of his muscle under her palm. It felt so good to be held against him.

Ian gently placed his cheek on the side of her head, and lightly kissed her temple. The feathery softness of his lips on her skin made Toni turn her face up to his. They stared at each other for what felt like an eternity. Toni wanted desperately for Ian to kiss her lips. Closing his eyes, he leaned closer and touched his lips to hers. What began as a tender kiss took on a sense of urgency as the passion between them overtook them. Ian rolled his tongue around hers awakening a need deep down in her. Toni had never been kissed like this before and it took her breath away. She hadn't had a man in a long time, and Ian was some kind of man.

Slowly pulling back, Ian ran his finger along Toni's jaw and smiled at her. "Wow," he breathed softly.

Smiling Toni said quietly, "My sentiments exactly."

"I've been wanting to do that since the moment I laid eyes on you. You have no idea how beautiful you are."

"I was hoping you felt that way. I'm not usually this impulsive, but there's something about you that disarms me. It generally takes a man many dates before he elicits a response like this from me," Toni said seriously.

"Does this mean that this was more than just a kiss?" Ian asked hopefully.

"That's up to you. Ian, I'm not going to chase after you but if you'd like to see me again I'm available." Toni felt vulnerable all of a sudden. She'd just put the ball in his court uncertain of what he would do next.

"Toni, you've lit a fuse inside me. You've touched parts of me no woman has ever touched before. I can't explain the effect you have on me, but I know I'd like to explore it further. I'm not looking for a one night stand." Ian said honestly.

"I'm not offering you one," Toni said flatly.

"I know that's one of the things I like about you. You have moral standards."

"I've been told my standards are too high," she said sighing.

"I'd like to show you that I can live up to them."

"That's the sweetest thing anyone's ever said to me," Toni said tilting her face up to his.

Ian kissed her again. Passionately. Toni didn't want this night to ever end, but she knew she had a tough day ahead of her. Reluctantly, she told Ian she'd like to head back so she could get home in time to get a decent amount of sleep.

Carlton didn't move from the couch for a full fifteen minutes. He wanted to be certain Toni wouldn't return unexpectedly and find him gone. His brain hummed with excitement as he thought about his next move. *Very cloak and dagger*, he thought relishing the feeling. With Toni and Ian safely tucked away at their quaint little restaurant, he felt he had plenty of time to conduct a methodical search of his grandmother's place. He pulled the new key out of his pants pocket and twirled it so it caught the light from the lamp. The glint of the metal was like a promise of future riches. *The key to my future*, he thought moving his eyebrows up and down.

Carlton was tingling with excitement as he unlocked his car and slid behind the steering wheel. It had turned into a chilly evening after the sun had gone down. *How did people live with this cold weather*, he asked himself. *I can't wait to get the hell out of here after the funeral.* Although everyone had been raving about the beautiful weather they'd been enjoying, to someone from Vegas, it was cold. Turning onto Antique Promenade, he decided to park behind the building.

No sense attracting attention to the fact that his would be the only car on the street at this time of night. He walked quickly up the alley keeping his head low, his shoulders hunched, and his hands in the pockets of his leather jacket.

Inside the shop with the front door relocked behind him, Carlton peered warily out of the large picture window to make sure the street was still deserted. He wanted to be certain no one had seen him. Since his arrival on Sunday, he'd spent much time in the office and the storeroom and was convinced the jewelry was not there. *Gram's too smart a lady to keep jewelry like that on the sales floor. It's probably with her personal belongings upstairs.* When he'd brought up the subject at dinner last night, Toni informed him firmly that she had other more pressing issues to deal with. "I'll look for them next week," she told him. "It's not like I'm getting married anytime soon. Besides they're probably still where Nana hid them and not going anywhere."

Carlton took the stairs two at a time and clicked on the chandelier above the landing. He immediately clicked it back off. Someone could see the light from the street. In the semi-darkness, he went from room to room, drew the drapes on all the windows, and then flicked on all the lights.

Debating where to start, he chose the bedroom. He stopped short just inside the door. A massive portrait of his grandfather hung above the queen size bed. Kurt DeWitt looked unsmilingly down at his grandson.

Carlton remembered the portrait had originally hung above the fireplace in his grandparent's house in the Estates. It was painted when Anna had given birth to the heir of the DeWitt name, Joel. Just as the women were supposed to give their daughters names that began with "A", the DeWitt men were supposed to have a portrait painted when their first son was born.

Good ol' dad, Carlton thought cynically. *Wonder why you never got yours painted when I was born?* He allowed his mind to wander back over the lowlights of his relationship with his father for a few minutes, then reminded himself of the reason he was here.

"Sorry Gramps, but I gotta do this," Carlton said out loud. "Hope you can forgive me." Moving farther into the bedroom, Carlton set to work. He opened the dresser drawers one by one. They contained panties, bras, slips, stockings, scarves, and handkerchiefs. He forced himself not to think about the fact that he was rifling through his dead grandmother's "intimates". He checked the inside of the dresser for any secret compartments, but found none. Pulling the dresser away from the wall, he checked behind it, and even looked behind the mirror. He got down on his hands and knees and looked on the underside of the dresser. Nothing.

Next, the closet. He opened the bi-fold doors and looked at his grandmother's elegant clothes hanging neatly on hangers. *She was certainly a clotheshorse,* Carlton thought. *Just like Toni. What is it with women and clothes anyway? At least she had good taste. This stuff's expensive.* He checked the pockets of every garment working his way from left to right. He found no jewelry, but he did come across Anna's full-length mink. *Well, I can always sell the fur. It should fetch a pretty penny.* Moving down to the floor Carlton looked under a shelf that held folded items. He then put his hand into all the shoes that were lined up neatly in a row on the floor. Nothing.

Carlton clambered onto the bed. That was the only piece of furniture he hadn't attacked yet. Crushing the pillows and shams with his feet he lifted the portrait with both hands and checked behind it for a wall safe. He didn't find one. He checked the headboard, slid off the bed, and got down on all fours to check under the bed. Nothing. Carlton sat back on his heels. He was beginning to get frustrated. He surveyed the disarray he'd created in his grandmother's bedroom.

"Damn it!" he cursed. "I was positive I'd find the jewelry in here." Carlton strode to the little kitchen and opened all the cabinets. He began slamming the cabinet doors shut. He no longer cared if he was seen or heard. He even checked the freezer and refrigerator. Nothing. He looked in the pantry and the stove. Couldn't leave anything out. Still nothing.

"Ahhh," he bellowed. His frustration was beginning to turn into anger. "Where the hell can the damn jewelry be?"

Carlton marched into the bathroom. Like a wild man he began turning this way and that not sure where to check first. The vanity yielded nothing but cleaning supplies. Nor did the medicine cabinet. He'd seen movies where people hid money or drugs in the toilet tank. But still he found nothing.

By now Carlton DeWitt was furious. He had only one room left, the living room. He stalked into it and sat down on the edge of the sofa trying to calm himself. He knew he couldn't let his anger get the better of him. Although he was making a mess, he didn't want to actually damage anything. He was planning to put everything back in place after he found the jewels. Checking his watch, he realized he had been at it more than an hour and was running out of time. I've got to get outta here and make sure I'm back to the apartment before Toni gets home.

Carlton ran both hands through his hair, and threw himself backwards on the sofa to stare at the ceiling. Taking a deep breath, he dropped his head to the right. His attention was caught by the array of photographs displayed in elegant silver frames on the empire style drum table next to the couch.

He sat up and using his hands, slid closer to the table. Looking at the still images, Carlton felt a pang of regret for what he had done. There was of course a photo of his parents, and one of Toni's parents. *Boy, does Toni look like Aunt Ashley*, he thought. There were also photographs of Toni in various stages of her life. But the ones that touched him the most, were the ones of him. His grandmother had lovingly placed his photos among those of her beloved family. Yeah, he knew he was family too, but their relationship had been cordial at best. Just when he was convinced his grandmother had written him off, he sees this. *Man, she even kept my wedding picture up*, he thought. *I looked so happy. Hmph. Seems like a lifetime ago.* Again, he found himself playing back scenes from his life.

Carlton stood up abruptly. "I don't have time for this!" he yelled at the people in the photographs. The anger he had managed to set aside, came back twofold. He felt like knocking all the frames onto the floor with one swipe. Instead, he turned his back on the memories and scanned each piece of furniture in the living room. He moved around checking under the sofa cushions, the credenza where the linen was stored, and the cabinet the television sat on. Every place he could think of. Nothing.

A sense of complete desperation gripped Carlton. He felt like he had gambled again and lost big time. He was beyond anger. Beyond rational thought. He needed to take his frustration out on something. He swung his leg back and, with a primal scream, hurled a kick at a brocade covered antique chair. The chair flew across the room and landed on its side with a loud thud. It rocked from side to side. Carlton knew he shouldn't have kicked the chair that hard, but man it felt good. His foot was throbbing, a dull pain that took his mind off his situation.

Rational thought set in. He walked cautiously toward the chair. *Oh no,* he thought hitting himself in the forehead, *I ripped it. I ripped the damn chair.* Sure enough, the fabric on the underside of the seat was torn. Kneeling to inspect the fabric, he pulled at it and realized it was not torn but it was loose because some of the upholstery tacks were missing. Carlton didn't know much about antiques or upholstery, but this looked like it was intentional. Maybe he wasn't responsible for this damage.

Breathing a sigh of relief, Carlton stood grabbing the legs of the chair in order to set it right side up. That's when he heard it. Something was shifting around inside the chair. Maybe he had damaged it after all. He dropped to the floor, and reached behind the loose fabric. His hand fell on a bulge. Slowly, carefully, he pulled out a royal blue velvet drawstring bag. Carlton's heart began to pound wildly as he opened the bag. He turned it upside down, holding out his other hand to catch whatever fell out of it. An emerald and diamond necklace, matching earrings, and a diamond bracelet tumbled out. Carlton gasped. They were the most amazing things he had ever seen. He examined each piece closely, totally mesmerized by its sparkle and size.

Gently, Carlton put each piece back into the bag and replaced the bundle in the chair. He didn't want to risk having anything happen to them until he was ready to meet Rashovsky. No need to take chances. He stood the chair up and put it back into position in the room. He quickly returned to the bedroom and straightened up the mess he'd created. He took one last look to be sure nothing looked disturbed. Tomorrow, he would call the Russian who wanted to buy the jewels and arrange the sale ASAP. By Friday, he hoped to be on his way back to Las Vegas. He could now pay off the Tropical Casino and then some.

Carlton DeWitt had finally broken the bank.

CHAPTER 17

Covington, Rhode Island
Thursday April 15th, 1999

Carlton, wearing a new black suit, stood to Toni's right and Joyce to her left. They were inches from the mahogany casket that held Anna's body. Ian, realizing this was a family moment, held back. He stood a short distance from them with his hands in the pockets of his black suit. They were the only four people who had remained; the other mourners had long since driven away. Her face hidden under a black veil and a pair of dark sunglasses, Toni really just wanted to throw herself onto the casket and say one final goodbye to her Nana. Instead, she allowed herself to be guided away from the gravesite to the waiting limousine.

During the making of the funeral arrangements, Toni had asked Mr. Chapman to come up with a way of making clear to the mourners that there would be no gathering after the burial. To comply with her request, he had given everyone a white rose instructing them to place it on the casket as a goodbye tribute to Anna DeWitt. One by one each placed their rose onto the casket, briefly stopped to give Toni their condolences, and then left the cemetery. Toni was shocked to see Mr. Rashovsky paying his respects. She would have asked him what the hell he was doing there if circumstances were different. However, she was beyond caring at that point.

Toni had watched them until it was her turn. She was last; holding a beautiful white rose she laid it carefully on the top of the casket. She placed her hands on the casket and leaned closer to it and kissed it lovingly. She turned her face and ever so gently placed her cheek against the cool, smooth wood.

Carlton was momentarily struck with the guilt of knowing he was responsible for this. But, only momentarily. He reached for Toni's shoulder, and pulling her back, held her right elbow and supported her as they walked along the carpet covering the dirt that had been excavated. Joyce instinctively held her other elbow. Ian brought up the rear of their silent procession.

The chauffeur had opened the back door of the limousine, and stood waiting for them to get in. Looking back one more time before she entered the limo, Toni saw the cemetery workers starting to lower the coffin into the vault. It was more than she could bear, and she collapsed. Carlton's grip tightened to stop her from falling. He then got her settled into the spacious back seat of the limo, and turned to Joyce. "Instead of dropping you off at home, can you come back to the apartment for a little while? I think it would help Toni to have another woman there with her," he said, trying to play on Joyce's motherly instincts. *I need to tread carefully around her,* he thought. *Especially after that call she made to Pratt.*

"I don't know. Maybe another time would be better," Joyce responded hesitantly.

"Joyce, please come, you're like family. I know she'd want you with her," Carlton almost pleaded. He was not in the mood to deal with a weepy woman on his own, and he wanted to make Joyce believe he had Toni's interest at heart.

"Well, alright. But, only for a little while. I need to be by myself also," Joyce said as she got into the limo.

Ian wondered if Carlton would invite him too. The detective in him thought he wouldn't; the human in him thought he would.

"Monroe?" Carlton looked at Ian as if asking him why he hadn't left with the other mourners.

Well, that answers my question, Ian thought. Out loud he said, "Absolutely, Carlton. I will meet you at Toni's apartment." Ian turned and walked to his car before Carlton could protest.

It was a sunny spring afternoon; not a cloud in the sky. The green fields flew by as the limousine headed back towards town. The ride seemed long. Silent. No one spoke. Each one lost in their own thoughts. One could guess Toni and Joyce's thoughts; Carlton's were a different story. *I've got to figure out a way to get back to the shop to meet Rashovsky. It would have been easy with just Joyce and Toni there. But now her cop invited himself over. I wonder why? Does he know? Or does he just want to be with Toni? There's something between them now, and it's going to complicate things for me. He obviously has feelings for her, any idiot can see that from the way he doted on her at the viewing. Damn it! Think, Carl, think. How can I get out of there without looking like I'm up to something? Oh hell, I'll figure something out.*

The limo pulled up to Toni's apartment complex. The chauffeur came around to their side of the limo to help them out. Silently they walked the short distance from the limo to the building. As the limo pulled away, Ian's car purred past the complex, and into visitor parking around the corner. A stab of jealousy ripped through Carlton as he imagined Ian's Corvette parked next to his old Mustang.

Carlton squinted in the bright sunlight and attempted a little smile. "Hey, Ton, how about I go get us some food? Your friend Monroe is on his way, and maybe others will show up also."

Joyce shot Carlton a look of disdain. "Apparently you misunderstood the whole point of the roses. No one is going to show up here, Carlton. And, this is hardly an appropriate time to be thinking about food."

"Joyce," Toni's voice was barely a whisper, "I'm sure Carl is only trying to be helpful."

Carlton opened his mouth to send a scathing remark in Joyce's direction, but stopped himself when Ian walked up.

"Why is everyone standing out here?" Ian questioned the group as he walked up.

"Carlton here thinks food is needed right now. So he suggested he go and buy some," Joyce said with obvious sarcasm.

"You trying to get away, buddy?" Ian pinned Carlton with one of his detective looks. It worked even though he was wearing sunglasses.

"What and leave this loving group?" Carlton shot back.

"If the two of you insist on acting like little boys, please do it somewhere else. I'm really not in the mood," Toni stated flatly.

"Sorry, Cuz. It's a guy thing. No harm meant. Right?" As if to give credence to his words, Carlton play punched Ian's right arm.

Ian responded with a stronger than normal clap on Carlton's back. "Right."

Joyce shook her head, "Come on, honey," she said to Toni. "Let's get these boys inside before they make public fools of themselves."

Once inside, Toni sat down on the sofa and kicked off her black pumps. She leaned forward and rubbed her toes, instep and ankles. She wasn't used to standing for long periods of time in heels. She massaged her lower legs; careful not to snag her pantyhose on the bracelet encircling her wrist. Toni wanted to get out of the black suit she was wearing, change into her favorite sweats, and curl up on the sofa. She felt numb and in a trance like state. She couldn't feel anything, no emotions, no tears; the shock had re-reared its ugly head. After all, Nana was dead a week now. She had just started getting used to the idea when the funeral brought it all back.

Ian had not spoken to Toni at the graveside service. Although they had established an unspoken commitment to seeing each other, he felt advertising his affection for her at this time was inappropriate. He had hovered near her at the viewing as a show of support, but he knew not to smother her. Besides it seemed that all of Covington had come out, and Toni needed to greet the mourners as they paid their respects. He sat down next to her, and wrapped his arm around her shoulders. "How are you holding up?"

"I'm here. Not great, but hanging in there," Toni said trying to speak without choking up. She realized if she didn't talk, she wouldn't cry. It was when people spoke to her that she became emotional and tears welled up in her eyes. Instinctively that was probably why she had wanted to be alone.

Ian pulled Toni into a hug, and kissed her neck. It was more than she could handle and she broke down sobbing in his arms. Becoming self-conscious, she stood up suddenly and said, "Excuse me. I'll be back in a few minutes."

Carlton had gone to the kitchen to get himself a glass of water. He shed the jacket of the suit Toni had bought him for the funeral, as well as the tie. He had to come up with a way of leaving the apartment. When Toni rushed to her bedroom to gather herself, he debated whether he should follow her. Joyce beat him to it. Carlton knew he should leave the kitchen and join the cop in the living room. However, he was worried about being alone with Ian Monroe. *This is not going to be as easy as I thought it would be.* Looking up at the ceiling, he wished for divine intervention. It came in the form of a phone call from Mr. Chapman. Anna's Death Certificates were ready for pick-up.

After taking the call, he knocked on Toni's bedroom door, told her who had called, and assured her he would be more than happy to handle this for her. Trying to contain his euphoria, Carlton bid Ian a hasty goodbye and hightailed it out of the apartment before anyone noticed how happy he was.

"I think it's going to rain," Ian stated flatly looking out of the open living room window. He had felt the need to say something to break the deafening silence. It was obvious Toni wanted to be alone, but he couldn't bring himself to leave her. He wanted to hold her and make the sadness in her eyes go away. Instead, he found himself wandering over to the window and talking about the weather.

Joyce, who had been hovering around Toni for the past half hour, left the seat she'd been occupying and joined Ian at the window. "What makes you say that?" She couldn't see past Ian's broad shoulders.

"The sky darkened up rather quickly, and the temperature has dropped a few degrees. Plus, it smells like rain."

"Oh dear me. I think you're right." Joyce turned back toward Toni with a worried expression on her face. "Oh dear me."

"Joyce," Toni said, "you'd better get going before it starts coming down. It's okay, really. I'll be alright."

Joyce felt a little guilty about being relieved to hear Toni say this. She had sensed that Toni wanted to be alone, but she couldn't figure out how to leave respectfully. She wasn't put out by Toni's not offering to give her a ride home. Anyone who knew Joyce Parsons knew she preferred to walk everywhere. "Alright dear. If you don't mind. I'll be going now. Call me tomorrow if you need me."

Toni stood and walked Joyce to the door. The women exchanged a hug.

"I think I'll be going also," Ian said tentatively. When Toni didn't protest, he realized he was doing the right thing. As Joyce went to call the elevator, Ian gathered Toni to him and gave her a soft kiss. "Call me if you need me," he whispered.

Toni smiled up at him, but said nothing. He waved to her as he and Joyce entered the elevator.

Always the perfect gentleman, he offered Joyce a ride home as they exited the apartment building.

"Thank you, my dear," Joyce smiled warmly at Ian as he held the door open for her. "But I've always preferred to walk. I live on Spring Street just off Antique Promenade. I'll be home in less than fifteen minutes.

"You're sure you will be okay?"

"Oh yes, yes." They parted ways.

Joyce watched Ian round the corner towards the visitor lot. When she was sure he could no longer see her, she turned and walked back into the building towards the wall of mailboxes. She quickly found the mailbox labeled with Toni's apartment number, and slipped a letter she had written to Toni into the slot. The letter contained thoughts and feelings that Joyce wanted to convey to Toni but couldn't bring herself to say in person. Her mission complete, she hastily left the building.

Joyce walked briskly down Village Way. *Yes, it definitely smells like rain. Good thing I only have a short walk home.*

The streetlights had already come on because of the overcast skies. Less than five minutes later she turned onto Antique Promenade, and wistfully looked at the lights shining from inside the shops at the beginning of the street. Saddened by the knowledge that *Anna's Attic* would be enveloped in darkness, she put her head down and resolutely promised herself to walk by quickly.

More than half way down the street, as she approached the shop, Joyce saw something unexpected out of the corner of her eye. The lights in the office were on. *That's strange,* she thought. *Did I leave those on when I left last?* Stopping to think, Joyce was almost positive she hadn't. After all, she had been turning those lights off religiously for many years. *I'd better go in to turn them off.*

Joyce fished for the shop key in her purse. She noticed that *Precious Collectibles,* the shop across the street seemed closed. *Sophie must not have opened today; she was rather upset at the funeral.* Upon further examination, she saw that more than half of the shops were dark. It was out of respect for Anna that they didn't open today. Joyce found the key, and inserted it into the doorknob. It was then that she realized the door was already unlocked.

Holding her breath, Joyce slowly pushed open the door. Her brain was telling her she should be calling the police, but her curiosity moved her into the showroom. She closed the door very gently behind her. Standing motionless she distinctly heard a man's voice. She was about to run out and call for help, when she recognized the voice to be Carlton's. Letting out the breath she'd been holding, Joyce intended to storm into the office and demand to know what Carlton was doing there, when the words he spoke stopped her.

"Listen Rashovsky, if you do not believe that I have the jewels then I will just have to find another buyer." There was a pause. Then Carlton continued. "Alright then. Give me an offer I can't refuse and let's set up an exchange and get this over with. I have to be back in Vegas ASAP." Another brief pause. "Well, I certainly cannot refuse that offer." A moment of silence, then, "Oh, you need a few days to get the money together? No problem. The Covington Suites. Tuesday at one o'clock. That gives you tomorrow and Monday to get the money together." More silence. "And it's a pleasure doing business with you too." Carlton hung up the phone, and placed the velvet jewelry bag he had retrieved from under the chair into the pocket of his leather jacket. He turned to leave the office, and stopped dead in his tracks. Joyce Parsons was standing in the office doorway, thunderstruck.

Perhaps Joyce hadn't heard what she thought she'd heard. Surely Carlton wouldn't be trying to sell jewelry to Rashovsky behind Toni's back. Maybe she'd heard wrong. Maybe this was a dream. Maybe a nightmare. Maybe she'd wake up. Maybe a lot of things. She didn't know if she should move, her feet felt heavy, cemented to the floor.

Carlton moved toward her. "What are you doing here, Joyce?" He didn't know how long she had been standing there.

Joyce cleared her throat. Her mouth felt dry. She swallowed hard. "I just left Toni's apartment to go home before the rain," she nervously explained. "As I walked by the shop I saw the office light and thought I'd left it on. I came in to turn off the light." Why did she feel like she had to defend herself for entering *Anna's Attic?*

"Oh, so you'll be on your way now. Let me walk you to the door." Carlton pressed closer but Joyce didn't budge.

She wished she didn't have to say what was on her mind. But, she had to know if she'd heard what she thought she'd heard. She took a deep breath, made eye contact with Carlton and mustered all the courage she could. "Carlton, when I came in I thought I heard you talking about selling jewelry to someone. Have you been upstairs? Have you taken some of your grandmother's jewelry?"

"What about it? What business is it of yours? It's not your jewelry." Carlton's face and voice changed in the blink of an eye to ugly.

"Carlton, Toni welcomed you back with open arms, and this is how you repay her?" Joyce's voice rose a fraction.

"I ask you again, what business is it of yours?" Carlton repeated through gritted teeth.

"I'm making it my business. I will not allow you to treat Toni this way." Joyce pulled herself up to her full height.

"Oh yeah? Let me see you stop me."

"So, I was right. You are trying to sell some jewelry. Well, you're not going to get very far. When I tell Toni what you've done, she will report the jewelry missing and you won't be able to sell it at all."

Carlton threw his head back and laughed without mirth. "She has no clue what it even looks like. How can she report it missing?"

"No clue…wait a minute. I heard you say Rashovsky's name. Oh my Lord! You found them. You found the jewels from the Grand Duchess. Carlton Joel DeWitt, how could you? And with your grandmother's body barely in the ground. Anna would never have sold those jewels. Not to anyone for any reason. They are a family heirloom. I know family means nothing to you, but it sure does to Toni and I know she wouldn't sell them either." Joyce was trying to stay calm, keep her voice from cracking and her emotions under control. But inside she was beginning to boil. *What right does this bum have to show up here after being away for years, steal the jewels and sell them out from under Toni? They're hers not his.*

"Yeah, but Toni doesn't have them and I do. And I plan to sell them. My ass is in deep shit in Vegas and this money is going to be my winning ticket." Carlton hadn't meant to go that far. He'd said more than he should have. Now Joyce would run back to Toni and he'd be dead meat. He had to shut her up.

"What kind of trouble are you in?"

"None of your damn business, Joyce!"

"Did Anna know about this? Is it gambling again?"

"Stupid, how could Anna know? She was dead when I got here," he shouted.

"Was she, or did you come here to ask for money for gambling and she turned you away?" She said as unemotionally as she could while keeping her eyes on him.

"You don't know what you're talking about old woman."

"I told Toni you hadn't changed. You've been doing the devoted loving cousin number but I know you, Carlton DeWitt." She poked her finger three times into his chest to make her point.

Carlton had had just about enough of this conversation. But, he couldn't let her leave now that she knew so much. He continued to talk while his eyes scanned the area looking for a way to silence her. "O.K. so you're right. I did ask Anna to help me. So what? She was my grandmother, and, had I been her favorite, she would have given me the money. Now I'm taking the jewelry instead. Indirectly she's still giving it to me." As he spoke, he flailed his hands and arms wildly to punctuate his words. The decibel level of his voice rose noticeably.

"Carlton, what did Anna say when you asked her for money?" Joyce had lowered her voice to barely above a whisper trying to calm Carlton. She figured if she kept him talking long enough she'd have a chance to get away.

Carlton stood inches from Joyce staring at her with a glazed look in his eyes. "What? What did you say? I didn't hear you." Joyce had caught him off guard.

"When you asked Anna, what did she say?"

"I don't know. Something about retirement. She had saved for her retirement."

"And then?" Joyce continued to press the issue. Her heart was thumping in her chest. Her brain registering the fact that Carlton must have seen Anna before she died.

"Goddamn it Joyce! What does it matter? She told me to get out. She saw through me. That I'd only come east to ask her for money."

"She was alive when you left?" Joyce's voice was trembling.

"No. Yes. I mean yes." Carlton realized he had admitted speaking to his grandmother before she died. It wouldn't be long before Joyce put two and two together.

Panic rose in Joyce's stomach threatening to choke her. She knew she was staring into the face of Anna's murderer. She couldn't keep the look of horror from her face.

"I didn't kill her. I mean I didn't mean to kill her." He hung his head and Joyce thought he looked relieved that someone finally knew the truth.

Joyce stepped quickly around Carlton and struggled to get to the desk phone to dial 911 before he regained his composure. She didn't make it.

"What the hell are you doing?" She had the phone up to her ear and had pressed the 9 and the first 1, when he stormed over, grabbed the phone out of her hand, and slammed it down; bumping against her in his haste.

"What are you going to do? Are you going to kill me too?" She swung around to face him. She wondered if the terror she was feeling inside showed on her face.

"I didn't kill Gram! She just died. She hit her head and died. I didn't kill her." He sounded like he was trying to convince himself more than Joyce.

Joyce didn't want to look at Carlton. She didn't want to know any more. She hated him and just wanted to get out of there. Easy to say, but not so easy to do. He was standing facing her and the backs of her legs were pressed against the desk. He easily towered over her and she knew he was strong. She had no chance against him physically. She turned away from him and began praying. Joyce Parsons knew she wouldn't make it home tonight.

Toni's bedroom door was closed by the time Carlton made it back to the apartment. She had turned on a lamp, and laid out sheets, pillows, and a quilt for him. There was also a note on the coffee table. *Carl, I've gone to bed. See you in the A.M. Love, T.*

Tossing his leather jacket onto the sofa, Carlton kicked off his shoes and headed for the bathroom. He stared longingly at the shower, wanting to scrub away the guilt, as well as the sweat. Knowing that the sound of the water would awaken Toni, he settled for a quick wash up. Turning on the faucet, he placed his hands under the hot running water. He was shocked to see his hands were blood red. He hadn't noticed the stains until now because this was the first well-lit area he had entered since leaving Joyce dead on the office carpet.

Frantically he searched for cleaning products. Anything that removed stains would do. He chose bleach that he'd found under the bathroom sink. Carlton stopped up the sink and let it fill with hot water. Pouring in the bleach, he scrubbed until his hands felt raw. Some of the stain came off, but his hands still had a distinct red tint to them. He wasn't sure what the stains were from. Maybe they were from the carpet cleaner he'd used when he tried to clean off the footprint he left. When he went to wipe off the telephone, he was forced to step over Joyce and managed to step in the blood that was pooling around her head. Either way he would try to keep his hands out of sight as best he could. He let the bleach water drain out of the sink, watching the red and white form swirls as the sink emptied.

As he leaned down on the sink to wash his face, he caught a glimpse in the wall mirror of blood on his shirt. *Oh shit. I'm glad no one saw me come in.* He quickly stripped off the shirt, balled it up and threw it on the floor. He splashed water on his face and stared in the mirror in disbelief. He had a five o'clock shadow, and his hair looked like it hadn't been combed in days. His eyes looked deep set and dark. His pupils dilated so his eyes looked almost maniacal. This was not the suave impeccably dressed guy who lived in Vegas. He wished he'd never left Vegas. He wished his life were different. But it wasn't and this was the mess he made of it. He was responsible for all of it. If only he'd done things differently, but in life there were no do overs. Although he'd screwed up big time, all he had to do was keep cool until Tuesday. Then he was home free.

The smell of bleach permeated the bathroom. Carlton hastily washed his face and upper body. Drying off, he opened the window to let the room air out a little. Clicking off the bathroom light, he bent down and picked up the shirt and quietly opened the door. In his socks, he tiptoed to the kitchen in the dimly lit apartment careful to not bump into anything. Pulling open the trash compactor, he shoved the balled up shirt under the garbage into the bottom of the bag. He gently pushed the compactor door closed and rinsed his hands in the sink.

Making his way back to the living room, Carlton retrieved the small velvet bag from his jacket pocket. He bounced it up and down in his hand a couple of times. Deciding his duffle bag would be the most private place to hide it, he tucked it into the inside pocket. Since he doubted Toni would look through his things, he retrieved the receipts from his jacket that Sandoval Pratt had given him and stuffed them in with the bag. They would all be safe there for now.

Carlton stripped off his pants and slid under the covers. The cool sheets felt good on his skin. He interlocked his fingers and put his hands behind his head. Staring up at the ceiling he tried to calm the storm of emotion that was raging inside him.

CHAPTER 18

Covington, Rhode Island
Friday April 16th, 1999

Ian starred blankly ahead of him. His mind was racing in a hundred different directions; the mug of coffee he poured himself earlier had turned cold. The conversation he'd just had with Mayor Boyce left him with a bad taste in his mouth. Ian had managed to avoid the mayor at the funeral yesterday, however he found him sitting at his desk when he got in this morning. Captain Kirk had cowered in his office and left Ian to fend for himself. Both men had tried to get the Captain's attention, but he'd tended not to notice. Ian knew that Mayor Boyce would have charged into Kirk's office if he'd wanted to. It was obvious, however, that the mayor wanted Ian and Ian alone.

The conversation was one-sided and redundant. It's been one week, no leads, no suspects, etc., etc. Mayor Boyce had left the precinct with a blatant warning: find the killer now!

Ian turned his attention to the list of Anna's customers that Joyce had given him. He hadn't gotten any useful information from the people he had already contacted. No one seemed to know why someone would want Anna DeWitt dead. He entered Abigail Beauchamp's phone number onto the keypad of his phone. As he waited for an answer, he twirled a pencil in his fingers.

"Hello," answered a female with a southern drawl.

"Good morning, may I speak to Abigail Beauchamp, please?"

"And who might I say is calling?" the southern drawl asked.

"Sergeant Ian Monroe, Covington P.D. I just have a few questions to ask her."

"Oh my," breathed the voice.

Ian was getting frustrated. "Is she there or not?"

"Well, Sergeant Monroe, there's no need to be snippy. How can I help you?"

"Mrs. Beauchamp?"

"That's right."

Well, why didn't you say so in the first place? Out loud he said, "Mrs. Beauchamp, I understand you were a regular customer of Anna DeWitt's. I was hoping you could provide me with some information."

"Oh, Anna, what a terrible tragedy. Such a wonderful lady. I will truly miss her…" Abigail droned on while Ian felt like banging his head against the desk. This is why he disliked Covington society. "I'm not sure I can tell you anything. It's been a few weeks since I've even spoken to Anna. I am recovering from a bout of influenza that just left me bedridden for the past month or so."

Influenza my ass. You were drinking yourself into oblivion because your husband is about to leave you for his much younger personal assistant, Ian thought recalling the conversation he had with his mother on the phone last night. She had regaled him with the latest country club gossip.

"Well, if you can think of anything, no matter how trivial, please call me at the police station."

"Actually, you would do better by speaking to Roslyn Smythe-Burns. She and Anna were close friends and I know Roslyn bought from Anna often. I could give you the number."

If you hadn't been in a drunken stupor you'd know Roslyn was in Europe. "I already have it. Thank you for your time Mrs. Beauchamp." Another dead end. He pressed the switch hook buttons, and entered the next phone number when he heard a dial tone.

"Treadwell residence."

"Good morning. Ian Monroe for Mr. Francis Treadwell," Ian wasted no time with the butler. Francis had told him years ago to be direct and identify himself right away if he intended to get past the butler.

"Just one moment, Sergeant."

There was a brief moment before Francis's booming voice came on the line. "Ian, so good to hear from you. What can I do for you?"

"Hey Fran, how's it going?"

"Oh Ian, if you only knew. I have enough money to buy whatever I want, but I can't seem to find one good man."

"What happened to Luis?"

"Oh Luis! That two timing SOB! Would you believe he was also screwing that waiter at the Peppermill."

"You mean the waiter that's been trying to get into your bed, not to mention your bank account?"

"Oh the perils of being handsome and rich. They all want me, Ian. Problem is I don't want any of them." Francis sighed. "Any chance of your coming around to my side?"

Ian rolled his eyes and shook his head. "Give it up, Fran. It's not going to happen, it'd break my mother's heart. Besides, I think I just met the mother of my children."

"Ooh, do tell. Who is the lucky lady?"

"Antonia Stanton."

"Ooh fabulous choice. I approve, I approve. Such an awful thing to happen to her grandmother."

"That's why I'm calling. I need any information you can give me about Anna." Ian didn't hold out much hope for anything useful.

"Don't know what to tell you. Good woman. Excellent reputation. Honest. Well-liked. Why anyone would want her dead I don't know. You know, if you can reach Roslyn Smythe-Burns, she could probably tell you more. They were good friends, you know."

"Yeah, I know. Anyway, thanks, we'll do lunch soon."

Ian hung up and stretched his shoulders and back. It felt good to expand his chest that way. He rolled his neck from side to side and returned to the phone list. One of the junior patrolmen placed a fresh cup of coffee on his desk. "You look like you could use this, Sarge."

"Thanks, McConnelly." Ian sipped the coffee as he waited for the next person on his list to answer their phone. Ian counted seven rings before hanging up. Marjorie Fulton was obviously not home. He would have to try her again later. His next call was to Deidre Vissing, the wife of Dennis Vissing, DMD. Dr. Vissing was currently being sued for sexual harassment by several of his female patients. Apparently, when he put them under, he performed more than oral surgery. Deidre was desperately trying to hold her head high, but she knew she was the laughing stock of the Covington Society.

"Greetings," Deidre Vissing's voice was not friendly.

"Mrs. Vissing, please."

"Speaking."

"Good morning, Mrs. Vissing. This is Sergeant Ian Monroe of the Coven…"

"Sorry, Sarge. My lawyer has advised me not to speak to anyone. Good day." The line went dead.

Ian wasn't offended by Deidre's brusqueness. She was most likely inundated with calls from police, lawyers, and reporters since her husband's arrest. He could understand where she was coming from. Ian took another sip of his coffee, and pushed the redial button. Before Deidre Vissing could hang up on him again, he told her the reason for his call. She was unable to provide him with any new information. However, she did mention Roslyn's name.

Ian decided that it was more than a coincidence that the three people he spoke with referred him to Roslyn Smythe-Burns. Without Captain Kirk's approval, he'd make the call to Roslyn on the ship. Hopefully, the call would yield useful information, justifying the expense to the Covington P.D. as well as Mayor Boyce. He consulted his worn notepad for the cruise information the Smythe-Burns housekeeper had provided.

A voice belonging to one of the patrolmen called out, "Monroe! Line 2."

"Sergeant Monroe."

Toni was on the phone, and she was frantic. "Ian! Oh my God! Joyce! Someone's killed her. There's blood everywhere." Her voice was hysterical. "Come quickly. Help me!"

Ian was on his feet like a shot. "Where are you?"

"At the shop. Hurry!"

"I'm on my way."

Ian's Corvette came to a screeching halt outside *Anna's Attic*. Behind him were two police cruisers, their lights flashing and their sirens blaring. Toni was on the sidewalk before he'd even opened the car door. She ran into his arms sobbing hysterically.

"It's horrible. Horrible. Who would do this? What am I gonna do?"

"Let's go inside, it's chilly out here." Although Toni was dressed in sweats he could feel her shivering as she leaned against him.

Once inside, Ian led Toni to the nearest antique sofa and gently got her settled. Carlton was standing near the picture window with his hands in his pockets. To Ian he looked too calm for a man who'd just discovered Joyce dead. "Take care of her," he ordered, motioning for Carlton to sit next to Toni. By this time the forensic photographer John Meadows, the fingerprint duster, Barry Cabot, and two patrolmen, Dan Williams and Matt Reynolds, were inside the showroom waiting for orders from the detective in charge. When Ian asked where Joyce was, Carlton pointed in the direction of the office.

Ian was a seasoned detective. He had investigated many gruesome crime scenes in his years with NYPD. What he saw in Anna's office turned his stomach. He had to turn away for a couple of seconds to regain his composure. It was obvious by the looks on the other policemen's faces that they were feeling the same. To see your kindergarten teacher bludgeoned was more than they could comprehend.

Putting their personal grief aside, they got to work. Joyce was lying on her back, close to the desk. She was missing the right side of her skull. Blood and brain matter were spattered on the wall, the desk and the carpet. Her eyes were squeezed shut and her jaw was clenched, almost as if she had been anticipating the fatal blow. It had come in the form of an ornate marble table lamp, now on its side near the body. The base of the lamp had what looked like remnants of hair and tissue on it. The purse she must have been carrying when she'd been hit was on the floor, it's contents spilled. Keys, a compact, a wallet, and a comb, were now covered in blood. The camera's periodic flash accentuated the morbidity of the scene.

Ian reached for his cell phone and called Captain Kirk. This crime was obviously connected to Anna DeWitt's murder and Ian knew the press would be here soon. He wanted his commanding officer to be involved especially since Mayor Boyce had been breathing down the department's neck. Knowing this could turn into a public relations nightmare, Ian wanted the brass there. He instructed the men with him not to touch anything until Kirk arrived. Meadows continued to photograph the scene, while Cabot, Williams and Reynolds stood outside the office.

Ian returned to the showroom and pulled a chair up to the sofa Toni and Carlton were sitting on. A wad of used tissues was on the sofa next to Toni, as Carlton held the tissue box for her. When he saw Ian he placed the box in Toni's lap and shoved his hands into his pockets.

"Toni, I know this is difficult, but I need to know how you found Joyce." Toni couldn't speak. She couldn't stop sobbing and wiping her face with tissues. She looked toward Carlton to speak for her.

"We arrived shortly before 9:30," Carlton began. "Toni asked me to come with her so we could begin cleaning out Gram's personal belongings upstairs."

"Were both locks on the door locked?"

"Yes." Carlton realized he had screwed up by locking the deadbolt before leaving last night. It wouldn't be long before Dick Tracy here figured out that the killer had his own key.

"Toni, who has keys to the shop?"

"Between sobs Toni managed, "As far as I know just Nana, Joyce, and I."

"What made you go into the office?" Ian asked, placing his elbows on his knees. He couldn't take his eyes off Toni. She looked so frail and delicate. Toni shrugged and took a steadying breath. "Habit, I guess. When I would visit Nana I always left my coat and purse in the office." Ian reached for her hand. Squeezing it he asked, "Did you touch anything?"

"Oh, no. I screamed...I think. Then I called you from my cell."

"And you?" Ian turned an icy stare at Carlton.

"What...Huh...What do you mean?" Carlton dodged the question.

"Did you touch anything?" Ian repeated as if speaking to a child.

"Uh...no. I ran into the office when Toni screamed and quickly pulled her outta there."

At the sound of car doors slamming, they looked out of the window to see Captain Kirk striding towards the shop with Officer Ryan McConnelly at his heels. Curious bystanders had begun to line the sidewalk outside *Anna's Attic*.

Flinging open the front door, Kirk barked, "Monroe, I need a uniform on crowd control outside pronto!"

"Williams, Reynolds," Ian called. "Clear the sidewalk."

As the two men strode towards the front door, Kirk bellowed, "And no press!" As Ian escorted Kirk and

McConnelly to the office, Carlton stood abruptly. He raked his hands through his hair and paced.

"Carl, you're making me more nervous. Please. Sit." Toni said quietly. She had gained control of her crying for now.

"I can't take all these cops. They make my skin crawl. Can we just get the hell out of here?"

"Why are you so agitated? What's gotten into you?"

"Maybe it's all this death. I don't know about you but this place is beginning to give me the creeps." Toni stared at Carlton in disbelief. She couldn't believe he was being so selfish. What happened to the kind, concerned cousin that showed up here last week? She was about to reprimand Carlton for his insensitivity to the situation when Ian reappeared.

"Toni," Ian began. "There's not much else you can do here. I think Carlton should take you home."

"No, I want to stay. Maybe I can remember something helpful." In reality she just wanted to be with Ian. She felt safe when he was around.

Oh hell no, Carl thought. *We're not staying here another minute.* He placed an arm around her shoulder revealing his red stained palm. Too late he realized that Monroe had noticed. "C'mon Toni. Ian's right, there's nothing more we can do here. Chances are we'll just be in the way."

Toni wanted to ask Ian to come home with her but she knew he had a job to do. She hugged him and gave him a quick kiss before allowing Carlton to usher her out.

Ian watched them drive away. He wanted to be with Toni more than anywhere else. However, Captain Kirk had instructed him to go to Joyce's house and see if he could find anything there.

Using one of the keys on the key chain he had retrieved from next to Joyce's body, Ian entered the little house. Officer McConnelly followed him quietly. They stood in the living room surveying the area, neither one relishing the task at hand. Ian divided the rooms between them; he would take the living room, kitchen and dining room. He deliberately left the two bedrooms, bathroom, and the den to McConnelly. Let the younger officer sift through Joyce's personal effects. McConnelly gave Ian a sideways glance but said nothing. Removing his policeman's hat and parka, he placed them on the coat rack and disappeared down the hall.

Ian removed his windbreaker and hung it on the coat rack. The only other pieces of furniture in the small living room were an old sofa, recliner, side table and floor lamp. Joyce was obviously not a television watcher since there wasn't one in sight. Sighing, Ian sat gingerly on the sofa not wanting to make himself at home. It creaked under his weight. From the indentation in the recliner he surmised that that was Joyce's preferred seat. He could hear the wooden floors creaking as McConnelly moved from room to room. Since he hadn't called him over he must not have found anything of significance.

The side table had a pile of papers and letters stacked neatly on it. *Might as well start there*, Ian thought. Picking up the stack with one hand he planned to sort through the papers quickly and then move into the kitchen. The paper on top was a computer printout of what looked like all the antique dealers closest to Covington. One of the entries had been circled over and over and had *Y128* written next to it. Ian planned on calling the number as soon as they left Joyce's. He placed the printout next to him and sifted through the remaining papers. Nothing but Joyce's unpaid bills, a couple of newsletters, a clothing catalog and a postcard from her son.

"McConnelly. Anything?" Ian called out.

McConnelly's voice was muffled. "No Sarge. Just the usual. I think the phone in here is older than I am."

Ian's curiosity peaked. He walked towards McConnelly's voice until he was staring at the phone on the nightstand. He was expecting to see a vintage 1940's model. Instead he was faced with a rotary beige desk telephone similar to one he'd had growing up.

"See I wasn't kidding. Try picking it up. It's darn heavy man."

"I remember these phones, McConnelly. Watch what you say."

"Sorry sir. No offense."

"None taken. Let's wrap this up. There's nothing here."

Ian locked Joyce's front door as McConnelly returned to the cruiser he'd driven them there in. Once in the passenger seat, Ian flipped open his cell phone and entered the circled number on the printout. McConnelly waited for Ian to give him the okay to drive away.

"Hope Valley Antiques and Collectibles. How may I help you?" A man's voice answered on the third ring.

"This is Sergeant Ian Monroe of the Covington Police Department. Your name and phone number were found during a search conducted for an investigation. Who am I speaking with?"

Ian's question was met with a long pause. On the other end of the line Sandoval Pratt was having a minor panic attack. His mind reeled as he tried to tell himself that this had nothing to do with Carlton and the antiques he'd bought from him. "While I am a supporter of the police, I am hesitant to answer any questions over the phone."

"Then I'm on my way there. Don't close early." Ian slammed his phone shut and barked the address to McConnelly. "Run lights if you have to. I want to be there now."

As they drove with their lights flashing, Ian placed a call to Captain Kirk's cell phone to let him know they were on their way to Hope Valley.

The little bell tinkled as Ian and Ryan entered *Hope Valley Antiques & Collectibles.* It seemed that Sandoval Pratt was waiting for them. He looked agitated and was ringing his hands nervously. There were no other people in the shop. "Detective Monroe, I presume?" he asked, extending his right hand.

Ian ignored his outstretched hand. "Where can we talk privately?"

"We can talk here," Pratt gestured towards a dining room table surrounded by six matching chairs.

Both Ian and Ryan took out notebooks from their pockets and sat side by side at the table. Pratt took one of the chairs opposite them.

"How can I be of assistance?" The elderly man asked.

"Your reaction to my phone call was most unusual. Instinct tells me you are hiding something. Care to explain?" Ian spoke in a low but firm voice.

"Ah. Um. Ah. I was quite taken aback. It's not everyday one receives a call where one is told their name came up in an investigation. Perhaps you can tell me what this is all about now that we are face to face."

Ian waited a few seconds before continuing. He wasn't convinced, but he had so little to go on that challenging Pratt's integrity would serve no purpose. Producing the printout he found at Joyce's, Ian pointed to *Y128* and asked, "Does this notation mean anything to you?"

Pratt peered at the printout and saw the notation was right next to his name. He had two choices: plead ignorance, or be truthful. He wisely chose the latter. The last thing he needed was a full blow investigation that could produce bad press. "That is the authentication number of a Quezal perfume bottle I purchased from a private seller a few days ago."

"What is its significance?" Ian asked as McConnelly took notes.

"It's almost like an identification mark. When a manufacturer makes a limited amount of an item they number each one. It's also a way of knowing that the perfume bottle is authentic."

"Has anyone asked about this bottle since you acquired it?"

"I did get a call earlier this week," Pratt responded shrugging his shoulders.

"Who was the call from?"

"A woman named...let me think...Janet, Janice, Joy, something like that?"

"Joyce?"

"That's it!" Pratt snapped his fingers.

Ian and McConnelly looked at each other. Pratt's attention went from one to the other. He'd had a feeling Carlton's dead aunt story was suspicious. Should he tell this detective everything? If Carlton had stolen the items, he, Pratt, could be indicted for dealing in stolen property. However, if he pleads ignorance and cooperates fully, they may let him go with a slap on the wrist.

"Did she say why she was calling about the bottle?"

"Yes. She asked me about the authentication number and how I acquired the bottle. She said she was working for a collector who was looking to expand a collection of perfume bottles. Really Detective, it was a usual request made between antique dealers for special customers."

"Is it usual for another dealer to ask after a specific authentication number?"

"No. I must say that was a little unusual."

"Weren't you curious at all?" Ian asked.

"I am far too busy to be curious about such things."

"Oh, yeah. I can tell," McConnelly mumbled eyeing the empty shop.

Pratt shifted in his seat, he was getting uncomfortable. He wished they would just leave. Ian sensed Pratt's uneasiness. If he pressed on maybe the man would be more willing to talk and they could be on their way.

"Mr. Pratt, I need the name of the private seller."

"I'm afraid that's confidential information. My business would suffer if my private customers found out I gave their names to the police."

"Mr. Pratt, I don't think you understand…"

"Detective Monroe, I don't think *you* understand. All I did was buy a few items from a private seller, something I do regularly. Now if you don't mind, this interview is over." Pratt began to stand.

"Sit down, Pratt. This is a murder investigation. I will leave when I'm finished with you." Ian's voice brooked no argument.

Not that Pratt was about to argue. The word *murder* had sent his heartbeat through the roof, and he plopped back down in the chair, expelling a breath. "Who's been murdered?"

"Joyce Parsons. The woman who called you about the bottle."

"Oh, my. Oh, dear. I had nothing to do with that. I've never even met the woman. Surely I am not on your list of suspects."

"You won't be if you tell me everything about the bottle, seller and those other items you mentioned."

"All right. I'll tell you everything you want to know. But, the transactions were legitimate on my part. If there was anything untoward about the antiques, I had no knowledge of it. The seller came to me twice. The first time he had the perfume bottle for sale. He returned a few days later with a hair comb, gold watch, and a stickpin. All were authentic and worth a pretty penny. He told me his aunt had died and left her antiques to his cousins and him."

"Sellers name, Pratt."

"Carlton, I don't remember the last name."

McConnelly's pen stilled. Ian stopped breathing for a second. The silence in the room was deafening. Recovering, Ian spoke slowly and deliberately, "I need to see your *dated* receipts immediately."

"Yes, yes. Detective. Right away."

As Pratt went to retrieve the receipts Ian and McConnelly shared a knowing look. Carlton was obviously engaged in suspicious activities. To what extent neither could guess.

Pratt returned and handed Ian two pink receipts, one dated Friday, April 9, the other Wednesday, April 14. Both bore the name of Carlton DeWitt.

Ian's mind was beginning to reel with more questions than answers. Where did Carlton get the bottle from? Why was Joyce so concerned about finding the bottle with the same number? Why was Carlton in Hope Valley two days before appearing in Covington on Sunday? Where was he coming from? Where was he going? Where was he for the weekend?

McConnelly's voice cut into his thoughts. "Detective, Mr. Pratt has kindly offered us the original receipts. He's made a copy for himself."

"Thank you, McConnelly. Mr. Pratt, can you think of anything Carlton said to you about where he had come from or where he was heading?"

"No. I'm sorry. Our conversations were limited to the antiques I was purchasing."

"Here's my card in case you think of anything else," Ian said as he and McConnelly headed out of the door. They were buckling their seatbelts when Pratt appeared at the passenger window. Ian lowered the glass and looked inquiringly at Pratt who seemed excited.

"Detective, I just remembered something else. When Carlton came in the second time, I mentioned the call I'd received from Joyce. He was quite insistent that I tell him all about it. I got the impression it made him nervous." Pratt made that last statement to throw suspicion away from himself and onto Carlton.

Ian reached through the open window and shook Pratt's hand. "Thank you, sir. You've been most helpful."

Ian, Captain Nicholas Kirk, and Officer Ryan McConnelly were huddled in the Captain's office staring at each other. Their small, quiet town of Covington, Rhode Island, had had two murders within two weeks. It was inconceivable.

Darkness was beginning to fall. Through the window, the three men could see the lights blazing in the *Covington*

Chronicle building across the street. No doubt the reporters were feverishly embellishing a story that would hit newsstands tomorrow morning. While Ian and Ryan were away, Kirk had held a press conference where he gave a brief statement, and refused to answer any questions. Although the only reporters in attendance were two from the *Chronicle*, two from the local news station and a cameraman, they made enough noise to attract the attention of anyone within a five-block radius.

When Toni and Carlton had tried to leave, a police escort was required. Williams and Reynolds did their best to keep the reporters and bystanders at bay. It was a scene right out of a movie.

"Captain, I just don't know what to make of this," Ian was shaking his head as he paced the small office. He rubbed his hands over his eyes and up both sides of his head ending on the back of his neck. "All this trouble seems to be centered around Carlton DeWitt. I don't trust the guy. He has a sneaky way about him that makes me think he's knows something that he's not telling. Shifty. That's it. He's shifty-eyed."

"Well, Ian, if you have a gut feeling, how about running a background check on him," Kirk nodded to Ian.

"I ran him on the NCIC and it came up that he has no criminal record with the Feds," Ian shrugged. "All we have on him is that he sold some antiques to a dealer in Hope Valley two days before arriving in Covington. We have no leads on where he spent those two days, who he was with, if anyone, or what he was doing. It's damn frustrating. Whenever I feel as if we've uncovered something, a million new questions are raised. I know there's a connection here. I just can't put my finger on it."

Ryan McConnelly, who had said very little on the car ride back from Hope Valley and had opted to sit quietly while his superiors conferred, piped up. "Sarge didn't you say he was from Vegas?"

Ian threw McConnelly a quizzical look. "And?"

"Isn't Sergeant Ross in Vegas for his niece's wedding?"

"So."

"Well, his brother is on the force out there. Shouldn't we call to ask him to check Carlton out at the local level?" McConnelly suggested.

"Yeah. That's a great idea kid. You'll make a great detective one day."

"In the meantime," Kirk interjected surveying the crime scene photographs, "what do we know about Joyce Parson's murder?"

Ian sat down next to McConnelly. Time of death was between 4 P.M. and 5 P.M. She must have stopped at the shop right after she left Toni's. Damn it, I wish I'd insisted on taking her home."

"Any theories?" Kirk asked.

"Just suspicions. DeWitt's the only one that I can think of," Ian responded. "If you look at one of the photos you'll notice a smeared area on the carpet about a foot away from the body that looked like someone had tried to clean something up."

"And I know you're going somewhere with this," Kirk said sarcastically.

"When Joyce died from her head injuries, the blood oozed out around her head and body. I figure the killer stepped over her for some reason. He probably stepped in the blood leaving a bloody footprint. It looks to me like he tried to clean the carpet."

McConnelly fidgeted in his seat trying to get a word in between the Captain and Ian. "I remember my wife used carpet cleaner after one of the kids cut his foot and tracked blood into the living room. She worked at it for a long time but you could always see the outline of the footprints until we had the carpet steam cleaned. It took a week for the stains on her hands to finally wear off too."

"What?" Ian perked up.

"Yeah, her hands were stained bright red from scrubbing the carpet. She tried everything but nothing would remove the stain on her palms. The house smelled like bleach for days."

"Oh shit! I love you, McConnelly," Ian exclaimed.

"Oh, Sergeant Monroe, I didn't know you felt that way."

"Knock it off you two. What's going on, Ian?" McConnelly had gotten Kirk's attention too.

"When I saw Carlton DeWitt this morning, it seemed like his hands were always in his pockets, which I thought was strange. But one time he took them out to console Toni and I noticed his palms were a reddish color. I didn't think anything more about it until just now," Ian explained excitedly.

"Did you ask him about his hands?" Kirk asked.

"No, I didn't think it meant anything at the time. I kinda had my hands full with the crime scene."

"Are you making that call to Vegas?" Kirk asked, pushing his phone toward Ian.

"I'm making it right now."

Ian hung up with a look like the cat that ate the canary on his face.

"Well, what did you find out?" Kirk prompted.

"According to Adam's brother a source on the street says they're looking for Carlton DeWitt. They know he has family back east and they may be headed this way."

"Why are they looking for him and who are 'they'"? Kirk asked.

"He has a reputation as a high roller who got into trouble. Word is he's into the Tropical Casino on a note for

$100K. And I don't know who 'they' are." Ian wondered if organized crime in Las Vegas was after Carlton DeWitt. They could be bad news for Covington if they came here looking for him.

"Woo hoo! That's a $100,000." McConnelly let out a low whistle.

"Yup."

"No foolin'," Kirk chimed in.

Ian continued, "Okay, the guy owes someone a lot of money, right? So, he comes to his rich grandmother to ask for help. Only she's dead. The guy doesn't know that. So, he latches on to the cousin hoping she'll help him. But, he has to make it look good. I mean she's not gonna hand over a hundred grand just like that, right? So, he pretends to be the good loving cousin mourning the loss of their grandma."

McConnelly jumped in. "But, Joyce doesn't buy the act. So, she tells him to get the hell out of Covington. He gets pissed at her and in a fit of rage bumps her off," he finished with a flourish. He looked at his superiors expectantly. He was greeted with complete silence.

Then Ian and Kirk looked at each other, looked at McConnelly, then looked at each other again. "That's enough motive for me," Captain Kirk announced.

"Should we bring him in for questioning?" Ian asked, giddy with frustration.

"Why the hell not," Kirk stated emphatically.

Minutes later, sanity set in. Ian was thinking about Toni and how she would react if he had to arrest Carlton. At this point everything was still circumstantial. But, he knew Carlton was involved. He wished he had confirmation from an eyewitness, someone who had seen Carlton. His frustration level was building.

CHAPTER 19

Covington, Rhode Island
Friday April 16th, 1999

As Toni slipped the key to her apartment into the lock, she was feeling more alone than she could recall in her whole life. Carlton followed her into the apartment carrying a few days worth of mail for her. Once inside the apartment he threw the stack of envelopes and catalogs onto the coffee table. He sat on the couch that had been his bed for the past week and clicked on the television. Toni stood in the living room doorway staring at him.

"What?" Carlton asked shrugging his shoulders.

"Nothing, Carl," Toni answered, shaking her head.

"What? I can't watch TV now?"

"I thought after the scene we'd just witnessed, TV would be the last thing on your mind."

"Maybe I need something to take my mind off finding Joyce dead, rather than wallow in misery," Carlton lashed back at her.

Toni was taken aback. She didn't know what to say. She knew she was wallowing in misery, but who could blame her. Silently she withdrew to the sanctity of her bedroom. She sat on her bed and began unlacing her sneakers. A wave of nausea came over her. So as not to give in to it, Toni lay back on her bed and stared up at the ceiling.

Being a child when her parents died, Toni had relied on her grandmother for comfort and all her material needs. Understandably inconsolable at first, with Anna's nurturing care and having a child's ability to adapt, she had come around and returned to school, activities, and friends. Albeit she never returned to being the outgoing cheerful little girl she once was. It was clear the simultaneous deaths of her parents influenced her developing personality. She never told anyone, not even her Nana, that she cried herself to sleep every night, and told God she hated Him for taking her parents away and would never forgive Him.

Now as an adult, she was trying to cope with and understand the loss of her precious Nana. If Anna had been sick or older or had died naturally, she would still mourn losing her. However, it would have been easier to handle. But for Anna to have been murdered, and now Joyce too, Toni was feeling a deep pit of emptiness inside. She feared the pit would remain forever. She would literally be alone when Carlton returned to Vegas, and would have absolutely no family near her.

This morning she had asked Carlton to accompany her to *Anna's Attic* to help with the readying of the shop for its reopening on Tuesday. Joyce was to meet them there. Just before entering, Toni sensed something wrong. She wasn't sure what. She remembered voicing her concern to Carl, half expecting him to play protector and announce he would go in first to make sure it was safe. Instead, he simply stood on the sidewalk behind her with his hands in his pockets. A stab of disappointment struck her and she couldn't help thinking that Ian would not have let her go in there first. The shock of finding Joyce lying in a pool of her own blood was too much for her to handle. She ran screaming from the office and called Ian on her cell phone. When Ian arrived, Toni was too shocked to say anything. Ian seemed more concerned about her than her own cousin. *Maybe Carl was just trying not to lose it in front of me,* she mused. *I mean we are just getting to know each other again.*

Carlton called to her from the kitchen. "Hey Toni, do you want anything?"

"No, not now. Thanks," she answered. She could hear him opening the refrigerator and moving things around, probably to get to the beer bottles at the back of the shelf. The fridge was nearly empty since she hadn't been grocery shopping in a while. Then she heard the distinctive 'pop' from the carbonation as he twisted off the cap. She finished taking her sneakers off and padded to the living room in her socks.

Carlton came around the corner from the kitchen and stopped. He saw Toni next to the living room window staring outside.

"What do you see?" he asked as he walked towards her.

"Nothing. Absolutely nothing. Everyone is going about their business as usual," she lamented in a low voice.

"Well what do you expect?"

"I don't know," her voice drifted off. She had thought after Anna's death Joyce would be there for her. Maybe to help run the shop. Maybe just to be a friend. She would have been there to tell Toni funny little trivia about Anna. Stories. Memories. Those were all lost now. She felt a lump forming in her throat and tears welling up in her eyes. "It's funny."

"What's funny?" Carlton looked puzzled by her comment.

"They both died in the place they dearly loved." With that she couldn't hold back the flood of tears, and broke down sobbing.

Carlton could see her shoulders jerking up and down as she cried. He made no attempt to console her. "Come on Toni, cut it out. You've got to get a grip on yourself. Look at you. You're a mess," he said insensitively.

Toni spun around to look at her cousin in disbelief. "I can't believe you. Nana's barely gone a week, and now Joyce, and you want me to act as if nothing happened," she shouted at him between sobs and sniffs.

"Toni, what's the point? They're gone. Nothing you do can bring them back," Carlton said as he stared expressionless at Toni.

"I know that. But that doesn't mean I'm carrying on as usual. I want to know what happened. Why did they have to die? Who decided to play God with their lives? What kind of person would kill two helpless old women?" She snatched a couple of tissues forcefully out of their box.

"Perhaps what happened had to happen," Carlton said.

"And what do you mean by *that*?" Toni asked looking him in the eye.

"Maybe the killer was left no choice," Carlton said as he nervously walked away from Toni and sat down on the sofa sipping his beer. He was beginning to feel uncomfortable around her. She was thinking too much and looking for answers to questions that could only lead to trouble. For him. Maybe it was time to split. *I could go back to Atlantic City until Tuesday when I meet Rashovsky. Then head back to Vegas. Maybe not head back to Vegas. I'll have enough money to live the rest of my life in luxury, in a foreign country.*

"What do you mean the killer had no choice?" Toni asked breaking into his thoughts.

"Motive and opportunity. Ask your cop. He'll explain it to you," Carlton said abruptly. He was short with Toni, bordering on rude. No evidence here of the earlier loving cousin. Several minutes elapsed then Carlton broke the silence, "I'm hungry. We didn't get lunch. You planning on skipping dinner too?"

"Carlton! What the hell is wrong with you? Why do you bring up food at the most inopportune times?"

"Because I'm hungry," Carlton stated flatly.

Toni stared at him in disbelief. She couldn't understand this change in him. *Why was he acting like this? Why is he being so insensitive?* "You wanna eat, eat. I have lost my appetite."

"Then how about a movie? I can get some popcorn, a hotdog, something," Carl said hopefully.

"A movie! Are you crazy?"

"Listen. I understand you are upset. But, I need to get out of here. I am not a homebody like you. Plus, it's a Friday night. Not a night for staying home with your cousin. I need to be around other people. Try not to be so selfish and expect me to behave like you."

"You're calling *me* selfish?" Toni shot back.

"I'm going for a shower."

"Carl, what's wrong? Why are you treating me this way?"

"I'm not treating you anyway. I'm just tired of all this. I think it's time for me to head home."

"Carl, no. Not now. Not yet. Please stay a little longer. I need you." Toni remembered a time when they were younger and he had taken advantage of her, borrowing money and never paying her back. At that time, she couldn't wait to be rid of him. Now she found herself begging him to stay.

"You don't need me anymore than I need you. You've got your cop buddy, I have Las Vegas. Covington wasn't my style years ago, and it sure isn't now."

"Alright. Something I've done is obviously bothering you. Why don't we sit and discuss it like adults? I don't want you leaving like this."

"Tell you what. I'm gonna drive over to Providence and look around. It'll help me cool off. Don't wait up. Tomorrow we can have our little chat."

"Whatever you say, Carlton." Toni turned her back on him.

Carlton had no intention of talking to Toni. He had hatched a plan. He would find some chick in Providence and stay with her until his scheduled meeting with Rashovsky on Tuesday. If worse came to worse he could get a hotel room. He debated whether to take his bag with him, but decided to leave it. Taking it right now would only open the door for more hassling. Besides, the jewelry was safer here than on the road with him.

Without another word, he left the apartment, slamming the door behind him.

CHAPTER 20

Covington, Rhode Island
Saturday April 17th, 1999

The Saturday *Covington Chronicle's* headline said it all. ANTIQUE ANTICS IN COVINGTON. *Who writes this stuff?* Ian snorted disgustedly.

The rest of the article did little to help his mood. The reporter, Tom Kaneda, an old friend from high school, had intimated that the Covington PD was inept. How could someone murder two defenseless old ladies right under the noses of the police and get away with it? The article questioned. And what was Captain Kirk doing about it? Ian looked at the small black and white photograph of the reporter. "Well, you're off my Christmas card list, buddy," he said to the picture. He threw the newspaper on the couch next to him, and ran his hands through his damp hair.

Ian's weekend morning routine was simple. Shower, paper, coffee; after sleeping in as late as he wanted. This morning he couldn't sleep in. Captain Kirk wanted him at the station by seven o'clock.

It was 6:45 A.M. Ian should be in his car by now. He knew he was stalling, and he knew why. Ian Monroe was feeling helpless. Frustrated. Angry. What the hell was happening to him? Why was he taking all these events so personally?

Sighing, he answered his own questions. He had grown extremely fond of Toni, and didn't want any more crap dumped on her. He wanted the two of them to be able to explore their developing relationship, but how could they with a murderer on the loose. And what if the murderer came after Toni next? Abruptly, Ian stood and walked into his kitchen. He didn't like the direction his thoughts were going, so he stopped them. He emptied the cold contents of his coffee mug into the sink, grabbed his keys and reluctantly made his way to work.

Ian parked his car in its reserved space in the City Hall parking garage under the building. He was glad he didn't have to go in through the main doors. He knew what would be waiting for him if he did. Covington had been rocked by two murders and the press was having a field day. The Department had been able to fend off the local press after Anna's death, but now their bloodlust was insatiable. Even the major Providence papers that rarely mentioned Covington in their coverage had picked up on the last two weeks' events, and had sent reporters to his small town. Captain Kirk was fit to be tied. Although he loved seeing his name in print, he hated it when it was connected to bad press.

The police station was once again buzzing when Ian entered it through the stairwell door. Captain Kirk's office door was open but he was not inside. *Must be dealing with the press*, Ian mused. *Better him than me.* He exchanged "good mornings" with the other policemen that were already there. The work on his desk was sitting just as he'd left it the night before. He opened the file containing the list of phone numbers he'd been making his way through, and scanned it. His eyes fell on the notes he had penciled in next to the people he had managed to get a hold of already. *Call RS-B,* they said. He remembered he was about to call Roslyn Smythe-Burns when he received the frantic call from Toni. He quickly jotted a note for himself on his desk calendar so he wouldn't forget. He fully intended to make the call, but he had to finalize his report on Joyce's murder first.

Ian went over the report with a fine toothcomb. He did not want to leave anything out. It was embarrassing enough that Anna DeWitt's murder had originally been ruled an accident when it wasn't; he could not afford to make any mistakes with Joyce's death. It was obvious to even an amateur that the two murders were probably related. Ian's gut was once again telling him that Carlton DeWitt had something to do with this. What, he wasn't sure. However, Carlton's behavior yesterday was suspicious. The mere fact that he kept trying to hide his hands from view, coupled with the nonchalant attitude towards Joyce's death told Ian that Carlton was not the person Toni thought he was. Add to that information he had gained from his visit with Sandoval Pratt, and Carlton had a lot of circumstantial evidence piled against him. Ian knew he needed more if he was going to get an indictment from the Prosecuting Attorney.

Ian pulled out the Verizon Yellow Pages, and found the number for Gateway Cruise Lines. After a brief conversation with a woman named Barbara, he learned how to make a call to a ship at sea. It was easier than he had expected. All you had to do was call long distance to the telephone number assigned to the Gateway Cruise Lines ship the Gateway Star.

"Monroe! Line 3."

"Monroe," Ian said into the mouthpiece.

"Ian?" A woman's voice inquired.

"Ye-es," he didn't recognize the voice by the one word.

"This is Julianna."

"Oh, hi," Ian said. This was the last person he expected to hear from. "How are you? What's going on? It's been a long time since we've talked," Ian was attempting pleasantries. Even though Julianna had broken off their engagement, they'd parted on friendly terms.

"Ian, I know it's been a long time since we've spoken, and I know this is going to sound like it's coming out of left field, but I don't know who else to call."

"Julianna, are you alright?" Ian was concerned. He hadn't spoken with Juli since she had left Covington. She must be in trouble or she wouldn't be calling.

"Yes, yes, I'm fine. I had a problem here last week, and the police tell me they've done all they can. They've just left me hanging. So I figured you might have some pull with them. You know, one cop to another," Julianna's voice trailed off.

So she still sees me as just a cop, Ian thought. His voice became a little distant when he said, "I'll see what I can do. What happened?"

I've called you several times and missed you. I really need your help. I wish you had caller ID or an answering machine," Julianna sounded frustrated.

Now why is she bringing all that back up again, Ian wondered. Out loud he said, "You can always call me at the station. I do have voice mail here." Ian thought he sounded more sarcastic than helpful. Obviously Juli was upset, and needed his help. He took a deep breath. "Juli, talk to me. What's going on?" he encouraged in a more pleasant tone.

"You know I've been working in The Gold Key Casino in Atlantic City as a dealer since I left Covington."

"Yes, go on."

"I was on the late shift last Friday at one of the Black Jack tables. Around midnight this good looking guy shows up and starts playing and winning. Whenever he'd win a hand, he'd give me a tip. I didn't think anything of it since many of my regulars tip me. As the night wore on he started flirting with me and making suggestions about getting together after work. I didn't want to turn him down flat; I mean he was kinda cute. But the casino is very strict about dealers not dating customers, and I told him so. He told me he wasn't from New Jersey and was only in town for a couple of days. He also told me he probably wouldn't be back in the casino again so technically he wouldn't be a customer. But I still refused.

"Somehow he found out when my shift ended and was standing in the lobby waiting for me after I had cashed out. I told him again I didn't think it was a good idea. I could lose my job. He said he couldn't see how a cup of coffee would hurt. I guess I was feeling a little lonely, so I said okay."

"Oh, Juli, Juli…"

"I know, Ian. I should have known better. But, he was so charming, and seemed harmless enough."

So does Carlton DeWitt, Ian thought wryly.

"Anyway," Julianna continued, "we went to a local coffee shop near my apartment. We had coffee and talked and one thing led to another and he came home with me. I was having such a good time with him that we ended up spending the next two days together. I know what you're thinking, but honestly I don't do this all the time. I don't know what came over me. But I tell you, he was a perfect gentleman. Nothing clued me in to his real intentions."

"Oh God, Julianna. Please tell me he didn't rape you."

"No, no. Nothing like that. I mean I do feel violated but not in that way, thank God. So, like I said, he was a perfect gentleman, we had a blast, yada, yada, yada. He had told me he was only in town until Sunday, so I expected him to leave. It was the way he left that threw me for a loop."

Ian had been interjecting uhus and hms when it was necessary, but he couldn't help wanting to end this conversation quickly so he could go on with his investigation. He was getting impatient. "Juli, I'm in the middle of a major investigation I have to get back to. You still haven't told me what the problem is."

"I'm getting there, Ian. As I was saying when I woke up Sunday he was gone. No note. No goodbye, thank you very much. That wasn't the problem. The son-of-a-bitch took all the cash I had when he left. I hadn't had a chance to stop by the bank so he got a tidy sum. After kicking myself for being such an idiot, I called the police. They were so rude to me. They basically called me an idiot, gave me a case card and said that was all they could do. One of them even told me scammers like this come in and out of Atlantic City all the time hoping to find a dumb victim like me, and I should have known better than to get involved with someone I didn't know well. They didn't even think this warranted a police report." Julianna stopped.

Obviously Ian was supposed to speak now. Problem is, he didn't know what to say. He actually agreed with the Atlantic City policemen. How could she have been so stupid? "Juli, I hate to tell you this, but they're right. There *is* nothing else they can do. If this guy had broken in to your house, it would be different. You got taken in by a bum. Chalk it up to experience and move on."

"But Ian, he seemed like a rich, good-looking, nice guy, no bum. He was neatly dressed and a looker."

"Julianna, I'm sorry to hear this. But, you know better than to take someone at face value. I know you must be devastated that this guy robbed you but quite honestly I don't know what I can do."

Julianna's voice became high-pitched, "Can't you call in some favors? I don't know. You cops always scratch each others' backs. Get them to ask questions. Investigate. Something. Can't you call Adam's brother in Vegas?" she was shouting by now.

"Vegas? Aren't you in Atlantic City?" Ian asked in a deadpan voice.

Julianna lowered her voice a little. "Oh. I guess I forgot to mention that this guy is from Vegas."

Ian's heart skipped a beat. Then it began hammering wildly in his chest. Carlton DeWitt was from Las Vegas. He steadied his voice as best as he could when he asked, "Juli, what was this guy's name?"

"Carlton something or other. I didn't get his last name."

Ian's spirits were soaring now. Finally, a break in the case. "What else do you know about him? Does he have any distinguishing features? Anything you can tell me will be helpful."

"Oh, all of a sudden you can do something about this?" she said cattily.

"Do you want my help or not?" Ian responded sharply. He heard her intake of breath.

"Honestly," she began in a softer tone, "I don't know much about him except his first name and his penchant for the finer things in life. Which is funny since I paid for almost everything," Julianna finished with a snort.

"Did you happen to see his car?"

"Oh, yeah. A 1988 Mustang Convertible. That should have tipped me off. If he had as much money as he let on, he'd be driving a newer car. I guess all the signs were there, I just ignored them. You must think I'm a real idiot."

"No, Juli, I don't. We all make mistakes. Listen I'm glad you called me. I will definitely check into this and get back to you."

After getting her phone number, Ian hung up barely containing his elation. He wanted to jump around the precinct like a little boy. Little ol' Carlton DeWitt was in Atlantic City the day after Anna DeWitt was killed, after stopping in Hope Valley that same morning. It certainly could not be a coincidence.

Ian snatched up the receiver he had just hung up and went through the calling process Barbara at Gateway Cruise Lines had given him. He checked his watch and noted that it was about five o'clock in the afternoon in Europe. He hoped he'd be able to catch Roslyn on the ship. The ringing sounded like it was coming from very far away. Eventually, a man with a slight Scandinavian accent answered. After identifying himself, Ian asked for Roslyn's cabin and prayed she'd be there.

"Hello?" a female answered.

"Mrs. Smythe-Burns?"

"Yes. Who's calling?"

"Mrs. Smythe-Burns, this is Sergeant Ian Monroe calling from Covington. I am sorry to bother you while you are on vacation, but I must get some information from you."

"Oh, my. Is everything all right?" Roslyn sounded concerned.

Ian chose his words carefully. He did not want to have to tell Roslyn that her close friend Anna Dewitt was dead. Not over the phone; and certainly not while she was on vacation. "Everything is just fine. We've just had many complaints about transients roaming Antique Promenade. One may be responsible for some burglaries that were perpetrated on the shops on that street. I am investigating one in particular that occurred on the Thursday before you left for your cruise. Since your house overlooks Antique Promenade, I was wondering if you had seen or heard anything that night." Ian hoped his spiel sounded plausible enough.

"Thursday before I left...Oh I remember, that was the day I bought Winston his table. I hope Anna was not the victim of this burglary you're investigating."

If only you knew, Ian thought. "Oh, no. No she wasn't. You mentioned you saw her that night. You don't by any chance remember the time do you?"

Roslyn paused a moment, "Oh, I remember. She was closing up. So it must have been around five, five thirty in the evening. That's usually when she closes. Anna'd know what time I was there. She keeps immaculate records you know. Have you asked her?"

If only I could. "I *have* checked with her records. But I was hoping you could add more. Did you see anyone that night?"

Ian's heart was hammering as he waited for Roslyn's response. "No. As I explained earlier I was Anna's last customer that day. When I left her shop there was no one else there. I'm sorry Sergeant Monroe. I don't think I am much help."

Ian's spirits plummeted. He was so sure this was going to be the final piece of the puzzle. Well, might as well end the call. "Thank you Mrs. Smythe-Burns. I appreciate your taking the time to speak with me. If there's anything else you can remember, please call me here at the precinct."

"Oh, Sergeant, you sound so disappointed. I wish I could have been more helpful. It was a typical quiet evening in Covington. There really was no one around besides myself, Anna and her grandson."

Ian almost fell out of his chair. "You saw Carlton DeWitt?" he all but shouted.

"Well yes. Didn't I mention that?" Roslyn asked innocently.

Uh, no you old bat! "No ma'am. You sure didn't." Calming himself, Ian asked, "Where was Carlton when you saw him?"

"Going into Anna's shop with her. Oh, she was so excited when she saw him. It really made her day to see him. Such a nice young man to surprise his grandmother like that, don't you think so?"

Oh, yeah. Real nice. "I thank you again Mrs. Smythe-Burns. You've been most helpful."

"Oh, I'm so glad. Have a good day."

Ian replaced the receiver. He was stunned. Carlton had been in Covington the Thursday Anna was murdered. Roslyn was probably the last one to see her alive. The police in Atlantic City were wrong. Carlton wasn't a scammer looking for a dumb woman to rob; he was running away from a murder he had just committed. Only to waltz back into town a few days later pretending to know nothing of the murder of his grandmother.

Son-of-a-bitch! Carlton DeWitt killed his own grandmother. He must have also killed Joyce. She probably caught him doing something in the shop on her way home after the funeral. He was a cold blooded killer. Ian sat for a few moments, digesting all this information. He'd have to tell Captain Kirk. Then they'd have to get an arrest warrant and then arrest Carlton. Maybe once they question him, he'll confess and tell them why he did it. Why would he kill his own grandmother and then pretend to be the loving cousin to Toni? And that's when it hit him. Toni. Carlton has killed twice already. What's to stop him from making Toni his third victim?

Like a bat out of hell, Ian Monroe tore a path from the precinct to Toni's apartment.

CHAPTER 21

Covington, Rhode Island
Saturday April 17th, 1999

Toni bent down to pick up the *Covington Chronicle* that lay on her doormat. Slipping it from its plastic sheaf, she scanned the headline: ANTIQUE ANTICS IN COVINGTON. She stood in the open doorway reading the article. She was grateful to note that her name had not been mentioned in the story. She knew Tom Kaneda well, and had worked with him on previous assignments. Right now, she didn't much care for the spin he'd put on the story of the two murders. The swoosh of the elevator doors opening reminded her that she was standing there in her pajamas. Hastily, she stepped back into her apartment and closed the door behind her.

Toni found herself alone in the apartment when she'd woken up. From the way Carlton had behaved the night before she wasn't surprised. *I wonder what got into Carl,* she thought. *He did a complete one-eighty. What happened that he suddenly turned into the whack job of last night? I opened my home to him, let him stay here and this is how he thanks me.* Joyce's comments about Carlton haunted her, 'A leopard never changes his spots.' *Maybe she was right. Maybe this is the real Carlton DeWitt that others had warned me about recently. Short-tempered and inconsiderate.*

She was in an odd mood—couldn't concentrate or get interested in anything. Restless. *Maybe I've got cabin fever too and don't know it. Maybe Carlton was right; I should've gone out and done something last night. I've got to do something with myself today or I'll go crazy just sitting around here.* Frustrated by the situation with Carlton and her feelings about another death in her life, she decided to clean the apartment. During the last week, housekeeping had been the farthest thing from her mind; but now she could really dig in and clean to her heart's content with Carlton away.

Changing into an old pair of sweats, Toni decided to start with the bathroom. Opening the bathroom door she could still smell the odor of bleach. Carlton had told her he used bleach in the sink to cleanup some shoe polish he had spilled while polishing his shoes. She couldn't imagine why Carlton would polish his shoes over her bathroom sink. *Men. What are they thinking? He probably used one of my good bath towels to wipe up the mess and it will be stained forever. Ugh!*

Donning rubber gloves to protect her hands and manicure, she set to work cleaning the tub. She had found cleaning to be therapeutic. Just enough to keep busy but not requiring her to think too much. Distracting but not needing intellectual concentration. While she cleaned, she sang along with the songs playing on the oldies radio station she had blasting from the living room. They filled her mind with meaningless lyrics instead of allowing a vacuum for the sad thoughts she knew lay just below the surface. If she concentrated on the songs she found she couldn't also think about Nana and Joyce both being gone. At least it would get her through part of the day. She'd figure the rest out later.

Stretching, Toni admired the fruits of her labor. The bathtub was transformed to its normal sparkling condition. Satisfied, she wiggled her butt to the beat of the song on the radio and turned her attention to the sink. The mirror revealed her image. Pausing, she looked into her eyes and for a moment felt the rush of sadness begin. *No! Stop! I'm not going to do that now.* She willfully got a grip on her emotions. She sprayed foam glass cleaner on the mirror successfully hiding her face. It ran down in bubbly streaks. She quickly wiped the mirror and turned her back to it. She picked up some dirty towels Carlton had dropped inches for the laundry hamper, and threw them into it.

Hearing the first few words of *I Will Survive* by Gloria Gaynor, she danced her way out of the bathroom, down the short hallway and into the living room. She boogied around the furniture to the song and fluffed the row of pillows and dusted the tops of all the tables. She didn't feel like hauling out the little red vacuum and dragging it around. Maybe later. She was a little disappointed when the song ended. The DJ, who sounded like Wolfman Jack, gave the weather report and announced the next song: *I Am Woman.* Toni loved the feeling this anthem gave her and remembered seeing Helen Reddy sing it on a TV special. She grabbed the remote control, jumped up on the couch, and pretending it was a microphone, lip-synched the words.

Feeling a little silly but refreshed, Toni hopped off the couch. Her stomach growled just as a commercial for potato chips blasted from the speakers. Turning the volume down, she doffed her gloves and helped herself to a new can of chips and a soda. Toni curled up on the sofa with the stack of mail that had been sitting on her coffee table. Glancing through the catalogs, bills, and advertising, she saw a small square envelope with no stamp on it. Her name was handwritten in a perfectly formed cursive she didn't recognize. I wonder how this got in my mailbox? Apprehension filled her as she ripped open the envelope.

Dearest Toni,

I'm writing you this note to tell you some things that I know you won't want to hear. I have tried several times to talk to you but Carlton has been around and I want this to be for you only. By writing this note you can read it when you are alone and think about what it means to you.

As you know, I do not trust Carlton. I know you think he has been a blessing to you since Anna's death, and I know how much he has helped you. But, take it from an older, wiser person; he's up to something. You know the situation with Carlton and his parents, so I don't need to go into that here.

However, since he returned to Covington, he seems to have miraculously changed into a model cousin. I think you will find this to be an act that he will not be able to continue much longer. In fact, I think his true colors are already showing, you just haven't seen them yet.

I have reasons for my feelings. Since Carlton has been here, several small, but very valuable items have disappeared from the storeroom. Anna and I have always kept a very accurate inventory. We both know exactly where everything is, what we have on hand, and what we have sold. These items were in the storeroom when I left on Wednesday. Anna recorded only one sale on Thursday and none of these items were listed. I have been watching Carlton very carefully since his arrival. As I mentioned to you earlier, he has spent a lot of time in the storeroom. I decided to check the inventory yesterday, and found these items missing. I suspect Carlton has taken them. They are worth a sizeable sum. Attached is a list of the missing items.

I don't want to burden you with more grief, but I feel you must know my suspicions. Please Toni, be careful not to put too much trust into Carlton. I think you will be betrayed by him. I know you don't want to hear me say these things about your cousin, but I feel I must tell you how strongly I dislike him. He has never shown any regard towards his family. His recent behavior is very out of character. I feel Carlton's true intentions will surface soon.

As a close friend of Anna's I would be remiss in not reminding you to be wary. Let's talk.

Love,

Joyce

Toni sank back into the sofa cushions and closed her eyes. *We'll never get a chance to have that talk. This makes matters worse. On top of Nana's and Joyce's deaths, now I have Joyce coming back from the grave giving me warnings about my cousin. Maybe I should go through his duffle bag to see if he has any of those items in there. No. I can't invade his privacy and search his things. But what if she's right? I will talk to Carlton when he gets back. Maybe he needs money more than he's letting on. Maybe he's too embarrassed to ask me for help. Maybe. Maybe. Maybe.*

To take her mind off what she'd just read, Toni decided to get back to her cleaning. She didn't want to think anymore. Her soul had just gone from I am woman to I am nothing.

Once the kitchen was clean, she pulled open the trash compactor drawer to change the full bag. She hastily yanked out the black plastic bag and accidentally tore the bottom on the metal edge of the compactor tray. Some of the contents spilled out onto her just mopped floor.

Damn it! Now I'm going to have to mop again, she thought. She dropped the bag on the vinyl floor and watched it land on its side spilling out more of its contents. *Shit! Shit! Shit!* She screwed up her face as she surveyed the disgusting mess. *Well, this is good therapy, isn't it?*

Gingerly, she began picking up the bigger pieces and throwing them into the new bag she'd pulled out. She turned her face and held her breath when she came upon a rather smelly unidentified "thing". It was then that she noticed what looked like blue fabric hanging out of the tear at the bottom of the old trash bag. Sure enough, she pulled out the sleeve to the new blue shirt she had bought Carlton for Nana's funeral. *What the hell is this doing in here? Does he always throw his clothes away after he's worn them?* Toni pulled the shirt all the way out and held it up. Looking at the back, she saw no tears in it. Turning it around, she let out a gasp. The front had blood splattered all over it. Holding it in front of her in disbelief she stared at the blood. *This can't possibly be a shaving cut,* she thought. Carlton uses an electric razor. *Where did all this blood come from?*

She sat back on her heels and let her head fall back with a groan. *Why me? Why now?* Taking in a deep breath, Toni knew what she needed to do. Enough dilly-dallying. She dropped the shirt into the stainless steel sink and washed her hands. *If I'm going to do it I should do it now while he's away.* Toni strode purposefully to the living room where Carlton's bag sat on the floor. She bent down to unzip it; then stood up and walked away. She was torn between doing the right thing, and doing what would satisfy her curiosity. Circling the sofa a couple of times, she debated with herself and tried to justify what she was about to do. *Screw it! I'm going to look. I need answers.*

Kneeling down she unzipped the bag without moving it from its location on the floor. Her hands shaking, Toni carefully removed the items one by one from it and placed them on the floor next to her. It was almost empty and she had found nothing.

She allowed herself to breathe a sigh of relief at only finding Carl's belongings. Running her hand around the bottom of the bag to assure herself there was nothing else, she unzipped the inside compartment and plunged her hand inside the little pocket. She could feel a soft pouch.

Heart hammering again, she pulled it out. It was royal blue velvet and fairly heavy for something so small. Pulling on the drawstring to loosen it, she was dazzled by the shimmer of the diamonds as they caught the sunlight streaming through her window. For the first time, she saw the jewels that she had only recently learned about. Her inheritance. Passed down from her great-grandmother, to her Nana, to her mother. A pang of sentimentality began deep inside her heart. Thoughts of her mother and Nana flashed through her mind. Her eyes welled up with tears as she took each piece of jewelry out of the little pouch and lovingly examined it. The stories this jewelry could tell if only it could talk.

She sat back on her heels again and stared at the four pieces. No wonder Joyce was so adamant that Anna would never ever sell these to anyone. Still holding the jewels, she reached into the compartment again and felt some paper. Pulling her hand out, she opened two thin yellow papers that were folded together. Boris Rashovsky's business card fluttered onto her thigh. She cocked her head to one side thoroughly confused. *Didn't I leave this in the shop?* The unfolded papers read, *Hope Valley Antiques and Collectibles* across the top and had items listed on them that Carlton had obviously sold. These were all the items Joyce had written about in her letter.

A white-hot anger coursed through her veins. *That piece of shit Carlton. I can't believe he did this to me. The son-of-a-bitch. Stealing from his own family. Everyone was right, and I was too blind to see it.* The words in Joyce's letter swam through her head. *How could I have been such an idiot? How stupid am I?* She let out an audible, guttural sound. It did little to release the tension that had built inside her.

Toni was still kneeling in her living room holding the jewels and the receipts, when she heard the key in the door. It would be Carlton. She knew she was guilty of invading his privacy, but he was guilty of so much more. She didn't care if he saw all his things scattered on the floor and the jewels in her hands. She brought herself up to her full height, and tensed in anticipation of the confrontation.

"Toni, I'm back," he announced, as he came through the door. "What the fuck are you doing with my things?" Carlton spewed as soon as he saw Toni standing there holding the jewels.

"*Your* things? These aren't *your* things. These belonged to Nana and you took them. Along with all the other stuff you've managed to pawn," she shouted back, throwing the receipts in his direction.

"Are you telling me I have no right to them? What makes you think you have more right to them than I do?" He lashed back curling his upper lip.

"Nana left them to me in her will. They were meant for me to wear on my wedding day," Toni yelled, her eyes never leaving Carlton's face.

"So." Carlton's voice was so hateful. He was angry that his cousin had gone through his things; but angrier that she had found the jewels that he had planned to sell.

"So? What do you mean, 'so'. How could you steal these right out from under me?" she shrieked waving the jewels at him. "You went looking for them behind my back. And now that you've found them, what are you planning to do? Sell them too?" Toni was breathing heavily by now.

"Just give me the damn jewelry, woman," Carlton said raising his voice. "Before I come over there and take them."

"Are you threatening me? I could have your sorry ass thrown in jail for theft. These jewels belong to *me*. You will not see them again. Ever!"

Carlton took a menacing step towards his cousin. "Are *you* threatening *me*?"

"Oh no. This is no threat. I want you out of my apartment immediately. I took you in, gave you a place to stay thinking you had changed. They all warned me about you. But no. I wouldn't listen. I needed to believe I still had family here."

"Who are 'they'? Who have you been talking to about me?"

"Joyce, Mr. Jamison, even Ian. They all said you were up to no good. And I defended you. You believe that? I defended you, and they were right all along."

"Yeah, so what. I'm gonna say it one more time. Give me the jewelry." When Toni didn't budge, Carlton said roughly, "Don't make me come over there and get them. I will not be gentle."

Alarm bells began going off in Toni's head. He was threatening to get physical with her. "Tell you what. I'll think about it when I hear why you want them so badly."

"Are you really that stupid? Why the hell wouldn't I want them? They've gotta be worth a small fortune," Carlton's anger was building.

"Carlton, what do you need a small fortune for?" Toni was afraid of the answer, but she asked anyway. She tried to keep her voice even.

"I'm into the Tropical Casino for a hundred large. They're after me."

"Shit!"

"My sentiments exactly."

"When? How long have you owed them?"

"Since my birthday. Why? You gonna bail me out?"

"Maybe, maybe not."

"I think maybe not. So, give me the jewels so I can go back where I came from. Now!"

"Carl, who do you think is going to buy this kind of jewelry from you? These are heirlooms from the Romanov Dynasty. You can't just take these to a local antique shop." Toni figured if she kept him talking long enough she could calm him down.

"Don't you think I know that? I'm a lot smarter than you give me credit for." Carlton was obviously riled.

Toni gasped. "Rashovsky! That's why you took his card. My God. You're a bigger snake than I gave you credit for. I'm so glad Nana isn't around to see this. Now I know why she only left you a thousand dollars. She knew what a piece of work you really are."

The veins in Carlton's neck began to bulge. "A thousand dollars! A fucking thousand dollars is all the damn bitch left me?"

"*Damn bitch*? Carlton, that's your grandmother you're talking about."

"Grandmother? What kind of grandmother would turn away her only grandson when he came to her for help?"

"What?" The word was little more than a breath.

"She wouldn't help me. I begged her to give me the money to pay the casino back. She refused. She threw me out!"

Horror gripped Toni. If Carlton had asked Nana for money to pay back the casino, he must have spoken with her right before she died. Toni was reeling. Something inside her was telling her Carl had killed Nana. "Carl, let's sit down and have that talk now," Toni whispered trying to calm him down. She was no longer sure what he was going to do. He was desperate, and she now felt he was capable of taking someone's life.

Carlton strode towards Toni, grabbed her upper arms and bodily lifted her off the floor in one swift motion. He dragged her to the sofa and slammed her down onto it. She fell back and her feet kicked out in front of her. She was still clutching the jewels in her right hand. "We're not having that talk. Now, or ever," he growled at her.

Gasping for air after having had the wind knocked out of her, she struggled to sit upright. Screaming his name, "Carl," Toni moved to the edge of the sofa and attempted to stand up. "So Joyce was right about you!" she shouted.

"What the hell are you talking about?"

"Joyce said I shouldn't trust you. She said you would betray me. Joyce saw through your little act and warned me to be careful."

"Yeah. What difference does it make? It's all over now. That meddling old woman won't stick her nose in anyone's business anymore. Gimme those jewels." He made a movement towards her and she knew he meant business. Grabbing them out of her hand, he crammed them into his pant's pocket. "I don't care what you believe or what you think you know," he raged.

"Carlton, I don't understand why you're acting this way." She had almost managed to stand up, but he pushed her back down onto the sofa. Hard. She struggled to sit up again. "Carl just talk to me, tell me what's wrong." Toni knew she had to call the police. She was in danger and she had to get help somehow.

"Shut up! Shut up! Shut up! Stop talking! Stop trying to rationalize. You've been handed everything you've ever wanted your entire life. Everyone loves *you*. Not the black sheep Carlton. Antonia, Antonia, Antonia. It's all about you. Well, not anymore. Sit there and don't move for an hour. Then you can call whoever you want. Anyone comes knocking at my door, and I'm coming after you," his voice became more menacing as he spoke.

Toni realized he was being dead serious. Panic rose in her throat. She could taste the fear. *Is this how Nana felt moments before she died?* She slumped back into the sofa realizing Carlton might beat her or even kill her if she moved. She had never seen him this angry or violent. *Kill her. Oh no, Joyce. Carlton said she was a meddling old woman. Did she find out something and confront him?*

Toni couldn't let Carlton waltz out of the apartment. She believed he had already killed two people. As he turned to leave she hurled herself at his back. Her arms were locked around his neck as she desperately tried to hold on to his sides with her feet. Carlton twisted side to side trying to shrug her off. He suddenly threw up both his arms. Toni went flying across the room and landed painfully in her potted plant. The branches scratched her arms and face. She got up screaming like a banshee. "You're a thief and a murderer! You killed them both! You're a disgrace to the human race! You are beyond pathetic! You can threaten me all you want, I'm calling the cops!"

"The hell you are!" Carlton lunged at her. He fell on top of her with a thud and wrapped his big hands around her throat.

Toni fought for her life. She kicked him, she scratched, she punched. "Stop Carlton! Stop! Please!" she gasped. Carlton said nothing. He just continued to choke her. He meant to kill her. One of her kicks finally made contact with his genitals. Howling in pain, he let go of her neck and grabbed his groin rolling on the floor. Toni tried to catch her breath as she began crawling towards the front door.

"You little bitch!" Carlton grabbed Toni's left ankle and yanked her back towards him. She felt something pop in her ankle and a searing pain invaded her body. She almost passed out from the pain. But her will to live was too great. She twisted onto her back and kicked out as hard as she could with her right foot. She caught Carlton square in the face. Blood spewed from Carlton's nose. They both stopped struggling for a second. Then Carlton seemed to come to life. He hurled himself on top of her. Grabbing both sides of her head, he pulled it forward and then banged it back onto the floor several times. Toni was stunned. She could barely breathe. Waves of dizziness kept threatening to overtake her.

Carlton's face swam in front of her eyes. Then all of a sudden he rolled off her. Toni lay motionless for a few seconds trying to regain a sense of awareness. She felt, more than saw, Carlton move towards the kitchen. This was her opportunity to escape. Rolling over, she half crawled, half dragged herself to the door. Her head and her ankle were throbbing. She wanted to close her eyes and let it all be over. But Nana's death had to be avenged.

From the kitchen, Carlton saw Toni moving closer to the front door. *I can't let her live.* She knows everything. He slid the butcher knife from its slot in the wooden block.

Toni was inches from the door, when she saw Carlton coming at her with the knife raised. Out of the corner of her eye she spotted her umbrella sitting in the base of the coat rack. Using the coat rack for support she pulled herself up, snatched up the umbrella and swung it back over her right shoulder. She smashed it down on Carlton's head with every ounce of energy she had left. Carlton was taken completely by surprise, and folded over dropping the knife. She hit him again and again across the back and the head. "How do you like that? Now you know what it feels like!" Toni punctuated each blow with her screeching.

Carlton lay motionless on the floor. Toni prayed she hadn't killed him. She poked him with the tip of the umbrella. He groaned and unsuccessfully tried to grab at her. Instead, he managed to take hold of the tip of the umbrella. Terrified that Carlton would try to grab her again, Toni let go of the umbrella and unsteadily made her way to the door. She jerked the door open and limped down the hall towards her nearest neighbor. She prayed the Cobbs were home, and that Carlton wasn't following her. She glanced back over her shoulder to see if he had come out of the apartment.

The stairwell door flew open seconds before Ian appeared. He reached her just in time to stop her from falling.

"Toni, are you OK? Where's Carlton?" Ian asked frantically.

Toni was openly sobbing. "Back there. Inside the apartment. I think I killed him."

Ian gently placed her on the carpeted floor. He un-holstered his Glock just as Mr. Cobb opened his apartment door. Without explanation, Ian ordered the man to watch over Toni, and then gun raised, moved towards her apartment.

CHAPTER 22

Covington, Rhode Island
Tuesday April 20th, 1999

Boris Rashovsky sat in the Tea Room of the Covington Suites tapping his foot. He did not like to be kept waiting. He had made all the necessary arrangements. A briefcase full of money sat on the chair next to him. The chair Carlton DeWitt should be occupying. Checking his watch, Rashovsky noted that DeWitt was now twenty-five minutes late. *These Americans, they have no concept of punctuality*, he thought impatiently. Under normal circumstances, Boris Rashovsky never waited for anyone. But these were not normal circumstances. He was about to make the purchase of a lifetime, and his seller's late arrival, although annoying, would not deter him. He would wait here as long as he had to.

From his seat, Rashovsky could see the lobby of the hotel. He watched the bellhop who had taken his luggage upstairs for him when he'd arrived. The young man was in his early twenties, and had learned that if you take care of your customers properly, they will take care of you. Rashovsky was amused as he watched him offer new hotel patrons 'extra amenities.' Rashovsky himself had been offered, 'the *Covington Chronicle* delivered right to your door every morning with a steaming cup of coffee,' for a fee of course. Rashovsky had declined, saying he was uninterested in reading the local paper.

It was well after four o'clock in the afternoon when the Russian, still sitting in the Tea Room, came to the conclusion that Carlton DeWitt was not going to show up.

Boris Rashovsky knew he would never achieve the national recognition he had craved for so many years.

EPILOGUE

Covington, Rhode Island
Saturday May 1st, 1999

Toni tore a chunk off the piece of bread she was holding, and threw it into the pond. She watched a few ducks flurry towards it. Quickly she threw them another chunk. "That one's from Nana," she said to the ducks. A cool breeze danced through her long hair. Closing her eyes, she tilted her head towards the morning sun and took in a deep breath. Opening her eyes, she gazed across Mills Pond.

Toni was standing on the street side of her favorite place in Covington. Mills Pond was located in the center of town. It was actually larger than most ponds but was christened a pond since it was too small to be called a lake.

A few feet away from her Mills Bridge stretched across the rippling water. It was the only way you could get to the recreational side of Mills Pond. There the people of Covington spent their summers picnicking, bike riding, and playing. The town swimming pool had been built within walking distance of Mills Pond in the early eighties. Nana had told Toni that back in the thirties and forties, the residents of Covington had no problem swimming in Mills Pond. In the late seventies, when the world seemed to become environmentally correct, those same residents balked at the idea of wading with the ducks. They petitioned the town council to build a swimming pool. Mills Pool was one of the most beautiful pools Toni had ever swum in. Soon the pool would reopen for the summer season, and this whole area would be buzzing with throngs of people.

Two blue jays screeched as they chased each other in and out of the nearby trees. Toni drank in the quietness around her. For the first time in weeks, she felt serene. This place held, oh, so many memories. She recalled the first year Nana had brought her here. From that day on, it became a ritual. Every first Saturday in May, they would walk here arm in arm, laughing, talking, and gossiping. They would feed the ducks and enjoy each other's company. Even after she'd moved out of her grandmother's house and began her career, Toni always made sure she was in town on the first Saturday in May. Today was no different. Ian had offered to take her to his favorite place in Maine, but postponed the trip until next weekend after she'd told him her reasons for needing to be in town today.

Ian. Just the mention of his name brought a silly smile to her face. She would have never believed that her knight in shining armor lived so close. And he truly was her hero. Her feelings for him had flourished since that fateful day in her apartment two weeks ago. Toni was in love with a man for the first time in her life. She cared about him a lot. Who and what he was. She liked how he looked at her and how it made her feel. Ian Monroe was what she'd been waiting for but with all those emotions, and, now that he'd arrived, she was a still a little afraid.

A slight throbbing in her left ankle reminded Toni that she'd been standing on it a little too long. Dr. McGowen, her family physician, had instructed her to stay off her feet for a few days. She'd also recommended Toni keep the sprained ankle wrapped for a couple of weeks. Besides the injured ankle, Toni had suffered no significant injuries from Carlton's vicious attack. She'd been transported by ambulance to Covington Regional where her cuts and bruises were given a little medical attention. The emergency room doctor had insisted that she stay overnight for observation to be sure there was no concussion.

Ian had arrived at the hospital after she'd been settled into a room, and stayed by her bedside the whole night. The next morning, Ian relayed the events of the day before. Apparently, Toni hadn't killed Carlton although she'd 'done a number on him,' Ian had said with pride.

Carlton had sustained a broken nose, a concussion, and many contusions. Despite Carlton's obvious discomfort, Ian handcuffed him anyway. When back-up arrived, Carlton was placed in an ambulance with a uniformed officer and taken to the same hospital as Toni. He was convalescing in the Providence County Jail having been transferred there the following morning. He was expected to make a full recovery for his arraignment scheduled for later the same day.

When Toni had been released from the hospital, Ian had taken her home and ended up staying with her for a few days. Captain Kirk had informed them that on the advice of his public defender, Carlton had signed a full confession to both murders and pled guilty at the arraignment. He was awaiting sentencing. According to Captain Kirk, he was 'going away for a long time.'

The sound of a car pulling up roused Toni from her thoughts. She turned and saw Ian getting out of his Corvette. She waved to him as her heart did that funny little pitter-patter it did whenever she saw him. She watched him stride towards her and thought herself so lucky to have him in her life. God, but he is gorgeous.

"I thought I'd find you here," he said as he pulled her close to him. He kissed her gently on the lips.

"Mmm. Cinnamon roll," Toni responded smiling. "I thought you'd sworn off doughnuts."

"No one can swear off doughnuts," he said laughing. "They're too good to give up."

"No, you are," Toni said looking up into his blue eyes. She loved to make him blush. He didn't disappoint her. A warm, red flush slowly covered the rugged features of his face.

"Shouldn't you be sitting down? You know what Dr. McGowen said."

"I was just about to." They sank down onto the soft green grass next to each other. She leaned her head on his shoulder. "I still can't believe she's gone."

Putting his arm around her, Ian simply held her close. "You're a strong woman, Toni. You've been through hell this past month, but it's almost all over now."

"Well, most of it is over. I'll never forgive Carlton for taking Nana away from me the way he did. And I'll never get over losing her. But, I will get on with my life because that's what Nana would expect. All that's left is the liquidation of the shop."

"When is your Uncle Joel arriving?"

"He'll be here on Monday. I told him not to come. He needs to be with Aunt Jess, but he insisted. Deep down, I'm glad he's coming. He can help me make decisions about the auction and listing the property for sale. I've already taken the pieces I want, and I think there are some things that he'd want."

"By the way, does he know about the jewelry?"

"Yes. Apparently, I'm the only member of my family that was in the dark about them. Well, besides Carlton. I have them tucked away in my safety deposit box at the bank."

"You mean you're not going to wear them?" Ian asked.

"I'm not supposed to until I get married, remember?" she paused. "It's amazing to me how things so breathtaking could cause so much pain."

"But, when you finally wear them, it will be a joyous event."

"You're right. It'll be like having Mom and Nana there," she said sighing. "I was tempted to try them on just before putting them into the box. But, I held off. I didn't want to break with tradition. Guess I'm gonna have to wait until my wedding day just like Nana and Mom had to."

"You may not have to wait too long," Ian said as he looked at her and pulled her closer to him.

Printed in the United States
62219LVS00002B/19-27